Vintage Movie Classics spotlights classic films that have stood the test of time, now rediscovered through the publication of the novels on which they were based.

D1388283

Movie Adaptation of Davis Grubb's

THE NIGHT OF THE HUNTER

1955: Produced by Paul Gregory. Directed by Charles Laughton. Starring Robert Mitchum, Shelley Winters, and Lillian Gish. Screenplay by James Agee.

Davis Grubb

THE NIGHT OF THE HUNTER

Davis Grubb (1919–1980) was an American short-story writer and novelist. Born in Moundsville, West Virginia, he moved to New York City in 1940 to be a writer. His stories were published in magazines such as *Collier's*, *Cosmopolitan*, and *Woman's Home Companion*, and in three collections. *The Night of the Hunter*, the first of his ten novels, was an instant bestseller and finalist for the National Book Award. Some of his short stories were adapted for television on *The Alfred Hitchcock Hour* and Rod Serling's *Night Gallery*; his novel *Fools' Parade* was the basis for a 1971 film starring James Stewart.

BOOKS BY DAVIS GRUBB

STORY COLLECTIONS

Twelve Tales of Suspense and the Supernatural

The Siege of 318: Thirteen Mystical Stories

You Never Believe Me and Other Stories

NOVELS

The Night of the Hunter

A Dream of Kings

The Watchman

The Voices of Glory

A Tree Full of Stars

Shadow of My Brother

The Golden Sickle

Fools' Parade

The Barefoot Man

Ancient Lights

THE NIGHT
OF THE HUNTER

THE NIGHT
OF THE HUNTER

Davis Grubb

Foreword by Julia Keller

Vintage Books
A Division of Penguin Random House LLC
New York

FIRST VINTAGE BOOKS EDITION, JULY 2015

Vintage Books Trade Paperback ISBN: 978-1-101-91005-4
eBook ISBN: 978-1-101-91006-1

www.vintagebooks.com

Printed in the United States of America
10 9 8 7 6 5 4 3 2 1

FOREWORD

Davis Grubb's Lost Masterpiece

by Julia Keller

If you close your eyes and throw a stick while standing in the for-est of American popular culture, you'll hit a million serial killers, give or take. In novels and TV shows, in movies and comic books and ballads and video games, there are constant iterations of the ruthless, machinelike murderer who whips through a victim list with perverse efficiency and no residual guilt. From the Hannibal Lecter novels of Thomas Harris to the TV series *Criminal Minds* to the Wes Craven film franchise featuring that fiend-in-a-fedora Freddy Krueger, serial killers are everywhere—hiding in tool-sheds, penning come-hither Craigslist ads, serving you a sumptu-ous dinner while fingering the carving knife behind your back. The true-crime genre is similarly besotted with these rapacious, cackling masterminds, these damaged souls of diabolical intent, who kill again and again simply because they get a kick out of it.

But to see how a writer might, with originality and audacity, turn that stereotype into the catalyst for a penetrating, atmospheric exploration of Depression-era poverty and human depravity, read

The Night of the Hunter by Davis Grubb. First published in 1953, it's a neglected masterpiece, a gem that somehow got lost in the back of literature's kitchen drawer along with the stray buttons and the tarnished spoons and the spare pennies.

Chances are you're familiar with the title, but you may know it best as the moniker of the 1955 film version of the book. The movie stars Robert Mitchum, Shelley Winters, and Lillian Gish and is generally regarded as a noir classic. Dominated by Mitchum's slow-burn depiction of the sinister predator with *l-o-v-e* tattooed on the knuckles of one hand and *h-a-t-e* on the other, the movie is so stark, so viscerally menacing, that the novel upon which it is based has drifted far out of the spotlight.

That's a shame, because *The Night of the Hunter* is a gorgeous gut-punch of a book, a crime novel and ghost story and morality tale all rolled into one. It's an ugly-beautiful work that pays scant attention to narrative niceties such as proper punctuation. It's rough-hewn, melodramatic, and wildly entertaining, with some crucial social commentary tucked in there, too, like a precious coin smuggled in a raggedy old sock.

Pearl and John are a sister and brother being raised by their mother, Willa, in Cresap's Landing, a sorrowful speck of a town along the Ohio River near Moundsville, West Virginia. This is the Great Depression—a time, notes one of the book's characters, that has "turned up the undersides of some mighty respectable folks." The children's father, Ben Harper, has just been executed for a murder committed in the course of an armed robbery. No one knows where Ben hid the money he stole.

While Ben was in prison, his cellmate was a creepy, twisted, God-haunted wreck of a man who calls himself Preacher. Once Preacher is free, he seeks out Ben's children, certain that they know the location of the dough. Preacher woos and wins Ben's widow—while John watches in mounting terror, immune to Preacher's charms. Indeed, the man's very presence puts "the smell of dread in his nose" until "doglike his flesh gathered and bunched at the scent of it." Soon John and Pearl are on the run across the Ohio River Valley, desperate to escape what the novel calls "something as old and dark as the things on the river's bed, old as evil itself."

Grubb based *The Night of the Hunter* on the real-life case of Harry F. Powers, a serial killer who preyed upon middle-aged widows. Powers was hanged for his crimes in 1932 at the state penitentiary in Moundsville, West Virginia—Grubb's hometown—but the case continues to intrigue. Most recently, Jayne Anne Phillips imagined the inner lives of some of Powers's victims, a widow and her children from Park Ridge, Illinois, in her 2013 novel *Quiet Dell*.

There is often a timeless quality to great fiction, a sense that the story could be occurring anywhere, to anyone, but there is also fiction that belongs right where the author put it. *The Night of the Hunter* is set during the Depression, and it is soaked with a stain of urgent necessity, with the recklessness and sorry compromising brought on by lack of money. Like any good psychopath, Preacher takes advantage of the family's economic troubles; he knows that Willa is in no position to refuse his advances—not if she wants to be able to feed her children.

To a world that routinely gorges itself on lurid spectacles of fictional gore, *The Night of the Hunter* is a reminder of the power of the less explicit. Grubb doesn't need to show us shredded flesh or shattered skulls or writhing intestines to create revulsion and fear. He doesn't need the grotesque. Instead he relies upon the insinuating force of evocative language: "Something had moved in the dark and secret world of night: something like the quick soft break and gasp of a sudden blowing flame in a coal grate in the dead of a winter's night."

Serial killers come and go in popular culture, and rarely rise above the banal, but Preacher is something special. Eager for the next kill, he waits for God to give him the go-ahead—"Is it time yet, Lord? Time for another widow? Say the word, Lord! Just say the word and I'm on my way!" Sometimes, as when he surveys a prostitute whose pale neck seems to beckon the knife he keeps in his pocket, Preacher is overwhelmed: "There were too many of *them*. He couldn't kill a world."

Killing a world: Was there ever a better, more succinct mission statement for a serial killer, for the kind of criminal whose compulsions come in bunches and never let him go? Grubb's novel is about a dark soul in a dark time, and it is about, too, the solace of fighting back against that darkness, and of "knowing that children are man at his strongest, that they are possessed, in those few short seasons of the little years, of more strength and endurance than God is ever to grant them again." In other words: Game on. Let the hunter's night commence.

An earlier version of this essay was read on National Public Radio. West Virginia native Julia Keller is a Pulitzer Prize–winning journalist and the author of a series of novels set in Appalachia, the most recent of which is *Last Ragged Breath*.

THE NIGHT
OF THE HUNTER

To my mother

Where do murderers go, man!
Who's to doom when the judge himself
is dragged to the bar?

—MELVILLE, *Moby-Dick*

CONTENTS

BOOK ONE

THE HANGING MAN

Wilt thou forgive that sinne by which I have wonne
Others to sinne? and, made my sinne their door?

—DONNE, *"A Hymne to God the Father"*

A child's hand and a piece of chalk had made it: a careful, child's scrawl of white lines on the red bricks of the wall beside Jander's Livery Stable: a crude pair of sticks for the gallows tree, a thick broken line for the rope, and then the scarecrow of the hanging man. Some passing by along that road did not see it at all; others saw it and remembered what it meant and thought solemn thoughts and turned their eyes to the house down the river road. The little children—the poor little children. Theirs were the eyes for which the crude picture was intended and they had seen it and heard along Peacock Alley the mocking child rhyme that went with it. And now, in the kitchen of that stricken house, they ate their breakfast in silence. Then Pearl stopped suddenly and frowned at her brother.

John, finish your mush.

John scowled, pressing his lips together, while their mother stared out the window into the yellow March morning that flowered in the dried honeysuckle along the window. A cold winter sun shot glistening rays among the early mists from the river.

John, eat your mush.

Be quiet, Pearl! cried Willa, mother of them. Leave John be. Eat your own breakfast and hush!

Yet John frowned still, watching as the little girl resumed eating, and would not let the matter lie.

You're only four and a half, Pearl, he said. And I'm nine. And you got no right telling me.

Hush, John.

Willa filled the blue china cup with sputtering hot coffee and sipped the edge of it, curling her nose against the steam. And then Pearl remembered again the picture on the brick wall beside Jander's Livery Stable down at Cresap's Landing. Pearl made them listen to the song about the hanging man.

Hing Hang Hung! See what the hangman done! chanted the little girl, and Willa, whirling, slammed the sloshing cup to the black stove top and struck the child so the four marks of her fingers were pink in the small flesh.

Don't you ever sing that! Ever! Ever! Ever!

Willa's poor, thin hands were knotted into tight blue fists. The knuckles shone white like the joints of butchered fowl. Pearl would have wept but it seemed to her that now, at last, she might get to the heart of the matter and so withheld the tears.

Why? she whispered. Why can't I sing that song? The kids down at Cresap's Landing sing it. And John said—

Never you mind about what John said. God in heaven, as if my cross wasn't hard enough to bear without my own children—his own children—mocking me with it! Now hush!

Where's Dad?

Hush! Hush!

But why won't you tell? John knows.

Hush! Hush your mouth this minute!

Willa struck the child's plump arm again as if, in so doing, she might in some way obliterate a fact of existence—as if this were not a child's arm at all but the specific implement of her own torment and despair. Now Pearl wept in soft, faint gasps, and clutching her old doll waddled off, breathless with outrage, into the cold hallway of the winter house. John ate on in pale indifference, yet obscurely pleased with the justice. Willa glared pathetically at him.

And I don't want you telling her, John, she whispered hoarsely. I don't want you breathing a word of it—you hear? I don't want her ever to know.

He made no reply, eating with a child's coarse gusto; smacking his lips over the crackling mush and maple sirup.

You hear me, John? You hear what I said?

Yes'm.

And, despite the sole and monstrous truth which loomed in his small world like a fairy-book ogre, despite the awareness which for so many weeks had crowded out all other sentiments (even the present sweet comfort of breakfast in his mother's steamy kitchen), John could not help finding a kind of cruel and mischievous joy as the lilt and ring of Pearl's chant pranced like a hurdy-gurdy clown in his head: Hing Hang Hung! See what the hangman done. Hung Hang Hing! See the robber swing.

It was the song the children sang: all the children at Cresap's Landing except, of course, John and Pearl. It was the song that was made by the children whose hands had made the chalk drawing on the red brick wall by Jander's Livery Stable. John finished his milk in a single gulp and took the cup and plate to Willa by the sink.

Now, she said, I'm going up to Moundsville to see your dad. Lunch is in the pantry. I'll be home to get you supper but I might not get back till late. John, I want you to mind Pearl today.

John, already heavy with responsibility for his sister, saw no reason to further acknowledge this bidding.

Hear, John? Mind her, now. And you, Pearl. Mind what John tells you. He'll give you your lunch at noon.

Yes.

And mind what else I told you, John. Don't breathe a word about—you know.

No'm.

Hing Hang Hung, he thought absently. (Why, it was almost a dancing tune.) Hung Hang Hing! See the robber swing. Hing Hang Hung! Now my song is done.

Willa by the brown mirror over the old chest of drawers tucked her chestnut curls into the wide straw hat with the green band.

Can Pearl and me play the Pianola?

Yes, but mind you don't tear the rolls, John. They was your dad's favorites.

She caught her breath, choking back a sob as she powdered her nose slowly and stared back into the wild, grieving eyes in the mirror. Why, it was almost as if Ben would ever hear them again: those squeaky, wheezy old Pianola rolls, almost as if he had just gone off on a fishing trip and would soon be back to play them and laugh and there would be those good old times again. She bit her lip and whirled away from the face in the mirror.

—And don't let Pearl play with the kitchen matches! she cried and was gone out the door into the bitter morning. When the gray door was closed John stood listening for the chuckle-and-gasp, and then the final cough-and-catch and the rising whine of the old Model T. Pearl appeared in the hall doorway with the ancient doll in her arms, its chipped and corroded face not unlike her own just now that was streaked with tears in faint, gleaming stains down her plump cheeks. John listened to the old car whining off up the river road to Moundsville. Pearl snuffled.

Come on, Pearl, John said cheerfully. I'll let you play the Pianola.

She stumped solemnly along behind him into the darkened parlor amid the ghostly shapes of the muslin-draped furniture gathered all round like fat old summer women. The ancient Pianola towered against the wall by the shaded window like a cathedral of fumed oak. John opened the window blind an inch to shed a bar of pale winter light on the stack of long boxes where the music was hidden. Pearl squatted and stretched a fat hand to take one.

No, he said gently. Let me, Pearl. Mom said they wasn't to be tore—and besides you can't read what them names say!

Pearl sighed and waited.

Now this here one, he announced presently, lifting a lid from the long box and gently removing the thick roll of slotted paper. This here is a real pretty one.

And he fitted the roll into the slot and snapped the paper into the clip of the wooden roll beneath and solemnly commenced pumping the pedal with his stubby shoes. The ancient instrument seemed to suck in its breath. There was a hiss and a whisper in the silence before it commenced to clamor.

Wait! wailed Pearl, edging onto the stool beside him. Wait, John! Let me! Let me!

But her feet would not reach as always and so she sat and listened and watched in stunned amazement; dumbfounded before the glorious chiming racket it made and the little black and white keys jumping up and down with never a mortal finger to touch them. John thought somberly: That's Carolina in the Morning. That was one of Dad's favorites.

And he could remember the times when they had all listened to it when Ben was there, when they were together, and he knew where the tear was in the roll and the keys would speak out in a short chord of confusion and then go rollicking off again into the mad, happy tune. Pearl hugged the old doll close and sucked her finger in dumb amaze. And when the tune was done she sighed.

More?

No, sighed John glumly, shuffling away into the kitchen, his heart heavy with thoughts of the good old times that were gone. I don't feel like it, Pearl.

She followed in his footsteps like a lost lamb, hugging the old doll tight as if it might some day be her last comfort, and she stood beside him at the kitchen window, nose squashed flat to the icy pane. The hanging man. Yes, they could see him dimly even now—far away down the frozen road amid the winter mists—the little white man on the red bricks. He had not gone away in the night. When you looked one way at his angular arms and legs he quite resembled an airplane. But, of course, one knew better than that. He was a neat little man with stiff arms and stiff legs and a little pointed hat and there was a white scratch for the rope and two white scratches for the gallows tree.

Hing Hang Hung! whispered Pearl, softly.

For she knew that John would never strike her. It was only Mom who could not abide the song.

Hung Hang Hing! she crooned again; the breath of its music caught in her throat.

John scowled and sketched a hing-ing hang-ing man on the foggy windowpane.

You better never let Mom catch you singing that song.

Why won't she tell, John?

Because you're too little.

I'm not, John! I'm not!

He said nothing, sucking his lip. He would have loved nothing more than to tell her. Since the day when the blue men had taken Ben away the burden of this solitary knowledge was almost more than he could endure. It was not a knowing that he could share with his mother or with anyone. It was a secret that was a little world of its own. A terrible little world like an island upon whose haunted beach he wandered alone now, like a solitary and stricken Crusoe, while everywhere about him his eyes would find the footprint of the dangling man.

Ben lay back in the bunk and smiled. Preacher has stopped talking now. Preacher just sits there across the cell from Ben with those black eyes boring into him. Preacher is trying to guess. Not that Ben hasn't told Preacher everything that he told the others at the trial: Warden Stidger, Mister McGlumphey, Judge Slathers, and the jury. Everything, that is, but the one thing they wanted the most to know. Ben won't tell that to anybody. But it is a kind of game: teasing Preacher. Ben tells him the story over and over again and Preacher sits hunched, heeding each word, waiting for the slip that never comes.

Because I was just plumb tired of being poor. That's the large and small of it, Preacher. Just sick to death of drawing that little pay envelope at the hardware store in Moundsville every Friday and then when I'd go over to Mister Smiley's bank on payday he'd open that little drawer with all the green tens and fifties and hundreds in it and every time I'd look at it there I'd just fairly choke to think of the things it would buy Willa and them kids of mine.

Greed and Lust!

Yes, Preacher, it was that. But I reckon it was more, too. It wasn't just for me that I wanted it.

You killed two men, Ben!

That's right, Preacher. One day I oiled up that little Smith and Wesson that Mr. Blankensop keeps in his rolltop desk at the hardware store and I went up to Mister Smiley's bank and I pointed that gun at Mister Smiley and the teller Corey South and I said for Corey to hand me over that big stack of hundred-dollar bills. Lord, you never seen such a wad, Preacher!

Ten thousand dollars' worth, Ben Harper!

Then Mister Smiley said I was crazy and Corey South went for his gun in the drawer and with that I shot him and Mister Smiley both and while I was reaching through to get that green stack of hundreds out of Corey's dead fingers Mister Smiley got the gun and lifted up on the floor and shot me through the shoulder. Well, sir, I run and got scared and didn't know which was up or down before long and so I just got in the car and come home.

With the money?

Yep!

And then?

Ben Harper smiles.

Why, they come down the river after me about four that afternoon—Sheriff Wiley Tomlinson and four policemen.

And where was you, Ben?

Why, I was there, Preacher. You see I was done running. I was just standing out back by the smokehouse with them two youngsters of mine—John and that little sweetheart Pearl.

And the money, Ben? What about that? What about that ten thousand dollars?

Ben smiles again and picks his front teeth with his thumbnail.

Go to hell, Preacher, he says softly, without rancor.

But listen to me, Ben Harper! It'll do you no good where you're going. What good is money in heaven or hell either one? Eh, boy?

Ben is silent. Preacher walks away and stands for a spell staring out the cell window with his long, skinny hands folded behind him. Ben looks at those hands and shivers. What kind of a man would have his fingers tattooed that way? he thinks. The fingers of the right hand, each one with a blue letter beneath the gray, evil skin—L—O—V—E. And the fingers of the left hand done the same way only now the letters spell out H—A—T—E. What kind of a man? What kind of a preacher? Ben muses and wonders softly and remembers the quick-leaping blade of the spring knife that Preacher keeps hidden in the soiled blanket of his bed. But Preacher would never use that knife on Ben. Preacher wants something from Ben. Preacher wants to know about that money and you can't use a knife to get at something like that especially with a husky fellow like Ben. Now Preacher comes back and stands by Ben's bunk.

Set your soul right, Ben Harper! That money's bloodied with Satan's own curse now. And the only way it can get cleared of it is to let it do His works in the hands of good, honest poor folks.

Like you, Preacher?

I am a man of Salvation!

You, Preacher?

I serve the Lord in my humble way, Ben.

Then, says Ben Harper softly, how come they got you locked up in Moundsville penitentiary, Preacher?

There are those that serves Satan's purposes against the Lord's servants, Ben Harper.

And how come you got that stick knife hid in your bed blankets, Preacher?

I serve God and I come not with peace but with a sword! God blinded mine enemies when they brought me to this evil place and I smuggled it in right under the noses of them damned guards. That sword has served me through many an evil time, Ben Harper.

I'll bet it has, Preacher, grins Ben and presently Preacher goes up into his bunk and lies there a while longer muttering and praying to himself and scheming up new ways to get Ben to tell him where he hid that ten thousand dollars in green hundreds. It's a game between them. And in a way it is Ben Harper's salvation— this little game. In three days they are coming to take Ben up to the death house and a body has to keep busy with little games like this to keep from losing his mind at the last. A little game—a little war of wills. Ben Harper and Preacher around the clock— day after day. And Ben Harper knows that it is a game that he will win. Because Preacher can talk the breath out of his body and Ben will never tell a mortal, living soul. But Preacher keeps on; stubborn, unremitting. In the quaking silence of the prison night: Listen, Ben! Where you're goin' it won't serve you none. Tell me, boy! Buy your way to Paradise now! You hear, boy? Mebbe the

Lord will think twice and let you in the good place if you was to tell me, boy. Tell me! Have a heart!

Go to sleep, Preacher.

Salvation! Why, it's always a last-minute business, boy. There's a day of judgment for us all, Ben Harper, and no man knows the hour. Now's your chance. Mister Smiley and Corey South is both dead, boy! Can't nothin' change that! But if you was to let that money serve the Lord's purposes He might feel kindly turned toward you. Ben, are you listenin' to me, boy?

Shut up, Preacher! Ben whispers, choking back a giggle at the game, the furious little game that keeps him from thinking about the rope upstairs and his own shoes swinging six feet above the floor of the drop room.

Listen, Ben! See this hand I'm holdin' up? See them letters tattooed on it? Love, Ben, love! That's what they spell! This hand—this right hand of mine—this hand is Love. But wait, Ben! Look! There's enough moonlight from the window to see. Look, boy! This left hand! Hate, Ben, hate! Now here's the moral, boy. These two hands are the soul of mortal man! Hate and Love, Ben—warring one against the other from the womb to the grave—

Ben listens to the familiar sermon; shudders with a kind of curious delight as Preacher writhes the fingers of his two tattooed hands together and twists them horribly, cracking the knuckles as the fingers grapple one hand with the other.

Warring, boy! Warring together! Left hand and right hand! Hate and Love! Good and Evil! But wait. Hot dog! Old Devil's a-losin', Ben! He's a slippin' boy!

And now Preacher brings both hands down with a climactic crash on the wooden bench by the bunks. Then he is silent, crouched in the darkness, smiling at the glory of God in his evil fingers and waiting to see if his little drama has done anything to the boy in the lower bunk.

I could build a tabernacle, Ben, he whimpers. To beat that Wheeling Island tabernacle to hell and gone! Think of it, Ben. A tabernacle built with that ten thousand dollars of cursed, bloodied gold. But wait, Ben! Now it's God's gold. Thousands of sinners and whores and drunkards flocking to hear His word and all because you give that money to build a temple in His name. Listen to me, boy! You reckon the Lord wouldn't change His mind about you after that? Why, shoot, Ben! He wouldn't let them little old killings stand between you and the gates of Glory. Hell, no!

Ben rises on his elbow, tired of the game now.

Shut up, Preacher! Shut up and go to sleep before I climb over there and stuff your bed tick down your throat!

Silence again. Preacher up there in the darkness, in the thick, creosote silence of the vast prison. Preacher lying up there on his back with those tattooed fingers criss-crossed behind his sandy, shaggy head thinking how he can worm it out of Ben Harper with only three days to the death house. Ben stuffs his knuckles into his teeth till he tastes blood. The ropes beneath his straw tick squeak to the rhythm of his ague-like trembling. Ben Harper is quaking with agony beneath the little dream that the night's blue fingers reach out to him. Once more it is that winter afternoon on the river shore by the old house up the road from Cresap's Landing. He is looking into the moon faces of the children: Pearl stony and silent as a graveyard cherub and John's big eyes wide with everything Ben was telling him, while Pearl clutched the old doll against her body.

Where you goin' to, Dad?

Away, John! Away!

You're bleedin', Dad.

It's nothin', boy. Just a scratched shoulder.

But there's blood, Dad.

Hush, John! Mind what I told you to do.

Yes, Dad.

And you, Pearl! You, too. Mind now! You swore!

Now, from the corner of his eye, Ben sees the blue men with the guns in the big touring car coming down the road beyond the corner of the orchard. John's mouth is a white little line as his dark eyes follow the blue men. They circle and walk slowly in through the dead grass that rims the yard.

Now I'm goin' away, boy.

John's mouth breaks and trembles but then it tightens back into the thinness again. He makes no sound.

Just mind everything I told you, John.

Yes, Dad.

And take good care of Pearl. Guard her with your life, boy.

Yes, Dad.

Who's them men? whispers Pearl at last.

Never mind them. They come and I'm goin' off with them, children. Don't even waste time thinkin' about that now. Just mind what I told you—mind what you swore to do, boy!

Yes!

Swear to it again, John. Swear, boy!

I swear! I swear!

Ben Harper lies in his bunk now with the sweat beaded like morning dew on his forehead. He does not move lest Preacher may sense that he is awake, frightened beyond all reason or caution, and think that now is the time to break the seal at last and end his quest for the knowledge of the hidden money. But Preacher is snoring and mumbling in his sleep about Sin and Gold and the Blood of the Lamb, and Ben relaxes after a spell and watches the edge of the winter moon in the window, just the rim of it in the blue square of window with the corner of one of the wall towers black like a child's school cut-out with the sharp little machine gun sticking out. He closes his eyes, thinking of the day just ended. His wife Willa had been allowed to see him that morning. He looked at her there on the other side of the chicken wire and wanted to say things to her that he hadn't felt in a longer time than he could remember. Back in the spring of 1928 when they had run off to Elkton, Maryland, and gotten married and spent the first whole night together in a tourist cabin making love the way she had always wanted it to be instead of sneaking off somewhere to do it. He had thought about how all that honeymoon night they had listened to the whirr and roar of the roller skates in the big rolla-drome across the highway and that record that played over and over again, that one that went, Lucky Lindy up in the air! Lucky Lindy flew over there! and he had dreamed of the life they would have together in the house down in the bottomlands above Cresap's Landing and how he would get himself a raise at the hardware store and buy her a player piano. It was funny how it had always been a matter of money. Right up to the very end. Even that day at the prison she kept asking him about it—the ten thousand dollars he had hidden somewhere. She kept saying over and over that it wasn't going to do him any good and he had no right to leave her and the two kids without anything but that old bottomlands house her Uncle Harry had left her. Nothing but that and the clothes on their backs. But he would not tell. And it made him sick at his stomach to sit there on the other side of the chicken wire and see her mouth saying it over and over again until her face began to look for all the world like the face of Preacher; weak and sick with greed; the same greed that had led Ben to murder and the gallows. He watched her eyes all bright and feverish with hope of finding out, her little pink tongue licking her dry lips with the excitement of it and, at last her mouth gone slack with disappointment when she realized that he would not tell—that he would never tell.

That same afternoon Mister McGlumphey, his lawyer, had been to see him, too. There was no getting around it—they had all been mighty nice to him at his trial. Mister McGlumphey had done his very best to get him off with life imprisonment and the jury was as nice a bunch of people as you'd want to see and he thought to himself many times since: I wish them no harm nor vengeance in this world or the other. Mister McGlumphey had told him at the outset that it would sure go easier with him if he was to tell what he'd done with that ten thousand dollars and it was really then that Ben had made up his mind not to tell. Because any poor fool could see that it wasn't justice they were after—it was the ten thousand dollars. So Ben simply said that he wouldn't tell them even if they was to break his arms and legs to make him tell and Mister McGlumphey said they wouldn't do anything like that but they'd like as not break worse than that and he couldn't see any possible way to save him from swinging if he felt that way about it. And so Ben was more sure than ever that he was right. And he concluded with grim Calvinist logic that if he needed to tell them about the money to be spared the hanging then there was no real justice in the courts and so he would take his satisfaction with him to the grave. It was Sin and Greed that had brought him to Moundsville and it was Sin and Greed that was making them hang him. It was the face of Willa begging and wheedling behind the chicken wire. It was the face of Mister McGlumphey arguing. It was the voice of Preacher in the dark.

Where? Where, Ben? Where? Have a heart, boy. Where, Ben? Where?

He awoke. The corner of the moon was gone from the window. The blue square was empty except for the ragged thatch of Preacher's head inches from his own. Ben gathered himself slowly under his blanket and let his muscles coil like a steel spring and then lashed out with all his strength until he felt his hard fist crunch into the bones of the whispering face. Ben, you hadn't ought to have hit me! I'm a man of God!

You're a son of a bitch! Sneaking up and whispering in my ear whilst I'm sleeping! Hoping you could make me talk about it in my sleep! Damn you, Preacher! Damn you to hell!

Just the same you shouldn't have done it, boy! I'm a man of the Lord!

You're a slobberin' hypocrite, Preacher! Now get the hell back up in your bunk before I smash your head in! I'd as soon hang for three killin's as two!

Ben lies rigid now, listening as the other scrambles fearfully up into the rustling straw tick and falls back, mopping his bleeding nose and whimpering. Ben fell asleep and saw it clear as day: the little room and the rope. His Cousin Wilfred and old Uncle Jimmy John Harper got passes to a hanging back in 1930 and Wilfred got sick and had to be taken to a drugstore to be revived and cleaned up and Uncle Jimmy John wouldn't even talk about it when he got back home and every time one of Ben's kids would come to him with a rope and ask him to take the knots out of it he would shoo that youngster out the kitchen door. Ben could see himself plain as day: in the little room and a man was putting that rope over his head and he saw then that the man was Preacher and Preacher laughed when they sprang the trap and Ben was falling, falling, falling. He sprang up in the bunk, striking his head against the wall. What did I say, Preacher?

What, Ben?

Now he was scrambling up into Preacher's bunk and his fingers were around Preacher's throat like a ring of baling wire. I said something in my sleep just now! What did I say, Preacher?

Nothin'! My God, nothin', Ben!

You're lyin', Preacher! Goddamn you, you're lyin'!

He tightened his fingers—pressing his thumbs into the gristle of the man's windpipe until Preacher's breath came rattling and gasping. Then he took the hands away for a moment.

I said something! What did I say, Preacher? What! What!

Ben lifted him by the shoulders and flung him against the

wall and banged his head against the stone to the rhythm of his words. Now the other convicts were yelling and banging for silence along the row.

What! What! What! What!

Preacher gasped and choked.

You—you was—you was quotin' the Book, Ben.

I which?

You was quotin' the Scripture! You said—you said, And a little child shall lead them.

Ben let go then and got back down in his bunk again and rolled up one of his socks and stuffed it into his mouth before he went back to sleep, and next morning when he woke to the siren's vast, echoing contralto the sock was still in his mouth, foul-tasting and thick on his dry tongue, but he knew, at least, that he had not talked. He spat it out and grinned across the cell at Preacher, dressed and shaved long before the morning siren blew. His nose was swollen and his eyes were puffed and black from the blow Ben had given him. Ben laughed out loud. Nothing would ever stop Preacher. Already the glitter was back of those hunting eyes; already the question was forming again behind those thin, mad lips. A feller almost had to hand it to Preacher.

Ben?

What, Preacher?

I'll be leaving this place in another month. You'll be dead then, Ben. Dead and gone to make your peace with God! Now if you was to tell me, boy, it might go easier. Why, Ben, with that ten thousand dollars I could build a tabernacle that would make that Wheeling Island place look like a chickenhouse! I'd even name it after you, boy! The Ben Harper Tabernacle! How's that sound? It'd be the glory of them all, Ben! The finest gospel tabernacle on the whole Ohio River!

Keep talkin', Preacher.

The Lord might feel kindly turned toward you, Ben! The Lord might say: What's a little murder—

Would you have free candy for the kids, Preacher?

Well, yes, I would.

Would you give out free eats to all the poor folks that was hungry, Preacher?

Don't jest, Ben.

I ain't jestin', Preacher. Would you?

Yes, Ben. If you say so, boy. It'd be your tabernacle. All them poor souls out there wanderin' around hungry in this terr'ble depression—all them folks driven to stealin' and whorin'! Just think, Ben! They'd come there and bless your name!

Ben Harper bends and searches under the bunk for his other sock.

Keep talkin', Preacher, he chuckles. Keep talkin'!

And the other one had his dreams, too. He would lie there in the dark and when he wasn't thinking about new ways to make Ben talk he would think about the women. He could never be exactly sure how many there had been. Sometimes there were twelve and sometimes it was only six and then again they would all blend together into one and her face would rise up in the wavering chiaroscuro of his dreams like the Whore of Sodom and not until his hand stole under his blanket and wound round the bone hasp of the faithful knife did the face blanch and dissolve into a spasm of horror and flee back into the darkness again. He was bad at remembering facts, dates, places, names. And yet fragments would return with shocking verisimilitude: the broken chards of forgotten times, lost names, dead faces; these would return and he would know for that instant what he had felt toward the time, the name, the place, and how God had spoken clear to him and told him what he had to do. The knife beneath the wool, the Sword of Jehovah beneath his wrathful fingers. God sent people to him. God told him what to do. And it was always a widow that God brought to him. A widow with a little wad of money in the dining-room sugar bowl and perhaps a little more in the county bank. The Lord provided. Sometimes it was only a few hundred dollars but he would thank the Lord just the same when it was all over and done with and everything was smoothed over and there was not so much as a single scarlet droplet on the leaves in the pleasant woods where it had ended and the Sword of God was wiped clean again—ready again.

Through the leafy, tranquil decade of the twenties he had wandered among the river hamlets and the mill towns of Ohio and Kentucky and Indiana doing God's work quietly; without fuss or ostentation. Perhaps it was his very indifference to being caught—his inability to imagine that anyone would even want to interfere—that kept them from ever nailing him for anything but the car theft in Parkersburg that had sent him to the state penitentiary. Sometimes he found his widows in the lonely-hearts columns of the pulp love story magazines. Always widows. Chuckling, pleasant, stupid widows who would want to sit alone with him on a dusty, bulging davenport in a parlor not yet aired free of the sickly-sweet flower smell of the dead man's funeral. Fat, simpering, hot widows who flirted and fluttered their eye-lashes and fumbled for his hand with plump fingers still sticky from the drugstore chocolates; soft corpse hands that made him retch and hold himself in while he turned to the powdered face and smiled and spoke of the provident God that had brought them both together. And afterward there was the little roll of money; money to go forth and preach God's word among a world of harlots and fools.

Wandering the land he preached. He would take a room at the cheap depot hotel where the drummers sat out the long sum-mer twilights and watched for the evening train and after a bit he would spread the word that he was in town and get himself invited to preach at a meetinghouse and presently he would announce a big open-air revival by the river for the last week in August. It never brought him much money. But it helped him spread God's glory. God took care of the money. God brought him widows.

His name was Harry Powell but everyone called him Preacher and sometimes that was the only word he would scrawl in the smudged hotel registers. Spring always found him back in Louisville because that was the town of his birth and because with the burgeoning of the ripe season upon the river he liked to feel his whole spirit come alive with holy rage and hatred of the spewing masses of harlots and whoremasters he saw in the crowded April night streets in that swarming river Sodom. He would pay his money and go into a burlesque show and sit in the front row watching it all and rub the knife in his pocket with sweating fingers; seething in a quiet convulsion of outrage and nausea at all that ocean of undulating womanhood beyond the lights; his nose growing full of it: the choking miasma of girl smell and cheap perfume and stogie smoke and man smell and the breath of ten-cent mountain corn liquor souring in the steamy air; and he would stumble out at last into the enchanted night, into the glitter and razzle-dazzle of the midnight April street, his whole spirit luminous with an enraptured and blessed fury at the world these whores had made. That night in his dollar hotel room he might crouch beneath the guttering blossom of the Welsbach flame above the brass bed and count his resources and think to himself: Time to go out again and preach the word? Or is it time for another one? Is it time yet, Lord? Time for another widow? Say the word, Lord! Just say the word and I'm on my way!

And then like as not he would hear God's voice in the haunted, twitching boards of the hotel hallway; above the giggle and whisper and soft, wet fumble on the creaking bedsprings of the room beyond his, the gagging of the drunkard over in the bathroom by the stair well. Down in the night, in the Louisville streets, the April tinkle of the cheap music and the coarse night voices were not loud enough to drown out his God's clear command.

Once he had nearly been caught, though it is not likely that he knew how close he had come to it nor would have cared much had he known. He had been solicited by a prostitute along Frey's Alley in Charleston, West Virginia, and had followed her into the house and, smirking at the madam, paid his money and followed the girl up the steps past the roaring, rollicking player piano, and when the girl had lain back upon the worn gray spread and wearily awaited him, her jaws not relinquishing even for this brief business the gum between her teeth, he had merely stood watching, smiling, his eyes alight with the Glory of God.

Well?

Well what?

Don't you want it?

He said nothing, his head bent a little, one eyelid fluttering almost closed, listening, harking. God was trying to say something and he could not quite hear the words.

You paid your money. Don't you want it now? Say, what *do* you want, mister?

He had his fingers around the bone hasp and he was already fumbling for the button that held back the swift blade but God spoke to him then and said there wasn't any sense in bothering. There were too many of *them*. He couldn't kill a world.

But the knife had been halfway out of his pocket before God had finished speaking and the girl's short, hoarse screams had brought a big Negro handyman up the steps and he had been kicked and beaten and thrown out into the alley among the cats and garbage pails. Another night he had taken a young mountain whore drunk to his room in a cheap boardinghouse in Cincinnati

and she had passed out naked on the bed and he had taken out
the knife and stood by the bed with it unopened in his hand for
a while, looking at her and waiting for the Word and when it did
not come he pressed the button and the steel tongue licked out,
and, bending by the bed on the worn rug, he delicately scratched
a cross in the girl's belly beneath the navel and left there with that
brand so frail and faint upon the flesh that it did not even bleed;
and when she woke in the morning alone she did not even notice
it, so lovingly and with so practiced and surgical a precision had
he wrought it there.

The faces troubled him at night; not with remorse but with
self-rebuke at the imprecision of his arithmetic. Were there
twelve? Or was it six? Was this the face of the gaunt, boney
India Coverley from Steubenville or was it the other one—her
ancient, senile sister Ella that he had had to kill because she
had surprised him burying the old woman in the peach orchard
behind the barn. The faces ran together like the years; like the
long rides in the yellow-lit railroad coaches through the clicking
river midnights as he wandered from town to town. Lord, won't
I never settle down? Lord, won't you never say the word that my
work is done? Another one, Lord? All right, Lord!

And he would plunge into the lonely-hearts column again or
search the faces at a church picnic and when he came to the right
one, the one the Lord had meant for him all along—he *knew*.
Then they arrested him for stealing that Essex in Parkersburg and
sent him to the state penitentiary for a year and the fools never
even knew that the pair of cheap cotton gloves in the glove com-
partment had belonged to the one that everyone had made such
a fuss about because it was in all the papers: that Stone woman
in Canton, Ohio—the fool with the two children that had been
so much trouble because the girl had been so fat and hard to
manage on the stairs that night. But the Lord sure knew what he
was doing, all right. He had sent him to the state penitentiary

to this very cell because a man named Ben Harper was going to die. A man with a widow in the making and ten thousand dollars hidden somewhere down-river. Maybe this would be the end of it, then. Maybe after this one the Lord would say: Well, that's enough, Harry Powell. Rest now, faithful servant. Build thou a temple to praise my Holy Name.

He was tired. Sometimes he cried in his sleep he was so tired. It was the killing that made him tired. Sometimes he wondered if God really understood. Not that the Lord minded about the killings. Why, His Book was full of killings. But there *were* things God did hate—perfume-smelling things—lacy things—things with curly hair—whore things. Preacher would think of these and his hands at night would go crawling down under the blankets till the fingers named Love closed around the bone hasp of the knife and his soul rose up in flaming glorious fury. He was the dark angel with the sword of a Vengeful God. Paul is choking misogynistic wrath upon Damascus Road.

The day they came and took Ben Harper up to the death house Preacher stood screaming after him, his knuckles white around the shaking bars of the cell.

Ben! Ben, boy! It ain't too late, boy! Where, Ben? Where, boy?

But Ben Harper did not call back. The game was over.

Bart the hangman lighted his pipe. He stood puffing and waited as the footsteps of his comrade rang closer down the cold, wet bricks of the prison courtyard. The other said nothing while Bart stamped his feet and shivered. They looked at one another for a moment and then moved through the prison gate into the deserted street. They walked in silence under the winter trees.

Any trouble?

No.

He was a cool one—that Harper, said the man in the old brown army coat. Never broke—game to the end.

He carried on some, said Bart the hangman. Kicked.

But he never told, did he? said the other.

No.

What do you figure he done with it?

I never talked with him, said Bart. But I figure he was a feller that wasn't used to killin'—a good sort at heart, what I mean to say. I figure he done it and what with being shot in the shoulder and half scared to death at what he had done he just went to pieces and throwed it all in the river.

Ten thousand dollars! In the river? In times like this, Bart? Aw, come off it! Ain't no man ever got that scared!

Well maybe not. But whatever he done with it he took the secret with him up there tonight when we dropped him.

It began to rain suddenly, like tears: a soft, thick river rain that blew in gusts from the dark hills around the valley. Bart the hangman and the other prison guard hurried up Jefferson Avenue toward their homes at the edge of the town.

They say he left a woman and two kids, said the man in the army coat.

I never heard, said the hangman, bitterly. My old woman's sister knowed the girl's mother, continued the other. She was a Bailey from Upshur County. Good country folks, Mabel says. And for that matter I never heard nothin' ornery about his folks. Lived in Marshall County for three generations. River folks.

The hangman hurried on a little, uncomfortable at this discussion of the family and affairs of the man he had just killed. And yet he knew of no reasonable way of silencing the man in the army coat.

Wonder what gets into a feller to make him do such a thing. I declare, this Goddamned depression has turned up the undersides of some mighty respectable folks, Bart! Yes, Yes.

I was talking to Arch Woodruff here a while back. He's captain over in that new block where they first had Harper. Arch says his cellmate was a short-termer from down in Wood County—feller folks call Preacher. Arch says that Goddamned preacher liked to talked poor Harper's ear off—hounded him night and day to get him to spill it—what he done with all that money!—kept hollering after him even when he was up in Death Row.

He paused and thought about it a while. Bart moved on through the rain in silence.

I be dogged if I wouldn't take a sniff after that money myself if I had me a lead to go on! Well anyways this short-termer—this preacher feller—he's gettin' out next month. I reckon he'll go huntin' after it with the rest of the hounds.

How about his missus? muttered the hangman. Don't she know nothin'?

Nary nothin'! cried the man in the army coat. He wouldn't tell a livin', mortal soul!

Can't say as I blame him.

Why?

Well just look where it put him tonight—all that money!

They parted at the corner and the hangman walked wearily up the wooden steps under the naked winter sycamores toward the cottage with the light in the parlor window. His wife looked up from her darning when he came in and rising, moved toward the kitchen.

I hope your supper ain't dried up, Bart, she said. I'll go heat up the coffee.

Bart was hungry as a wolf. It always shamed his soul: the vast and gnawing hunger that consumed him the nights after hangings. He hung his wet coat and cap on the antler in the hallway and tiptoed up the stairs to the bathroom to wash up. He could not remember whether he had washed his hands that night after work. At any rate, they seemed cleaner as the bitter, lemony smell of the glycerine soap touched his nostrils and he dried them briskly on the coarse towel. Through the open doorway to the bedroom he could see the sleeping forms of the two children on the big brass bed by the window. He was very quiet as he tiptoed into their room and stared down at the yellow curls of the two little girls asleep on the long bolster. It had stopped raining now and a cold winter's moon had moved into the night's arena. The pale light shone on the sleeping faces of the children. Gently, Bart the hangman adjusted the bright quilt which covered them, pulling it down an inch or two so that the edge of the quilt would not cover their mouths, so that the crisp white sheets would not touch their throats.

Now eat! cried his wife when he sat at the table and tugged his napkin from the thick silver ring which bore his name. It's been waitin' since ten o'clock.

Bart sat for a moment staring at the napkin before he tucked it into his stiff collar and seized the fork.

Mother. Sometimes I think it might be better for us all if I was to quit my job as guard and get my old job back at the mine!

The gray-haired woman sat back suddenly in the straight chair and laid two fingers alongside her pale lips. It was a dread thought.

Yes mom, he said, with his mouth full of the boiled cabbage. I sometimes wish I was back under the hill at Benwood.

And leave me a widow after another blast like the one in '24? Not on your life, old mister!

He ate in silence, chewing his food slowly and heavily, his face clouded over with speculation.

I don't wish to be no widow! cried his wife again. With them two growin' kids to raise!

No woman does, he said.

After a moment he rose and went to the pump and bent, searching for something.

Where's the laundry soap, Mother? I forgot to wash up.

Three weeks after Ben Harper's hanging Walt Spoon gave Willa a job waiting on tables and counter at his little ice-cream parlor at Cresap's Landing. The job paid five dollars a week plus meals. The Spoons needed no help. It was a kindness. The first morning Willa left for work she fed the children their breakfast and told John there was lunch in the pantry—corn-bread and a stone pitcher of cold milk and some leftover sausage. The children watched at the window as Willa walked the short stretch of river road to the Landing. John was gravely and silently dubious of the entire business.

John, can we get candy at Mister Spoon's?

No.

Why?

We ain't got no pennies is why. And besides Mom don't want us hangin' around when she's working.

Oh.

Come on, Pearl, he said patiently. Get your hat and coat.

Where we goin', John?

Out of doors.

Pearl scampered off to the hall closet to get her things. John, dressed and ready, stood waiting for her return. Pearl stood patiently while he buttoned up her ragged brown coat and tucked her silly brown curls into the little goblin's cap. Pearl clutched her doll Jenny throughout and snuffled wearily with an old winter's cold until John fetched out his own handkerchief and tended to her nose.

Now, he said properly. That ought to keep you warm. Come on, Pearl!

He paused on his way to the kitchen door and glanced out the window, up the river road to Jander's Livery Stable. The picture of the hanging man had been washed away in a warm March rain on a night weeks before and yet he could never look at the red bricks of the old lichen-stained wall without hearing the chant again. The picture was gone from the stone and no one sang the song at him on the road but still he could hear it. Though, quite providentially, he was vague in his thinking about what really *had* happened to his father. There was the feed-store calendar in the kitchen, above the pump, and the red circle of lipstick that Willa had made around that number, that day, and that crimson eye had fixed them all for days until Willa, in tears one night, had torn the month away and burned it solemnly in the stove. In the red circle was a knowledge that he did not fully know. It had to do with the blue men who had taken his dad away that day. It had to do with the hanging man on the red brick wall by Jander's and with the song the children sang.

Hing Hang Hung! he hummed softly and shivered when he opened the kitchen door and the March air, piercing and drenched with river cold, swept among them on the threshold. The morning air was thin with winter—sour as lemon. The smoke of morning chimneys rose from the stacks of the houses down at Cresap's Landing and hung for a moment before curling under the gray sky and dragged to earth again like cheap fur collars on old coats. John and Pearl stumped silently along up the dirt road, aimless before the long morning.

Howdy, youngins.

John's eyes turned and stared across the street. It was old Walt Spoon, stamping on the stoop of his ice-cream parlor and blowing on the fingers of one hand while the other waved two green lollipops at them. Through the window, under the pale flower of gaslight by the soda fountain, John saw Willa sipping a cup of hot morning cocoa. He caught Pearl's hand and moved off again, pretending that he had seen neither Walt Spoon nor Willa nor the green lollipops. Now the children paused before the window of Miz Cunningham's secondhand store. John made no sound. Because there was no sound in the world that one might sensibly make while staring through this particular window. For there was no word for total wonder and one could only breathe lightly and in silence against the sorcerer's glass and watch the faint, tiny cumulus of breath vapor come and go upon the pane.

What's that? What are you looking at, John?

He said nothing, had not really heard.

John? Are you going to buy it, John?

But she would not have understood even if he had tried to tell her and so he continued to stare through the window into the dusty shelf where the silver pocket watch lay, winking dully among the gimcracks and buttons and fake diamond stickpins and the old Bryan campaign badges. Then, abruptly, there was a motion among the vast panoply of miserable and tired coats and vests and pants that served as backdrop to the window shelf and without further warning this gray curtain parted and the cunning and dissipated face of an old woman appeared and blinked down at the children in the street. Behind the winking lenses of her bent and crooked spectacles the face of Miz Cunningham was that of an ancient and querulous turkey hen. Her dirty hands fluttered in appalling gaiety to the children and then disappearing momentarily she scurried around to the door which presently opened with the single cry of a little bell, like a ragged golden bird.

Ahhhh! If it ain't the poor little Harper lambs!

John said nothing. Pearl was pleased and put her forefinger coyly to her lips.

And how is your poor, poor mother this sad winter?

She's up at Spoon's, said John, quite cold and matter-of-fact about it, yet uncomfortable lest some of the old woman's coarse and maudlin sentiment brush off on his fingers like the greasy, gray dust of certain miller moths. He let his eyes stray again to the wonderful silver watch.

Hing Hang Hung! the words rang faintly through his day-dreams like echoes of Miz Cunningham's tart little doorbell. Then he looked again at the old woman herself. Why, she was really quite wonderful—this old fat woman! In the end, she got her hands on nearly everything in the world! Just look at her window! There by the pair of old overshoes were Jamey Hankins's ice skates. There was old Walt Spoon's elk's tooth. There—his mother's own wedding ring! There was a world in that window of this remarkable old woman. And it was probable that when Miz Cunningham like an ancient barn owl fluttered and flapped to earth at last, they would take her away and pluck her open and find her belly lined with fur and feathers and the tiny mice skulls of myriad dreams.

I'll just bet my two little lambs would like a nice hot cup of coffee! cried the old woman, fidgeting at her iron spectacles with three fat fingers. Eh, now?

I don't care, said John gravely.

Willa never served them coffee at home; partly because it would stunt their growth and partly because it was so dear at the store.

Miz Cunningham's kitchen, like her show window, was like the nest of a thieving black crow. Old clothes hanging on the water pipes and stove door handles. Old shoes in boxes by the door. Old hats in apple baskets beneath the window sill. And because old hats, old shoes, and old clothes bear forever the stance and shape and bulge of the mortal flesh that wore them once the house of the old woman was a place of reflective ghosts, of elbows and bosoms and shoulders long gone into the dust or wandered away down Peacock Alley to count their pennies on Poverty's own lean palm. John and Pearl sat moon-eyed at the littered table while Miz Cunningham fetched her blue-speckled coffeepot and poured them each half-cupfuls.

Now! she exclaimed heartily, settling down for a bit of dandelion wine for her stomach and a breath of gossip for her dusty ears. Tell me how your poor, poor mother is enduring.

John shrugged.

I don't know, he smiled thinly.

Ah, now! I mean about the poor father and all. Ah, poor little lambs! The Lord tends you both these days.

At this poetic outburst the old face screwed suddenly awry, one eye twitched as water appeared above the rheumy lid, trembled, and trickled in unabashed emotion down the sagging, powdered cheek.

There now, she snuffled, rising gruffly and scratching off to the pantry again for her fruit jar of summer provender against winter's griefs. There now, my pets. I'm all right. It's all over in a minute. It's nothing! It's just that it tears the heart out of a body's very breast to see young lambs fatherless and that pretty mother widowed at thirty. Ah, and I knowed your dad. Yessirree, my lambikins! I knowed him like my own. Many and many is the night he sat right yonder on that hair trunk by the stove and drank coffee with my own dear, late-departed Clyde.

John did not listen as the old woman's voice rose in anguished retrospect. He thought again of the watch in the window. It had twelve black numbers on its moon face and there was magic to that. For these were numbers that were not really numbers at all but letters like in words. He shivered at the possibilities of such untold magic. But now Miz Cunningham's hen voice came picking its yellow bill through the dream that covered him.

Has the cat got your tongue, boy? She smiled, dreadfully.

Pardon, ma'am?

I said didn't they never find out what Ben Harper done with all that money he stole?

She grimaced and squinted in cunning speculation as if she were bargaining for a pretty gold pin.

Poor, poor Ben! Gracious me, such a lot of money he took that day from poor dead Mister Smiley! And to think that when they caught him—why, there wasn't so much as a penny of it to be seen! Now what do you make of that? Eh, boy?

John sighed. He stood up and took Pearl by the hand.

Pearl and me, he said. We have to go.

Eh? What's say? What? Why, you ain't even touched your coffee!

John gathered into his fingers the soft little pads of Pearl's hand and led her back the way they had come, through the mournful forest of dangling coats and through the dusty beaded curtains and empty gray dresses with ghosts of perfume about them like the memory of old and far-wandering loves. Away in the dusty shadows shone the door, the light of winter in the street. Behind him John could hear the old woman wheezing and snuffling among the fusty garments in his wake.

Great day in the morning! she exclaimed. For a boy who don't know nothin' about that money you sure pick up and run right quick when a body—

He squeezed Pearl's small fingers till she whined in pain and pulled them free and ran ahead, hugging her old loose doll tight against her. At the doorway threshold Miz Cunningham could contain herself no longer. The fat, ring-crusted fingers clamped tight on John's quaking shoulders and swung him around full face.

If you was to tell *me!* the old voice croaked, all guile and oil gone from it now. Why, then there wouldn't be no one to know but us three, boy! Eh, now? Do you know where the money's hid? Did your dad tell you where? Does your mother know? Eh, boy? Did you see where it was hid?

No! cried John, and twisted free.

The iron bell uttered its harsh and broken cry and the chill March air flowed among them as they hurried out onto the road again. The old owl face squinted again from among the dusty sleeves in the window racks. The children wandered off down Peacock Alley toward the river.

She's bad, observed Pearl. I don't like Miz Cunningham.

John stumped on ahead, quaking with fright.

John! John, wait for me!

He stopped by the corner under the gun and locksmith's shop where the great wooden key creaked hoarsely over the pavement at every whim of river wind. John took out his handkerchief and held it again for the little girl to blow.

Hing Hang Hung! See what the hangman done! Hung Hang Hing! See the robber swing! Hing Hang Hung! Now my song is done!

Was it the children singing in Peacock Alley that morning in Cresap's Landing?—the song of the hanging man? No, he knew then, it was the rusty chant of the swinging key above his head. Yet in a flash he had caught Pearl's hand and begun walking her swiftly up toward the river road and the solace of home. It had begun to snow and the wind grieved in the stark river trees—a wind like a moaning song—a wind like a hunter's horn.

River dusk drifted like a golden smoke among the trees of Cresap's Landing. At six Walt Spoon fetched a kitchen match from his vest and lighted the two gas lamps behind the marble counter. There were no customers in the place now but when the first movie let out at the Orpheum two or three couples would drift in for some of Icey's home-made vanilla cream. Now Walt heard footsteps echoing up the bricks of the sidewalk and turned. It was Willa, her nose cherry-red with cold.

Git them two kids fed and bedded down did ye? cried Walt.

Yes, Mr. Spoon, she smiled.

Better go back to the kitchen and let Icey give you a cup of hot coffee!

All right. Thanks, Mr. Spoon.

He followed her with his gaze, wondering what kindly thing one might say to a woman whose husband had been hanged for murder. She was so remote; going about, doing her work well and yet so hidden away from everything that happened around her. He wanted to tell her that it would all turn out for the best; that it hadn't really mattered what had happened; that each cloud had a silver lining. He followed her miserably to the kitchen and watched from the doorway as she helped herself to coffee at the stove.

Here, honey, scolded Icey. Let me git you that. Set down and give your feet a rest.

Icey Spoon was fat and pleasant. Most of her sixty years had been spent cooking good things: tasting pots of boiling fudge, sampling fingerfuls of cookie batter or thick ice cream on the wooden paddles of the old crank freezer. Her ideas of the world and of its people were as simple and even and unchanging as the little pastry hearts her cookie cutter made.

Willa! she snapped cheerfully. What you need is a little meat on your bones.

Willa smiled wanly. She sipped the black, scalding coffee in the thick steamboat china cup. Icey stood before her with fat, freckled fingers smoothing her apron. After glaring at Willa in mounting disapproval for a moment she shuffled off to the ice cream freezers. Presently she returned with a heaping dish of the chocolate cream and set it firmly at Willa's elbow.

There! A dish of that two or three times a day and you'll commence to shape into something a feller might want to look twice at.

Willa thanked her and glanced uneasily at the old woman's eyes, knowing well what it was all leading up to.

Honey, said Icey Spoon, waving her husband away from the kitchen and settling her thick, dimpled elbows firmly on the table, there is certain plain facts of life that adds up. Just like two plus two makes four.

Willa kept her peace, not lifting her eyes, knowing that part of her burden as a widow was to endure such preachments.

And one of them is this, Icey went on. No woman is good enough to raise growin' youngsters alone. The Lord meant that job for two. Are you listenin' to me, now, honey?

Yes.

Now, then! There ain't so many single fellers nor widowers in Cresap's Landing that a girl can afford to get too choosey. There's Charley Blankensop—he drinks. There's Bill Showacre—and he don't amount to much except doin' card tricks at socials but he is kind and he don't touch a drop and the old pap's got some farmland.

Icey, I don't want a husband.

Want nothin'! cried Icey, slamming her palm on the table till the sugar bowl chattered. It's not a matter of wantin' or not wantin'! You're no spring chicken with hot britches, Willa Harper. You're a grown woman widowed with two little youngins and it's them you should be thinkin' about.

Well, yes. Yes, I know that, Icey.

And I don't want you gettin' the idea that neither me nor Walt is buttin' in! the old woman added, pursing her lips and smoothing the tablecloth with swift outward strokes of her fingers. You're welcome to work here and even bring them kids in to live here if you've a mind to. But it's a man you need in the house, Willa Harper!

John—the boy, said Willa. He minds the littlest—Pearl. He takes awful good care of her, Icey.

Mindin' girls ain't no fit business for a growin' boy, neither.

Willa shrugged and looked away.

It's not so easy, she said softly. Finding someone—

I know! Ah, Lord, I know! cried the other woman, rising and sniffling her nose against the heel of her hand. Ah, men is such fools!

Not every man, Willa continued, her eyes grave with her thoughts, wants the widow of a man who—

—A man who done somethin' ornery and foolish! snapped Icey. Ben Harper warn't no common robber. Why, I knowed him as well as I knowed my own five boys and I'd have put him up alongside any one of them. It's these hard, mean times that ruins men, Willa.

Willa stared at the palms of her hands.

I never really understood Ben, she said. He was always think-ing things I never knew—wanting things I never knew about. He wasn't a bad man, Icey—he just wanted more than his share, I reckon.

Icey's gingham-blue eyes squinted shrewdly as she bent and pinched Willa lightly on the arm.

There hain't a one of them, she whispered hoarsely, that's walked into that Moundsville bank that ain't been tempted to do the same thing Ben done! And don't you forget it! Lordy, there has been times during this depression when I was afraid of what my own Walt would turn his hand to next!

She sat suddenly, subsided, hugging her fat arms against her bosom and reflecting upon the evil season.

That boy John, smiled Willa. He's so much like his dad it just naturally scares me sometimes, Icey. So serious about everything! He's took his dad's death hard, Icey.

Hmmph! He's took it like a little man if you was to ask me.

Willa scooped a tiny mountain in the spilled sugar by the bowl and her hand trembled. He knows something, she said in a low voice. It scares me, Icey!

How?

There's something strange—He knows something!

Knows what, honey?

Like there was something still between him—and Ben, said the girl and shivered as the river wind said something behind the window and a boat blew low on the river.

Between him and his dad?

Yes, said Willa. Sometimes I think about Ben lying there in that little plot of ground between my ma and pa and him being dead all these weeks and then I look into the boy's face and it's almost as if—

Off in the parlor they could hear Walt cranking the Victrola and waiting impatiently for the couples to come in for ice cream after the first show. Willa was as white as the linen on Icey's spotless kitchen table.

—As if him and Ben—as if they had a pact, said the girl at last.

About which?

About that money, Icey.

That money! snorted the old woman, pouring them both more coffee. A curse and an abomination before God! I hope Ben throwed it in the river wrapped around a cobblestone.

But he didn't, said the girl.

Pshaw!

I'm right sure of it, Icey. It's hid somewhere.

Well if it is—I don't want to know where! That money's caused enough sin and cursedness—

—And I think little John knows where it is, said Willa.

What? Great day in the morning! That child? Fiddlesticks!

Yes, Icey. I may be wrong. But I think Ben told him.

Then why—if he told the boy—why not you—his own wife?

Willa smiled sheepishly and plucked at a loose thread in the tablecloth.

He never thought I was fit to know, she said.

Fiddlesticks, now! Did he say that, now?

The girl nodded.

At the prison? Did you ask him when you visited him there?

Yes. I begged with him to tell. I told him it wasn't just for me—it was for them two kids as well. I told him that.

And what did he say to that?

He said if I got my hands on that money I would just go to hell headlong. He said I was a Bailey and there wasn't ever a Bailey or Harper either one that knowed the worth of a five-cent piece and he said there wasn't a one of them ever got their hands on money that didn't drag himself and all his kin down the fancy road to perdition.

Well, now, I never!

Icey pursed her mouth, considering it all.

But what did he say about them kids of his? What did he figure you to raise them on?

I asked him that, Icey.

And what did he have to say to that?

He said that money was where it wouldn't ever hurt nobody no more and then he shut up like a clam and wouldn't talk about it any more!

But you think the boy knows where it's hid?

Willa nodded and her eyes brimmed and filled.

Icey! Honest to God, I don't want that money! I just wish it was gone somewhere—lost forever—gone to the bottom of the river! When I think about its still being anywheres around us— it just makes me feel like folks is starin'—wonderin'—sniffin' around for it like dogs. Like somethin' awful was going to happen to me and them kids because of it!

Pshaw! Ben was talkin' out of his mind, Willa. The strain of it all! That money is rottin' at the bottom of the river right this very minute.

Willa did not answer, finishing her coffee in slow gulps while old Icey grumbled and speculated by the stove, rattling her pots and skillets angrily about.

And that's why I say, she exclaimed presently, that the sooner you get a man into that house the better, Willa! There's so much can happen to a widowed woman and two youngsters.

A glance at the girl told her that this final remark had frightened her even more. Icey's face lit up and she cracked her palms together sharply.

Ouija! she cried.

What?

The board! We'll just ask old Ouija where Ben hid that money.

No!

Willa's lips were trembling now, the color of cold ashes.

All right, then. We'll just ask Ouija about that man—the one you're going to meet.

Oh, Icey, I'd rather not.

Just you set down there, Willa, and mind your manners. I'll go fetch the board. You can mock if you will but me and Walt has found out more from Ouija than a body ever gets from them tea leaves and cards.

Willa sat solemnly, with her legs pressed tight together, listening as Icey's slippers shuffled off into the parlor after the board. She was back in a moment and slapped it on the table and sat down facing it, across from Willa. Walt came to the doorway to watch and stood puffing thoughtfully on his cob pipe. Icey's face grew solemn and properly awed as she rested the tips of her fingers on the little arrowshaped pointer.

It takes a spell for Ouija to get to workin' right, explained Icey, opening one eye to glance at Willa. And don't talk neither. It gets the spirits nervous.

Willa's nerves curled in her flesh as Icey addressed the beyond. Ouija! Please to give us the name of Willa's next husband.

Willa felt the sweat gather upon her quaking thighs. It seemed as if this were to tempt old ghosts to speak—to conjure from the blackness of that winter night the face of a hanged man who would tell her again with his ruined, strangled mouth that she was not fit—that she was weak—that she would drag them all down if she knew. Now the room was stone-silent but for the thick bubbling of the teakettle and the faint cold whisper of river wind against the sills.

Ah! Ah! There! whispered Icey. See, now!

And the little pointer scratched sharply and jumped beneath her fingers. Willa shut her eyes and pressed the trembling lids with the tips of her fingers. She listened to the dry little feet of the pointer scrabbling slowly across the board, spelling out the letters. Icey's sonorous voice called them as they came. C—L—O—

Willa thought: Yes, he was right! The money is bloodied and cursed and it would take us all to hell headlong. Because we were born in sin and in sin we have lived and God makes us suffer so we can be free!

C—L—O—T—H! Cloth! cried Icey. Now, Walt, whatever do you make of that? Cloth! What kind of sense does that make?

It's a word, said Walt, taking the stem of his pipe from between his long brown teeth. That's plain enough.

Well, sure it's a word! We all know that! But the question was: Give us the name of Willa's next husband. Now cloth ain't no answer to that.

Well, now, hold on here for just a while, said the man. That might signify a lot of things.

He sat solemnly at the table and regarded the board, scowling.

Icey reached out to pat Willa's cold knee and then winked.

Walt's right good at understandin' Ouija, honey. Just you wait, now.

—It might mean Willa was to meet a drummer, said Walt loudly. A drummer that sold bolts of yard goods.

Why, sure! *Cloth!*

But now Icey pursed her lips and frowned.

Well, shoot! A drummer ain't no bargain for a husband!

Willa smiled and shrugged.

I don't know any drummers, she said softly. What drummer would want to settle down with me?

Just you wait! laughed Icey. We'll try again another night. Ouija's mighty good at lookin' ahead, honey.

Now they heard the front door squeak out in the ice cream parlor and the soft laughter of young voices.

Gracious! Them's customers! cried Icey, springing to her feet. Better go tend them, honey.

Willa hurried off and took the orders while Walt put a record on the Victrola, and throughout the next hour they kept busy as other customers came and went and Walt stood by cranking and changing the records and Icey filled orders for sandwiches and coffee in the kitchen. By ten o'clock the town had gone to sleep. Outside the snow drifted past in big flakes and the dark wind had fallen. Willa sat alone by the cash box until Walt came and told her she could go for the night. He and Icey stood watching her move slowly down Peacock Alley toward the river road.

Poor, poor little thing, mumbled Icey, her handkerchief balled and pressed to her lips.

Walt said nothing as he moved about downstairs, locking windows. After a bit he came and stood beside her, staring into the dark that had swallowed up the tiny figure on the road at last.

Poor child, Icey said again, shaking her head. I wonder what will ever become of her. It's a story sad enough to beat them picture shows.

Because a pipeline ran through the Harper yard the gas company gave them a free lamp on a wooden post—a big box with a roof like a birdhouse with glass sides and a perpetual flame within. It stood by the great oak at the road's edge and when the wind tossed the branches of the tree the light from the gas lamp made pictures on the wall of the children's bedroom. The twisted, barren winter branches tossed stiffly in the golden light and yet with a curious grace, like the fingers of old men spinning tales, and John, lying snug in his bed beside the little girl, shut his left eye and squinted through the lashes at these weaving phantoms of shadow and light. There was a black horse prancing—lifting its feet to the winter galaxies. And now as the wind changed there came a three-legged peddler roistering to the mad wind's song. And now a brave soldier appeared; then a merry clown with toothpick legs.

John?

Yes.

Is Mom home?

Yes.

Is she in bed, John?

Yes. Go to sleep, Pearl.

All right, John. Good night.

Good night. Sleep tight, Pearl! Don't let the bedbugs bite!

The little girl lay still for a bit, breathing thoughtfully into the matted wig of her doll.

John?

Yes?

What's bedbugs?

Hush up, Pearl! It's time you was asleep!

She lay still a moment more and then commenced scratching furiously and sat upright in bed.

Does bedbugs tickle when they walk, John?

Hush, Pearl. Go to sleep. That's just a joke when you say, Don't let the bedbugs bite. There ain't no such a thing. Now go to sleep!

Pearl watched the whirling pictures in the light the yard lamp made on the wallpaper.

Tell me a story, John. She sighed, her eyes lost in the fancies of the dancing shadow branches. John lay still and squinted his other eye.

All right. If you'll lay back down and keep the covers on you so's you won't catch your death of cold.

Pearl shot down under the sheets again and tucked her legs up tight against her breast, hugging the doll and waiting for the story to start.

Once upon a time—there was a rich king—

What's a rich king, John?

Never mind! You'll see what it means directly, Pearl. There was this rich king and he had a son and a daughter and they all lived in a castle over in Africa. Well, one day this king got carried away by bad men—

Pearl loathed the story now. But still she was silent, thankful enough to hear any story at all; comforted by the droning voice muffled beneath the quilt.

—And before he got carried off he told this son to kill anyone that tried to steal their gold. Well it wasn't long before them same bad men come back to get the gold—you see they missed that on the first trip—and these bad men—

The blue men? whispered Pearl, in a perfect faint of dread.

John stopped telling the story. He turned his head away from the dancing things and shut his eyes against the fresh, wind-smelling pillow.

John! What happened to the king's gold? Did the blue men—

Go to sleep, Pearl! I forgit the rest of that story.

He shivered silently under the warm covers, his fingernails digging into his palms. Pearl sighed and put her thumb in her mouth. Presently she took the thumb out again and blinked at the doll on the pillow beside her.

Good night, Miz Jenny, she said softly. Don't let the bedbugs bite.

And she fell asleep. But John lay still awake, heeding on the winter wind the blowing bawl of a steamboat whistle upriver at the head of the Devil's Elbow where the channel straightened and ran up straight through the Narrows. The dark tumbling wind was rollicking with river ghosts. John thought of some of the tales old Uncle Birdie Steptoe used to spin on the deck of his wharfboat on dreaming summer afternoons: of the dark river men—gone now and cursed and lost in the deep water's running. Simon Girty riding with the Shawnees against his own people; the soldier Mason running with the devil Harper to ravage the river from Cave-in-Rock clean to the sugar coast; Cornstalk and Logan and the young chiefs in the black buffalo robes. Old Uncle Birdie carried the tales down through the river years from a lost time, tales spun round the smoking oil lamps of a thousand wharfboats from Pittsburgh to the Delta. John rose from his pillow when he heard the thick, even breath of his sleeping sister. Slipping from bed John tiptoed across the frosty boards of the floor and fetched his broken cap pistol from the pocket of his jacket. For a moment his own shadow loomed vast and threatening in the golden arena on the wallpaper. The small boy scowled, clenched his chattering teeth, and brandished the little gun.

I ain't scared of you none! he whispered hoarsely and made a fierce devil's face at the shadow. And he watched in fascination as it mocked him. The shadow hunched down when John hunched down, it twisted when he twisted, and it bent grimacing to one side when he did. Blue man! Take that!

His mouth shaped the words as his finger pressed the trigger of the broken toy and in his mind the wonderful roar of powder filled the silence. But the shadow did not fall. When John lifted the pistol above his head and danced on his numb white toes the shadow danced and waved his pistol, too. John clicked the toy pistol once more, a *coup de grace,* and stumped grimly back to the bed. Now the shadow man was dead. He and his kind would come no more to drag the king from his castle by the sea. Beside the body of his sleeping sister John snuggled his face into the cold, sweet pillow and pressed the toy gun underneath where he could get at it in a moment. And then something in the wind's dark voice caused him to open one eye again to the square of yellow light on the wall. The shadow man: it was smaller than before but it was still there. He pondered it a moment, lying quite still, his heart thundering in his throat. Yes, to be sure it was the shadow of a man in the yellow square of light from the yard lamp: a very silent, motionless man with a narrow-brimmed hat and still, straight arms. John's tongue grew thick as a mitten at the growing dread within him.

I ain't scared of you, he whispered to the shadow man and the wind rattled the window like pressing hands.

The shadow could not really be there. John was not there to make it. And yet there it was: the neatest little shadow man in the world and he could see it unmistakably and it was not make-believe like the clown and the peddler and the prancing horse that the branches made. John slipped out of bed again and crept to the window. He pressed his nose to the icy pane and stared across the deserted snowy yard to the place where the single yellow flame bloomed in the glass box like a golden fish in a bowl of light. Then he saw the man by the roadside. The man stood in silence, motionless, staring speculatively toward the house like a traveler seeking a night's lodging.

Go away, man! whispered John, his flesh gathering for a paroxysm of trembling.

Off down the river the eleven-o'clock train of the Ohio River Division of the Baltimore and Ohio screamed twice and hurried off panting among the bottom farms. There was no regular depot at Cresap's Landing and often the late train from Moundsville stopped at the crossroads to let off travelers or drummers to make their way as best they could the half mile into Cresap's Landing and a room at Mamie Ernest's boardinghouse.

I ain't scared! I ain't scared! whispered John and saw after a moment that his dread had been unnecessary. It was really a most plain-looking man. He stood shivering for a moment longer in his cheap gray suit and his old gray hat and even as John watched he moved back into the shadows again and off up the road to Cresap's Landing. Now the old winter branches made the dancing horse again on the golden square and the clown with toothpick legs frolicked on the mad wind. John crept back into the bed and huddling close to the warm body of Pearl thought carefully to himself: Just a little gray man in a little gray suit and a little gray hat and he's gone. A pleasant man, too, one would guess. For even now as he wandered up the road for Mamie Ernest's he was lifting his high, clear tenor to the cold night and singing a sweet old gospel tune.

Willa said he was a dirty old man and used to forbid John to go there. But to the boy the old wharfboat at the landing seemed the most perfect kind of home. It wallowed against the lapping slope of the shore—a crumbling houseboat scarcely better than the cheap floating shacks of the shantyboat trash down the shore under the willows at the edge of Jason Lindsay's meadow. Willa had taken Pearl to work with her that morning and John had a few hours to spend as he chose. Uncle Birdie was just having morning coffee. When the old man spied John standing timidly on the bricks by the narrow gangplank he threw up his knotted hands and ran to the door.

Bless my soul if it hain't Ben Harper's boy John! Hop up, boy!

John smiled, and Uncle Birdie motioned him up the plank.

Come on in, boy, and have a good hot cup of coffee with me. Does your maw let you?

John's eyes fell.

By damn, it don't matter if she does or don't! We'll have ourselves a cup anyways. I say a feller ain't worth a hoot without his morning coffee. Hurry up, there, boy, and shut that door! It's cold enough to freeze the horns off a muley cow!

John crept into the narrow little cabin and sat on a salt box by the stove.

Now! cried the old man, fetching the coffeepot and pouring John's cup full. How you been? 'Deed, I hain't seen you for a coon's age, Johnny!

I been mindin' Pearl, said John.

Birdie cracked his old fist in his leathery palm.

Pshaw, now! Hain't it a caution what women will load onto a feller's shoulders when he ain't lookin'! Mindin' girls! Shoot! That hain't no job for a big feller like you!

Oh! said John promptly. I don't mind, Uncle Birdie. Pearl needs someone to mind her.

Well, now, yes, I reckon that's so. I reckon with your pap gone—that sorty makes you the man of the house, so to speak! 'Scuse me, Cap, while I sweeten up my coffee a little. A man of my years needs a little snort to get his boiler heated of a mornin'.

John watched as the old man reached under the bursting leather rocker in which he sat and fetching up a pint bottle of crystal liquid splashed generously into his coffee. He sipped it,

sucked his wet white mustaches for a moment, and then fixed
John with his twinkling blue eyes.

And how's your maw, Johnny?

Well she's fine. She's workin' up at Mr. Spoon's place now.

Go away, now! She is? By granny's, it hain't ever' boy in Cresap's Landing whose maw works in an ice-cream parlor! Bet she
can sneak you out a dish of tutti-frutti anytime you take a notion,
eh, Johnny?

Oh, no! She don't like me or Pearl hangin' around her at
work. She's took Pearl up there with her today but it's kind of
special.

And so you figured it was time you come down and paid old
Uncle Birdie a call, eh, boy?

John wriggled his cold toes in his shoes and moved closer to
the cherry-red woodstove. Beyond the dusty window the river
was flaked with shards of spring ice. The early thaw had begun
and in a month the cattails in the shallows would lift their brown
thumbs to test the first spring wind. John wandered to the window and stared at the half-sunken boat down the shore below
the landing.

Ain't nobody stole Dad's skiff, he observed softly.

Ain't nobody goin' to, neither! cried Uncle Birdie. Ain't
nobody hadn't better try! I keep my weather eye on them shantyboat trash down the shore. There hain't a one of them wouldn't
swipe that skiff if I was to let 'em. I figger another three–four
weeks the weather'll be fit for me to wade down and git her up
on the bank. Then I'll give her a good calkin' and a new paint
job and this summer I'll learn you how to lay as good a trotline as
ever your daddy did, boy.

John came alive at the prospect. He remembered the times
when his dad was home and on summer days that flashed with
dragonflies they had gone fishing for channel cats as far down
river as Middle Island Creek.

Ah! Look, boy! Looky yonder! cried Birdie, motioning up river through the windowpane. There comes the *Sarah T. Blake!*

A stern-wheeler had appeared small and white on the bend, trailing a dirty string of smoke up from her stacks to stain the pearly winter sky.

Ain't like the old times, Johnny, sighed Uncle Birdie, sloshing another helping of liquor into his morning coffee. Many's the forenoon I've cleared five big Pittsburgh packets at this very wharf.

John nodded gravely at the thought of these faded wonders.

Why just this mornin' at breakfast I was talkin' to the new boarder up at Mamie Ernest's and he—Daggone it, anyways, boy! I knowed I had somethin' to tell you and here it clean slipped my mind till just now. That new boarder! He knowed your dad!

John grew small and silent, crawling deep within himself, listening with every nerve of his body now.

Yessir! You see old Mamie's been sweet on me for years now and she gives me breakfast up at the boardinghouse ever' single mornin' and this very mornin' this stranger was here and we got to talkin' friendly-like and he said he knowed Ben Harper. Well sir, I piped right up and—

The blue men, said John.

Which? said Uncle Birdie. Why, no—he was a preacher and I'll swear to it. Anyways he wanted to know about you two little lambs—meanin' you and little Pearl—and he said he was just itchin' to do somethin' to help you folks out if there was anything at all you needed. Well now he was the kindliest-turned feller a body could ask for.

Where did he know Dad?

Birdie's face fell and he fumbled in his pants for his whittling stick and penknife.

Well, boy, I'll not hide the truth—it was up at Moundsville penitentiary when they had your dad there. This here feller was chaplain and that's how come he got to know Ben. But wait,

now! Don't get the idee he's one of these here glum-faced, fun-
killing old holiness preachers, now. Why, he was just as jokey and
pleasant as a Wheeling drummer with a easeful of samples.

John handed the coffee cup back to the old man unfinished.

I gotta go now, Uncle Birdie!

Aw, well, shucks now, boy! You just got here.

Well, I told Mom I'd be back for Pearl. She don't like us kids
hangin' around Mister Spoon's place too much.

All right then, Cap. But mind what I promised you now—
about the skiff. First nice day we git I'll haul her up and git to
work fixin' her up and then you and me'll go fishin'.

John did not turn back as he ran up the narrow board to the
landing and hurried against the wind that blew down Peacock
Alley from the hills. Behind him he heard the shrill whistle of
the little stern-wheeler as she passed Cresap's Landing in mid-
channel. Now as John rounded the corner by Jander's Livery Stable he saw them clearly through the window of Spoon's Place and
his heart rose thick and cold in his throat. There was the man in
the gray suit and the gray hat sitting at the soda fountain smiling and talking with little Pearl kicking her legs over the edge
of the marble counter and Willa standing flushed and pleased
with her hands folded in her apron while Walt Spoon and Icey
stood by with prim, pleased smiles on their faces as they harked
to the stranger's words. He was talking to them all and they were
just eating it all up like a kitten eats cream, and John thought
his heart would stop beating altogether because the stranger had
Pearl's old doll in his hands now and he was bouncing it up and
down on the little girl's knee like it was nothing but the plainest,
commonest doll in the world.

Miss Icey whipped the hot fudge till the black stove trembled.
God works in a mysterious way, she said, His wonders to perform.

Walt sat by the window puffing contentedly on his pipe. Willa stood in the kitchen doorway, weeping soundlessly into her handkerchief while Pearl, at her knees, buried her face in her mother's apron. John kept apart from them, pale and thin-lipped, his eyes cast to the feet of the stranger.

And it's a good man, Icey continued, letting a drop of the candy fall in cold water to see if it balled and was ready to pour. A mighty good man that would come out of his way to bring a word of cheer to a grieving widow! Preacher cleared his throat.

I was with Brother Harper almost to the end, he said in his clear voice. And I 'lowed as how it would cheer the soul of this poor child to know how brave her husband was—how humble in the face of Eternity and the final judgment.

Icey, despite herself, uttered a single sob and lashed angrily at a tear with her apron hem.

Preacher! There'll be a place for you in heaven for bringing them tidings to Willa here!

As one of the chaplains at the penitentiary, said Preacher softly, it was, of course, my sad duty to bring comfort to the unhappy man during his final days. And now that I'm no longer employed by the penitentiary it is my joy to bring this small comfort to his widow.

Pearl took her face from the apron and lifted her enormous eyes to Willa.

Where's Dad, Mom?

Hush! whispered Willa, checking her sobs at last and mopping at her swollen eyes.

Icey poured the black fudge onto the buttered pan, and when the pot was scraped at last held it out for John to finish with his thumb. But the little boy's stony eyes did not turn to see. Icey, guessing how such first-hand intelligence of his father's last days must have stung the child, hurried off and thrust the pan into the sink.

Ben Harper, Preacher said, sitting now at the table and folding his long fingers into a web of tranquil piety, was the last of the condemned men whose troubled spirits I brought comfort to.

You say you ain't with the state no more? said Walt.

No, brother. I resigned only yesterday. The heart-rending spectacle of these poor men was too much for me. I figure to move on down the river and find myself a little pulpit somewheres. Kentucky maybe. Maybe farther.

The fingers. John could not take his eyes from them. They rested together on the tablecloth in pale, silent embrace like spiders entwined. The fingers with the little blue letters. Now as the fingers stirred John could see them all. He supposed at first that the letters meant nothing; that perhaps each finger had a name and the name was a letter. H—A—T—E. The left hand. L—O—V—E. The right hand. Left hand and right hand and the fingers each had names. Now Preacher saw the boy staring and the hands sprang apart and he held them up.

Ah, little lad! You're staring at my fingers!

John said no word. His eyes fell back to the stubby black tops of Preacher's shoes.

These letters spell out the Lesson of Life, boy! boomed Preacher with a cozening and unctuous geniality. Shall I tell you the little story of Right-Hand-Left-Hand—the tale of Good and Evil?

John pressed his lips tighter.

Speak, boy! cried old Walt, nudging him. Preacher asked you a question!

Yes.

Ah, he's a shy one, poor little tyke! cried Preacher. And no wonder! Think, my friends, what life has already done to those tender years.

John would have none of him. But Pearl, who had come and stood by his knee, was wholly won now at the word story. And she pressed her head against his elbow till he noticed her.

Come set on Preacher's knee, little darling! he cried, and tossed her up and cradled her there while Willa's dark eyes watched, as spellbound as the rest.

Hate! roared Preacher, thrusting up the fingers of his left hand so that all might read. It was with this left hand that old brother Cain struck the blow that laid his brother low! And since that ungodly day, brethren, the left hand has borne the curse of the living and Almighty Jehovah!

Walt grunted approval and, scratching a match on his trouser seat, held it to his pipe and sucked the flame.

Love! cried Preacher, thrusting up the right hand now. See these here fingers, dear friends! These fingers has veins that lead right square to the heart—to the almighty soul of man! The right hand, friends! The hand of Love! Now watch and I'll show you the story of Life! The fingers of these hands, dear hearts!—they're always a-tuggin' and a-warrin' one hand against the other!

Now he thrust his fingers together, left hand and right hand, and now they wrung and twisted one another until the knuckles crackled horribly.

—a-warrin' and a-ragin', my friends! The soul of man a-fightin' against his own greed and lust and stinking corruption! Look at them, dear hearts! Old left hand Hate's a-fightin' and it looks like old right hand Love's a goner! But wait, now! Hot dog! Love's a-winnin'! Yessirree! Old left hand Hate's a goner! And at the last word he brought both hands down with a crash to the table top.

Hot dog, brothers and sisters! It was Love that won! Old Mister Left Hand has gone down for the count!

Icey sighed and sliced the crisscross squares of fudge with the long bread knife.

I declare! she said softly. I never heard it better told, Preacher.

Now! cried Preacher, bending to John with a smile. Did you catch on, boy?

John sighed.

Answer when you're spoken to, John, said Willa.

Yes.

Most folks, smiled Preacher, wonders about these here tat-toos. When a feller has tattoos on his hands it's generally some-thin' ornery like anchors and pistols and naked females and such. I tell you I find these tattoos mighty handy when it comes to preachin' the Word.

Well now, said Walt, between puffs of pipe smoke. It sure tells me the story.

That fudge, smiled Icey, will be cool directly and we'll all have some.

Thank you, sister.

I declare, Willa, sighed Icey with a hard stare at John. I never seen that boy of yours so quiet. Looks to me like he could use a good dose of salts.

John! Take your hands from behind you and act nice.

Yes, Mom.

Preacher smiled and patted the shaggy head with firm, quick movements.

Many and many's the time, he said softly, when I sat listening to Brother Harper speak about these youngins.

Now John's eyes flew to Preacher's face.

What did he tell you?

The room was silent. Outside the pale winter sun had appeared and they could hear the drip, drip of the melting snow on the roof.

Why, he told me what fine little lambs you and your sister yonder both was! cried Preacher, his washed-out-blue eyes twin-kling palely.

Is that all? John said.

Willa stirred uncomfortably and went over to gather Pearl from the stranger's lap.

Why no, boy, smiled Preacher, something new in his eyes now as if a game had begun between them. He told me lots and lots of things. Nice things, boy.

John lapsed into silence again, his hands pushing into his pockets.

Well, he said, without glancing at Willa. I reckon me and Pearl better go now!

Oh, but the fudge ain't hard yit! cried Icey warmly. I promised you a piece if you was good.

I don't want no fudge, said John, quite plainly.

Well, I declare! cried Icey, her mouth pursing angrily. Such impudence!

John Harper! When you don't want somethin' you're supposed to say, No thank you! cried Willa.

No thank you!

I'm sorry, Icey, Willa murmured, blushing with shame. I'll tend to him 'gainst I get him home.

But Preacher intervened.

Now, my dear! We all forgit how much these little lambs has endured. He didn't mean no impudence. Did you now, boy?

The fingers. John could not take his eyes from the fingers long enough to think about what it was Preacher was saying.

Did you, boy?

John stood quite still, his feet very close together, thinking about his dad that day in the tall grass by the smokehouse and he could not hear what they were saying because he was thinking back, trying to remember the hands of the blue men with the guns and sticks. But because the hands had kept moving he could not remember whether these had been the hands named Love or the hands named Hate or whether they had any names at all. Now Willa's breath stirred in his ear, hot and furious, choking with humiliation.

You just wait, John Harper! Just wait till I git you home!

BOOK TWO

THE HUNTER

Run, puppy, run! Run, puppy, run!
Yonder comes the big dog, run, puppy, run!

—Child's Rhyme

This was toward the end of March. On the Monday of the third week of Preacher's stay at Cresap's Landing he told Walt Spoon that he had made up his mind to stay on through the spring. And since he had no money it was his intention to wait until he could pick up a little work on one of the larger bottomland farms and pay off his debts and then in May or June he would hold a grand spring revival over in Jason Lindsay's orchard. Few country preachers work full time at it: most of them are farmers or they hire out for the harvest or do store work in the lean times and so to Walt Spoon this seemed a plainly sensible plan. Mamie Ernest, as much taken in by Preacher's grand manner as the rest of them, did not so much as mention the matter of board and room he owed her for and it was tacitly agreed that he would pay for these things when he could. Old Friend Martin, the regular pastor at Cresap's Landing's little frame Presbyterian Church, gave Preacher a perfectly good old black overcoat and invited him to preach at his own pulpit. Everyone was completely won by Preacher's flashing eyes and his rolling, booming voice, and the sermon about the right- and left-hand fingers had the congregation buzzing and chattering all the way home that Sunday. Willa kept on at her job at the confectionery and it was a fairly common thing before long for Preacher to come by of an evening to talk to her about Ben's last days and to enjoy cocoa and a platter of Icey's Potsdam cakes. There was never, of course, a breath of bad gossip about these casual attentions because everyone could see the two of them quite plainly through the window of the ice-cream parlor. Icey, however, had launched upon an all-out campaign to fan the friendship into the sort of refined interest that would lead to Willa's second marriage. But Willa resisted.

No, Icey. It's too soon after Ben's passing for me to be thinkin' about marryin' again. Besides—

Besides nothin'! cried Icey, popping a little frosted cube of Turkish delight into her mouth. That feller is just achin' to settle down with some nice woman and make a home for himself here in Cresap's Landing, Willa. I declare, I don't know what's the matter with you. Are ye blind? 'Deed, it ain't every day in the week that as nice a man as that comes down the pike. And you can bet your bottom dollar, my fine girl, there'll be some smart young sister between here and Captina will snap him up if you don't.

John don't like him much.

Pshaw! Youngins! It'll be a sad day when a sassy-britches like that John of yours can stand up and tell their elders what's right and wrong.

Well—I suppose—

Besides, honey! What about Pearl? She just *dotes* on him!

Yes. Yes, that's so, Icey.

Fiddlesticks! It's only natural for boys to feel sorty—well sorty *loyal* to the memory of the father. You mark my words, Willa, that boy wouldn't cotton up to no man you picked to marry.

Gracious, Icey! Here we are just talkin' about it like he'd gone and *asked* me.

Shoot, now! Ain't no man'll ever ask a woman if she don't find a way to let him know she's ready.

Willa had finished polishing the long silver soda spoons and now she was arranging them neatly in a long row behind the fountain. She sighed and lifted her troubled eyes to Icey's impatient scowl.

There's something else, she said softly.

Well! The only thing else I can think of is you just naturally can't see yourself in the same bed with him.

No, it's not that. I don't much care about that any more. I don't think I ever want to have those feelings about any man again. It's not love I'm huntin' any more. I reckon I've had my chance at that already. If I was to marry again, Icey, it wouldn't be for no other earthly reason than to give the kids a father and a provider—

Then what in heaven's name is wrong with Mister Powell? He wouldn't make much but it would be a comfort to your soul to—

It's the money, Icey! she breathed quickly, and commenced polishing one of the spoons over again, with swift, nervous rubs of the fragrant cloth.

Icey grunted.

Pshaw! That money! I declare you'll let that money haunt you to your grave, Willa Harper.

I reckon that's so, Icey, said the girl. It's always there—bloody and evil and covered with sin. My sin as much as Ben's, Icey! I feel like I ought to have to pay for it just as much as he done some ways. Like I'd driven him to it.

Such barefaced foolishness! It's gone—gone I tell you!

There's no way I can tell, said Willa, staring at her chapped hands, whether he knows about it or not.

Who knows?

Mr. Powell.

Well, shoot! I reckon he should know about it! Everyone in Marshall County knew. It was in the Moundsville *Daily Echo*— the whole story. I reckon it was even in the Wheeling papers, too. Folks talked about it all up and down the panhandle. But what in the world has his knowin' about it got to do with anything, will you please tell me that?

Willa shivered.

Maybe, she whispered, he knows where it's hid.

It's at the bottom of the Ohio River! That's where it's hid!

Maybe. Maybe not.

It was a warm night for the end of March. Walt had left the front door to the ice-cream parlor open when he went out after supper to gossip with the old men down at Darly Stidger's store. And yet it was not spring, although winter was dead and the moon was sickly with the neitherness of the time between those seasons: those last few weeks before the cries of the green frogs would rise in stitching clamor from the river shores and meadow bogs.

How would I know, said Willa presently, if Preacher was to ask me to marry him—that he wasn't just after the money? Maybe he thinks I've got it hid somewhere.

He's a man of God, said Icey, gravely. It's plain enough to me.

Oh, I know, Icey—

Besides. It was wrote plain enough in the papers—how Ben wouldn't tell—how Mr. McGlumphey said he might get him off with Life if he told and he still wouldn't tell.

Secretly, said Willa. He could have told me secretly. And give it to me to hide.

Well, did he?

No.

Well then why don't you just come right out plain and ask Mr. Powell if Ben ever said anything to him about it?

About the money?

Yes.

He'd think it was queer, Icey.

Fiddlesticks! A man never knows what a woman really means.

Besides—like you say—he's a man of God. I'd be ashamed to have him know I suspicioned him.

Hark! cried Icey, holding up a finger. That's him a-comin' up Peacock Alley now!

Yes! Yes! cried Willa, flushing. That's him a-singin'! Don't he have the grandest singin' voice?

They could have heard it moments before had they been still: Preacher's sweet, high tenor as he drew closer along the sidewalks, singing the old hymn.

Oh, Icey, I'm a sight!

Pshaw! You look grand. Now, fill him up with cocoa, Willa! Men can't think good when they're gettin' fed.

Icey ran off to the kitchen so she could listen at the crack. But the old woman's ears did not serve her well in these late years and she knew nothing of what the two had said until ten o'clock struck and Willa returned, flushed and happier-looking than Icey ever remembered seeing her.

Has he gone?

Yes, Icey! Yes!

Well, child, what's the commotion?

Willa flung herself upon the old woman's shoulder, hugging her and sobbing happily.

Here, now! Here! What's all this?

Oh, Icey! It's such a load off my mind!

Did he ask you to marry him?

No! No, it's not that, Icey! It's about the money!

Well, gracious sakes alive, stop fidgeting and tell me. What now?

Icey, I just come right out bold as brass and asked him straight.

Ask him about the money?

Icey, I just said: Did Ben Harper ever tell you what he done with that money he stole? And Mr. Powell just looked at me funny for a minute with his head on one side and directly he smiled and he says to me: Why, my dear child, don't you know? And I told him I didn't know and I said I'd asked Ben myself during those last days and he wouldn't never tell me because he said that money had the curse of Cain on it and if I was to have it I'd just go to hell headlong.

Well, then what—

Wait, now! I'll get to it, Icey. Then Mr. Powell just looked at me peculiar for a minute and then he finished his cocoa and he smiles and he says: Well now I'm mighty surprised he wouldn't tell you, my child. And I says: Why, whatever do you mean, Mr. Powell? And he says: Because the night before they hanged him he told *me* where that money was.

He told Mr. Powell?

Yes.

Then where—

Wait, now, Icey! I'm getting to it! He said Ben sent for him that night and said that the curse of that money had soured on his conscience long enough. He said he wanted to leave this world without leaving that gold behind for other poor, weak mortals to lust after and murder for—

Icey pursed her lips rapidly, her black eyes twinkling like hat pins in her flushed, plump face.

—and Ben told him that night that the money was gone where it wouldn't never do no one any more harm because of the sinful and greedy willfulness of poor mortals like himself—

The clock in the hall rattled suddenly and rustled like an awakening bird. It chimed the quarter hour.

Then where is the money?

At the bottom of the river, said Willa gladly. Wrapped around a twelve-pound cobblestone.

Ah, Lord! It's a blessing from God, Willa. A blessing from God.

Yes, Icey! Oh, yes! And I can mind the time when I would

have sold my soul to Satan himself to know how I could lay hands on that bloody gold. Oh, Icey, sin gets such a hold sometimes! There was nights when I'd want to know about that money so bad I'd even fergit the awful thing that was going to happen to Ben up there at Moundsville penitentiary. That's what sin and greed will do to a human soul, Icey.

Praise God! Yes, Willa! Yes!

But Ben took care of me, Icey. Even in death he kept me from the awful sin that money would have brought with it.

Yes! Yes! Oh, that's so true!

I feel clean now, Icey. My whole body's just a-quiverin' with cleanness.

I know! I know!

That money was cursed!

It was that! Cursed and bloodied! Praise God!

And now God has saved me from it!

They subsided, uttering little crooning cries of emotion and directly Icey bent forward in her rocker and shook a finger gently under Willa's nose.

And now! she cried softly. You'll know that when Mr. Powell asks you to marry him—that it won't be for *that*. You know well and good that a man of God like him don't give a whipstitch about money or not. It's a cinch he's not stayin' here at Cresap's Landing just for the fun of helping Jason Lindsay with his second plowing!

No, reflected Willa. I know that. But still—

Still what?

I just can't help wonderin' how little John will take the news.

About what?

About the money, Icey.

Pshaw! Why tell him at all?

Yes, said Willa. Yes, I'm going to tell him. He should know.

She was silent a moment.

It's all so strange, Icey.

Willa's eyes were bright with the old fear again.

All along, she said, I had the feeling that John knew something.

John thought: I will go with them because not going would make them think: What does he know? Why is he afraid for us to see him? Is he afraid we'll make him tell?

He thought: Because Mr. Powell knows. He knows I know where the money's hid. He has always known and that's why he told Mom that fib about Dad saying the money was in the river. That's so he can have me all to himself—get it out of me his own way. I am afraid of Mr. Powell. I am more afraid of him than I have ever been of shadows or the thunder or when you look through the little bubble in the glass of the window in the upstairs hall and all of the out-of-doors stretches and twists its neck.

Willa called: Pearl? John? You ready?

Yes, he thought. Yes, I am ready. Because I mustn't let them know I am afraid and I must keep on pretending I am brave because I promised I would be. When the blue men come and took him away that day I promised that I would take care of Pearl with my life and I promised I wouldn't never tell about what he made me swear not to. His name is Preacher. His name is Harry Powell. But the names of the fingers are E and V and O and L and E and T and A and H and that story he tells about the one hand being Hate and the other hand being Love is a lie because they are both Hate and to watch them moving scares me worse than shadows, worse than the wind.

Willa in a pretty new hat from Moundsville was busy by the pump tucking the last of the sandwiches into the picnic basket. Pearl's hair was brushed till the ringlets shone like dark, carved wood against the shoulders of her bright gingham dress. John waited, transfixed with his thoughts, on the back porch.

John? You ready? Have you got your hair brushed?

Yes.

She came to the screen door and glared at him.

Young man, just kindly wipe that pout off your face 'gainst I give you more of what you got the other night!

He sighed heavily and turned from the door, staring at the yard pump, at the smokehouse, and beyond the picket fence where the hills were peppered now with the first green smoke of spring. It had come overnight: a burgeoning and a stirring in the land that was tired and musty-smelling like the flesh of old folks after the death of winter; now the land was alive and the air was ripe and musky with the spring river smell like the ripe, passionate sweat of a country waitress. He could hear them preparing for the day's outing. It was to be a church picnic downriver at Raven Rock at the old Presbyterian graveyard where his father was buried and all the lost, forgotten progenitors before him. They were taking a little chartered packet down river and at nightfall they would return.

John thought: Is God one of them? Is God on the side of the fingers with names that are letters like the letters on the watch in Miz Cunningham's window?

There now! Willa was saying to Pearl. You look just grand. Aren't you happy we're all going on a picnic with Mr. Powell?

Yes. Oh, yes!

John thought: But I can't hate Pearl. Dad said I couldn't hate her because she is mine to protect with my life. But I am scared. I am scared more than I was ever scared of dark or wind or the twisting bubble world, but then I reckon Dad was scared, too, when the blue men took him away, but he was brave and that's what you have to be.

Preacher appeared in the hallway. Willa and Pearl ran to

greet him and John knew Willa would be holding Pearl and the doll up to kiss and be kissed by Preacher and there was nothing he could do to stop that.

John? John? Come on, now! We're leaving!

Off on the sweet morning wind he heard the foolish, womanly hoot of the little steamboat at the wharf. He turned and pushed through the screen door and into the kitchen to where they were. His hair was flattened and itching where she had wet it down and brushed it slick-flat and his thighs scratched and tingled against the harsh cloth of his good Sunday knickers.

Ah, there's my boy! There's the little man! Good morning, John.

'Morning.

He tried to smile because they might ask him questions if he didn't smile.

Willa, you were truly left a priceless legacy when Brother Harper passed on! These fine, fine youngins!

Willa flushed with pleasure and patted Pearl's curls more neatly against her shoulders.

Priceless beyond the worth of much fine gold, Preacher said, the laughter of these precious little children!

John stared. The finger named H reached over and chucked him under the chin. John thought: She says he is a man of God. And so God is one of them; God is a blue man.

Yes, Willa said. I'm right proud, Mr. Powell. Such a comfort they've been to me.

John thought: I wish it was night. I wish I was in bed under the comforter. I wish the wind was blowing and the darkness was being because I am not as much afraid of them as I am of the finger whose name is H.

Well, I reckon we'd best be gettin' down to the boat! boomed Preacher.

They followed him, the picnic basket in his hand, and in Pea-

cock Alley it was spring and the warped mossy bricks of the pavement were covered with little green wings from the silver maples
and they crunched under their feet, and the air was blue and
green and yellow with little broken soft pieces of sun that blew
on the river wind. At the wharf John spied the face of Uncle
Birdie, and Willa stiffened when the old man waved courteously
and she told John he should not speak to that dirty old man.
Then John saw Walt Spoon and Icey and a lot of other people
on the landing and by the wharfboat the little stern-wheeler
lay waiting, its stacks puffing white clouds impatiently into the
raspberry-cobbler sky.

Forevermore! What a pretty day! sighed Willa, her cheeks
pinched pink by the air, her eyes sparkling with happiness.

Well, sure! It's spring—that's why it's so purty, laughed Walt
Spoon and led them all through the wharfboat and up the little
plank onto the boat. There was really no cabin. They sat in the
shelter of the little boiler deck by the railings where they could
look out over the broad expanse of rich, motionless river and
the rolling hills of spring beyond the water and in its reflection
another spring, another world.

Here, John! Come and set by me and Pearl and Mr. Powell.

John obeyed, stiff with fright that had long gone beyond the
prerogative of anger or protest; moving now to the dumb bidding
of muscles he had set in motion from an earlier outset. He squatted by the borrowed folding chair (there were a dozen on the
deck, borrowed from the funeral parlor) beside his mother and
listened as Icey Spoon chattered on about a lantern slide show
some missionary fellow was going to give at the church and he
could smell the steam of the boat and the smell of Walt Spoon's
pipe and back in the wharfboat Uncle Birdie Steptoe was picking
out a silly tune on a rusty banjo.

Gracious! cried Willa, when the whistle blew again, sur-
rounding them for an instant in a shivering glass ball of sound.

Land's sakes! We're moving! cried Icey, and old Friend Martin, the preacher at the church, lifted his enormous palm as if on cue, and Nelly Bloyd, the choir leader, raised her sweet soprano voice in the hymn. They were all singing now: the voices of different texture and size mingling together into a curious and pleasant chord.

Shall—we—gather at the r-i-v-e-r! Where bright angel feet have tro-od!

John watched the land move, the wharfboat move, the world moving slowly away from them with the dark water's intervention stranding them somehow upon the river's implacable face, and he thought: It will be all right because Pearl is sitting on the other side of him and the doll is where he can't see it. Nothing will happen. It will be all right.

We—will—walk and worship e-e-ver! All the happy, golden d-a-ay!

So they sang on for an hour and between hymns Walt Spoon called out the river points and hamlets as they passed them: That's Sunfish yonder, folks! Over there is Petticoat Ripple! Yonder is Grape and Bat Island! We're passin' Sistersville already! I declare, Mother, this little boat makes right fair time, don't she?

Above them the chattering puffing of the steam engine and the occasional shrill scream of the whistle left stuttering echoes among the environing hills and set yard dogs bawling and howling in the bottom farms along the shore. The air was unbelievably rich and sweet with the temper of the season: the river smell like the incense of some primal pagan fertility.

Why are you so still, boy?

John lifted his eyes at the question, beyond the fingers, beyond the dead-gray vest and the stiff paper collar and the black tie. He shrugged swiftly as small boys do and then grinned, the perfect picture of a fool.

I'd figure a boy like you would be mighty excited—takin' a ride on a real steamboat.

Still he said nothing in reply. John, I don't believe you like me very much. He could not make the lie with his mouth and so he sat mute and blushing. Willa, chattering happily with Icey Spoon and Nelly Bloyd, did not overhear Preacher talking to the boy and Pearl was dreaming, her eyes lost in the magic mirror of the passing river, the doll's face pressed close against her pink bonnet brim.

Aw, have a heart, boy! I think you made up your mind not to like me from the first.

And John thought: When I walked on the tall fence in Jason Lindsay's meadow that time I walked with my feet going very carefully so that I wouldn't fall and that is how I must make myself be when he is looking at me. Eh, boy? What?

He lifted his gaze now and met Preacher's eyes steadily. Was there something quite calm and deadly in those eyes now? The glitter not of ice but of chilled blue steel?

Perhaps you better start trying to like me, smiled Preacher, ominously.

He paused a moment, letting the words sink in, before he went on.

—Because your mamma likes me, John! John clenched his teeth until his spittle tasted like pennies under the tongue.

—And your dear little sister Pearl likes me, Preacher went on, with a mock cajoling warmth. And if both of them like me and you don't—why, then that makes you different, John. Now, don't you think you might try to like me just a little? You don't want to be different do you? No—yes.

He thought: Because when you tell a lie it must be to keep from saying a worse thing. Then lying is not a sin and God will not punish you. (But what if God is one of them?)

Ah, that's the boy! boomed Preacher. Did you hear that, Willa my girl?

He turned and pressed his hand gently upon her shoulder so that she turned laughing, in mid-sentence.

Pardon?

John! cried Preacher. He says he likes me!

Icey intervened, her face flushed and kittenish.

Why, of course he likes Mr. Powell! she cried. He's a fine boy! He likes all his elders—don't you, John?

Now the boat whistle blew three shrill blasts and they moved from the channel toward the grove of trees on the West Virginia shore where in those pale, sweet reaches shone the white spire of a country church and, among the fences, the pale stones of the burying ground.

We're here! We're here! cried Willa with a child's happiness, and John sprang suddenly to her side, clasping her hand, having thought in one sudden, wonderful moment that she had cried: He's here! He's here!

Is Dad—

The picnic joy washed from her eyes for that moment and the smile faded on her mouth.

John, how could you be that mean? To mention *his* name to me today!

But I thought—I thought you said—

He stumbled away from her, foolish and clumsy among the braces and chairs and the steam and the stirring, stiff legs of the standing people and he kept thinking over and over: Because if I cry then they will know something is wrong and then they will guess that I know something that I would die before I would tell any of them.

Then the little boat scraped on the brick landing, the green and fair wind blew, and up in the meadow behind the grove the little country church woke suddenly as if in greeting and began striking soft golden notes of April sound.

They spent the morning solemnly trimming the grass on the little mounds of earth and wrenching winter weeds away from the carved names and the foolish sandstone angels and the little inlaid enamel pictures above the lost and faded dates. They set jelly glasses of Johnny-jump-ups at the headstones and carried little pails of water from the faucet at the edge of the grove. The wind blew gently all the morning and white clouds glided slowly across the blue sky like strange, grand frigates. And so until noon there was no other sound but the snip-snip of grass scissors and the hushing sigh of sickles and the occasional scratching cry of a spring bird soaring in restive and feral joy into the untroubled sky. They ate late in the afternoon. John had carried his share of water pails and stood by the unmarked grave of his father while Willa wept and Pearl stood beside her hugging the old doll until the older ones walked away again and then she began the questions again.

John?

Yes.

Where's Dad?

I don't know, he said truthfully and Willa intervened then with thick sandwiches for each of them: ham salad between thick slices of salt-rising bread fresh that morning from Icey's oven. John watched them eat but held his own sandwich untouched, still warm and yielding within the wax paper. He returned to his father's grave and stood for a moment perplexed and scowling at the fresh earth.

Listen here, now—he began clumsily, and then abandoned it because it was just a pile of dirt and he had been foolish enough for a moment to think that it was really *him* there and that maybe he could have made his dad say that it didn't really matter—that it was all right to tell them after all because it was more than he would be able to endure: holding it all inside. Then suddenly he could not believe that anyone alive or dead could be there no matter what the older people said or that any of it had any reality at all: the square eroded slabs with the little names, the numbers, the pictures of the sad, smiling ladies and the little dimpled stone babies. These were the great stone toys of a giant who had grown weary of his play and wandered away long ago. It was a joke of some kind. It was just letters—like the letters on Preacher's fingers.

John, are you sick? she said.

No, Mom.

Then why don't you eat your sandwich?

Not hungry, Mom.

Well, now, I don't want you pestering me going home on the boat this evening. There'll not be a drop of food to eat then.

He unwrapped his big sandwich slowly, regarded it with faint distaste an instant, and then dutifully bit into it. He did not like the smell of Icey's salt-rising bread. It had the sour smell like when someone is sick. But he ate valiantly, chewing the hunks of sandwich in his dry mouth.

Ah, here's my boy!

His mouth stopped chewing, then began again. He swallowed in dry agony.

How about a bite out of that sandwich, boy?

John said nothing, heard nothing but the vast and enormous clanking of the watch in Preacher's pocket: the gold watch of his dad's that Willa had given him.

Aw, have a heart, boy, whined the voice, and the hand named Love reached out for the sandwich.

John looked at the fingers and the blue letters of false love and thought: Which is more dangerous? Which is worse? When he is joking like this or when his eyes turn blue like the steel of the pistols in the hands of the men by the smokehouse that day. He held the sandwich out.

Tut tut, boy! I don't want your sandwich. That was just my little joke.

John turned suddenly, threw the sandwich into the rank winter grass, and moved off again. After a bit he found an Indian arrowhead in the sandy earth and brushed it clean and polished it and felt curiously safer with it in his pocket and then he saw them on a wood bench by the roadside: his mother and Preacher. The others had gone off, flushed and giggling, knowing how it was with lovers, letting them be alone. John looked at his mother's face—flushed and glowing the way it had used to be when Ben Harper came home from work and kissed her in the door. After a bit Willa called to him and stood up smoothing her skirts. She had seen the others moving again toward the landing with their baskets and garden tools.

Come along, boy! We're leaving now.

On the boat again he saw that it was nearly dark and there were black clouds over the Ohio hills and the faint grumble of thunder like a dog growling under a porch and he suddenly thought that he had forgotten something; felt suddenly as if there were still a question he should ask the man under the mound. But then he remembered again that there was no one really there.

Why are you afraid? he asked himself.

Because of the rain, he told himself. Because of the lightning and the thunder.

No, he answered himself. That's not why you are afraid.

In mid-channel, above the bend in the river at Paden City a swift and violent spring storm had overtaken them. Night had fallen as swiftly as a door slammed to by the wind. Then in an instant the river was lit by vast sheets of lightning like falling shivers of broken glass and the green water was lashed and riven by the mountain winds. The little river packet tossed and groaned in the passion of the torrential fury. John made no sound, holding Pearl's hand tightly by his mother's side.

Now, everybody just keep calm and collected! Walt Spoon was calling above the roar of the wind and rain. We'll be home in our parlors inside of twenty minutes!

In the shelter of the boilers they were protected from the tempest and the great gusts of rain that raced like sheep dogs across the torn, ragged waters of the river. John kept his eyes on the rough boards of the deck beneath him. Thunder boomed and echoed between the high hills in a giant and unremitting cannonade. Lightning flashed and shivered on the black, reflecting waters. Now Preacher stepped into the midst of them and held up his hands.

Brothers and sisters! The Lord is a-watchin' over us! But just the same I think we might keep our spirits up in the presence of His almighty wrath with a little hymn singing.

Well, yes! Yes, that's a mighty fine idea!

And Preacher commenced the singing, stamping his foot in a fierce, heavy rhythm on the boards and the little band began singing: their voices lost and wandering among the high keening shrills of the river wind and the bombardment of the thunder. John squeezed Pearl's hand and glanced sidelong at the doll in her arms. It was safe, close against her heart, its vacuous plaster stare unmoved by any terror such as theirs.

Brightly beams our Father's mer-cy! From His lighthouse evermo-o-ore!

But to us He gives the keeping—of the lights along the sho-o-re!

John felt Preacher against him and turned his eyes to the fingers on his shoulder and saw the one named H and the one named A and—

Why ain't you singin', John?

The hot breath was whispering against his face and the bad smell against his lips. He said nothing.

—Dark the night of sin has settled! Loud the angry billows roa-ar!

Eager eyes are watching, longing—for the lights along the shore!

Why aren't you singin', boy?

Now a single flame of lightning rent the river in a blinding sheet and while the night strained and creaked under the enormous blast of sound John lifted his eyes and in another flash saw the face of the man, glittering with rain and twisted with a fury as sudden as the storm itself.

Why aren't you singin', boy?

Trying now to make the harbor! In the darkness may be lost!

The fingers were tightening, like the steel pincers of a tool, on the soft flesh of the boy's shoulder. He tried to wrench free but the grip went under the tendons, around the shoulder bone.

Sing, boy! Sing! came the hot and furious whisper in his eyes. Goddamn you, sing the hymn!

I don't know no words! John cried out suddenly and the fingers sprang free. I don't know no words!

He wailed it and flung himself into the soft, scented vastness of Willa's petticoats, burying his face deep in the sweet, lavender-fragrant clothing, against the warm thigh, and trembled violently, not crying because he would have to learn again some day how to cry and Willa thought it was the wind, the dark, the thunder and the rain that had done it to him; made him scream and throw himself trembling against her.

I don't know no words! he stuttered again into the muffling calico.

But the thunder was so loud and Preacher's singing was so loud that no one heard what he was saying.

In the Ohio Valley it is the river that gives and takes the seasons. It is as if that mighty stream were the vast, alluvial artery of the land itself so that when the towns grow weary of snows and harsh fogs the great heart pumps green spring blood down the valley and the banks are warmed and nourished by it and soon the whole environing earth blossoms despite itself and the air comes alive and lambs caper and bleat upon the hillside paths. And so now it was the prime of spring in the bottomlands. Soon the redbone hound would kelt in the creek hollows on nights when the moon was a curl of golden hair against the shoulder of the Ohio hills. Soon the shantyboat people would join their fiddle and mouth-harp racket to the chorus of green frogs down under the mists in the moonlit willows. And that morning the showboat *Humpty Dumpty* had put in at the landing.

And if, in this urgent season of mating, Willa found the attentions of Preacher attractive and exciting, to Icey Spoon they were a challenging imperative. She was roused to a perfect fury of determination to make a match between these two. It seemed to the old woman that to instrument such a union would vindicate something lost in the dust of her own old, youthful, half-forgotten yearnings. Preacher was a man of God. Any woman should be proud to marry a man of God. The ideal aspect to this was that it had none of the sex—none of the nastiness—with which, for her, marriage had always been tainted. And so she persisted night and day, pressing Willa upon this prince of men. Even Walt grew tired of it after a while and would wander down to the grocery store to gossip and spit and whittle and be away from the smell of women which sometimes grew thick in his home. Willa waited, in warm awareness, biding her time while Icey kept on with this kind of ferocious schoolgirl energy.

It'll not be forever, my fine missy, that a man like that will wait around for a widow to make up her mind. You're not the only fish in the river, my proud girl!

Oh, I know, Icey. I just don't know what to say.

Say yes. That's all! How many times is it he's asked you now? Twice.

Forevermore! And you ain't said—I swear Willa if you ain't a caution!

They sat behind the marble counter that night; the gold blooms of the twin gas lamps flowering softly in the air above their heads, the whine of a Victrola somewhere off down the leafy street. Willa shook her head, eyes shut, as if she were trying to shake loose some key thought from among others.

If I was only sure it would—turn out, Icey—

A husband, grunted Icey, is one piece of store goods you never know till you take it home and get the paper off.

I know. That's why I—

But if ever I seen a sure bargain, cried Icey, it's Mr. Powell! A good, Christian gentleman!

Yes, Icey, but that boy of mine—

John? Well if you care for my opinion what that boy needs is the switch a little more often! He's growed just a little too big for his britches, missy!

Yes, I know that. But something happened on the picnic that day.

The storm?

Something more than that. Something between him and Mr. Powell. He won't tell.

Git in the habit of calling him Harry, honey. Men likes to hear a woman say their Christian name.

I didn't say anything about it to—to Harry, of course.

Maybe it was just seein' the father's grave and all, said Icey. Youngsters find it so hard to understand that the flesh is really there—under the stone—

Willa shivered and stared at the spring night outside: the street lamp glowing behind the canopy of young sycamore leaves in a misty green halo.

And John—I don't think he believes that about the money—that Ben throwed it in the river.

Nonsense! Mr. Powell wouldn't have lied. He's a man of God, Willa. Did you explain to the boy?

Yes. I told John yesterday. And then I made him come in the parlor and stand by the chair while Mr. Powell—while Harry told him.

And what did he say to that?

Nothing.

Without warning the still night was full of the piping notes of the calliope on the showboat down at the landing.

My, my! Hear that, honey! grinned old Icey. A body don't hear that sound every month in the year. That's the sound that says it's spring.

Yes, sighed Willa. It's spring.

And ain't it a caution how such a noisy thing as that can get in your bones and make you want to kick up and frolic!

Yes. Yes, I reckon, Icey—

Honey, what's wrong?

Willa plunged her naked arms into the blue dishwater and brought out a dripping ice-cream dish.

I don't think John believed Mr. Powell, she said.

Well, honey, don't *you* believe him? That's the important thing, after all.

Yes, I suppose. I just can't imagine why Ben wouldn't have told me—those days when I went to see him at the prison—pled with him!

Because Ben Harper was a good man, said Icey. That's why. He knowed that money wasn't nothin' but Sin and Torment and Abomination. And I reckon he thought he'd test you—let you think it was still somewhere hid—hopin' at last you'd say you didn't want it anyways and then maybe he'd be free of it—and you'd be free of it, too. Maybe you failed Ben, Willa! And maybe this is your chance to make it all up to him!

Aw, Icey, I know! I never doubt really—what Harry says is true.

Willa stared for a moment at her dripping hands and then pushed a lock of hair back with the heel of her hand and turned her anguished eyes to the old woman.

Icey, what shall I do?

Marry him!

But I don't feel—Icey, it ain't like Ben and me that summer—

Fiddlesticks! That wasn't love, honey. That was just hot britches. There's more to a marriage than four bare legs in a bed. When you're married forty years you'll know that all that don't matter a hill of beans. I been married that long to my Walt now and I'll swear in all that time whenever he took me I'd just lie there thinking about my canning or how I'd manage to git one of the boys new shoes for school—

That's another thing, sighed Willa. I kept that boy John out of school all last winter till the trouble was over. I just couldn't bear what they had to put up with from them other kids—mean, nasty songs and horrible pictures on the fences—

—a woman, Icey continued, heedless, is a fool to marry for that. Because it's all just a fake and a pipe dream to start with. It's somethin' for a man—the good Lord never meant for a decent woman to want that—not *really* want it.

Next winter, Willa said. If I married Mr. Powell—I'd send them both back to school. They'd seem more respectable some-how—

Pssst!

What?

Yonder he comes! Mr. Powell on his way here!

Yes. Oh, yes! Do I look all right, Icey?

Honey, you're as pretty as a picture.

That's good, Icey! she breathed wildly. Because—

Did you—Have you decided? Will you—

Yes! Oh, yes, Icey! If he asks me again tonight I'll say yes!

Icey scampered off to the kitchen, purple with excitement, and presently Willa and Preacher were alone at a table by the window.

Cocoa tonight? She smiled.

No, my child! I haven't eaten a smidgen of food all day.

Goodness! Are you sick?

Yes—no—

He rested his elbows on the table and fixed her with his burning eyes.

Willa, I can't sleep nights till you say yes, he murmured, reaching for her hand still damp from the dishwater. It's just as if the Lord kept whisperin' in my ear—This is the woman for you, Harry Powell!

He paused for an instant.

Have you thought about it, Willa?

Yes! she breathed, scarlet with her emotions. I have!

And have you got an answer for me?

Harry, I'll marry you, she stammered. If only—

If only what, my dear?

She sought to form the answer, but it was too vague, too lost. She did not know herself whose voice this was, deep in the vast river murmurs of her mind, that kept telling her not to do this thing. Something—the figure of a man—wandered in and out among the trees of her consciousness, through the white, blurring fog upon her mind's shores. Now it was the shape of a lover

and now something else—something frightful beyond telling—
something with the body of a child in its arms.

Old Uncle Birdie took his quid of tobacco out of his mouth long
enough to gulp down another choking throatful of the corn liquor
in the tin cup. John squatted on the threshold of the wharfboat
cabin watching him with a faint, admiring smile. The night air
was shrill with the enormous racket of the showboat calliope a
few feet above them.

I can't hear ye, boy!

I said, Did you fix Dad's skiff yet?

The skiff! Daggone it, Johnny, I've had such a misery in my
hip these past couple of days I've barely stirred from the boat.
Next week, now. I promise. We'll go fishin' first day of June if it
ain't too sunny.

John sighed.

How's your maw?

Oh she's all right.

How's your sister Pearl?

What?

Pearl? Pearl?

John nodded with grown-up authority.

Jist fine.

He ducked his head outside the door again and stared again
in consuming wonder at the blazing glory of the showboat.
She was little more than an enormous barn built on a raft with
a stern-wheeler to tow her. And yet she was a miracle from
stem to stern—strung with blazing electric lights and glittering white paint. Half the county had come to Cresap's Landing
that night to see her and pay their quarters and go on board to
view the show. John, of course, had no quarter and so he had
contented himself with the prospect of a half hour's chat with

Uncle Birdie and these stolen glances at the wonderful boat here within staggering earshot of her piping calliope. He had disobeyed Willa again—coming here. And he had, with much greater misgivings, left Pearl in bed alone. And it was this latter which itched his conscience until inevitably it got the better of him and so at last he rose and lifted his hand in farewell to the old man.

Leavin', boy?

Yep! Gotta watch out for Pearl, Uncle Birdie.

Well good night, boy. Come again—anytime. And mind, now—I'll have your paw's skiff in shipshape inside of a week.

John skipped up the plank and onto the bricks of the landing, already slick with evening mists. The water front was lined with buggies and old Model T's with ditch mud splattered clean to the windows. Country girls and their boys and the old folks lined the shore with their hands holding their money till the calliope stopped playing. Then they would go down and give Mr. Bryant their money and go inside for the show. John sighed and moved away along the tree-shaded darkness of Peacock Alley. He was wild with misgivings now about having left Pearl alone in the house. She was his trust, his pledge to Ben. As he hurried for the river road the voice of the calliope fell to a thin, faint chatter high in the spring night. Passing Spoon's he spied his mother and Icey at the fountain, and Icey was fairly dancing a jig and hugging Willa and kissing her cheek, and he moved on past, shaking his head, wondering what they were up to now, thinking that he would never understand the ways of woman. He hurried more, knowing that it was past ten, and he did not want his mother to overtake him on her way home from work. The house loomed silent in the faint shine of the young spring moon. The light of the gas lamp in the yard lit the peppering of new growth on the oak tree and he saw that the lamp in the parlor window was lit. He could not remember whether it had been lit when he left and that made him frightened because he was sure Willa would not have left it burning.

Is somebody there? he said to the house, as he tiptoed up the steps.

By the river, under the fog, the green frogs chanted their unending litany of love.

Is anybody there?

But there was no reply, no sound, and he opened the screen door and closed it softly and stepped into the shadowed hallway. He knew almost at once that Preacher was there or had been there not an instant before because there was a Preacher smell in the silent air and it was the smell of dread in his nose, and dog-like his flesh gathered and bunched at the scent of it.

Is anybody here?

Good evening, John!

So he had been standing there all along by the hall rack where Ben Harper used to hang his cap when he came in from the car of an evening. Preacher: standing there all along, letting him be scared, letting him call three times before he answered. Now Preacher moved forward and the light from the open doorway to the parlor threw a gold bar of light across the livid line of lip and cheek and bone beneath and one eye shone like a dark, wet grape and the lid crinkled over it nervously.

Does your mother know you go wandering alone at night, John?

No. She said—

But there was no way to explain, no excuse, no escape. And then he felt the anger rise choking in his throat and he thought: What right has he got?

Your little sister Pearl is asleep, then?

Yes.

Good, John.

Now he was in his genial, cajoling mood, and John knew suddenly that he liked this mood less than the other: the dangerous mood, because you never knew what was going on behind the coaxing, squinting eyes and the thin smile.

I have something to talk to you about, John.

Well, he sighed. I reckon I ought to be gettin' up to bed if you don't mind—

Really, my lad! You weren't worryin' about bed when you sneaked off to the wharf to waste your time with that evil old man.

And this had John dead to rights and so he sat down on a straight-backed chair by the door and wished for the sound of Willa's footfall on the tanbark outside because he was getting scared again like he had been that night on the steamboat. Then he heard the scrape of another chair as Preacher sat opposite him and laid a cold finger on his hand.

I had a little talk with your mother tonight, John.

John thought: Why don't he take me in the parlor to talk where there is light instead of out here in the dark hallway where I can't watch his face while he says it and know whether what he is saying is real or not.

We talked it over, John—and your mother decided it might be best for me to—let you know the news.

What news? What?

Your mother told me tonight she wanted me to be a daddy to you and your sister. We're going to get married, boy!

He thought: That is why it is all dark out there, because it is asleep and I am having a bad dream because I rolled over on Pearl's doll and it hurts my stomach and when I wake up I will see the light on the wall where the tree branch dances and then I will turn over and it won't hurt any more.

Did you hear what I said, boy?

What?

Your mother and I— Did you hear what I said?

He thought: She wouldn't do this to Dad because he loved all of us and because if she does it he will come back and kill her because he isn't really in that mound.

Married! Preacher's voice went on triumphantly. We have decided to go to Sistersville tomorrow and have a very simple wedding and when we come back—

You ain't my dad! breathed John. You won't never be my dad!

He was not scared anymore; his anger swung and blazed in the dark room like a pine torch.

—and when we come back, shrilled Preacher, we will all live here together in this house—and be friends—and *share our fortunes together, John!*

Afterward John could not believe he could ever have said so foolish a thing as he said next. At night, remembering it weeks later, he would sweat and clench his hands till the soft nails bit into the palms and the lips in his tossing face would deny it to the dark, to the dancing figures on the golden square, to the lashing wind and the river night. But it was true—he had said it.

You think you can make me tell! he had screamed, till the house was shrill with it. But I won't! I won't! I won't!

And then he hunched and gawked at his own folly. And the fingers of his left hand cupped over his aghast mouth; his fingers tasting of river and tar from the wharfboat, and his heart crying out like a little dry voice of dread: Oh, I shouldn't never have said that! Now he will guess! Now he will know! Oh, God, please don't let him know!

Tell me *what*, boy? said Preacher softly, and though the face had moved out of the bar of light again John knew the head was cocked and the mouth smiling.

Nothin'!

Are we keeping secrets from one another, little lad?

No. No.

Now the vast, dark figure straightened and relaxed, chuckling softly.

No matter, boy! We've got a long time together.

He held out the hand called Love but John did not move.

Will you shake my hand, boy? Will you wish me happiness with your mother?

John whirled then and raced helter-skelter up the creaking stairway to the bed where he had belonged all along and he knew God had done all this thing to him to punish him for being bad and leaving Pearl alone. He crouched by her sleeping face and listened to the house. He knew Preacher had not left, that he would be standing there still in the hall by the coat rack, stunned with anger and affront. But while John tore his clothes from his aching body he heard the fall of the door at last and then the footsteps going down the lane. Preacher was gone and yet he must be certain and so he stole to the window and spied the lonely figure moving into the mists toward Cresap's Landing. Once the figure paused and looked back but John could not see the face; could not know what fury rested there or what black resolutions already stirred in the clenched hand named Hate. John curled up in the darkness beneath the quilt and embraced the warm body of the sleeping Pearl while his hand sought for the doll's face and his finger traced the shape of one staring plaster eye over and over in senseless and iterant terror.

Tonight, chuckled Icey, patting John's head, you and your sister are going to sleep here with me and Mister Spoon.

Where's Mom, John? said Pearl.

Icey caught the little girl up and plumped her into the ample lap and patted a chubby knee.

Your ma has went to Sistersville, she said. With Mr. Powell! Why?

To git married is why! Ain't that nice, honey? Just think! 'Gainst she gits back tomorrow you'll have a brand-new dad.

Is Dad comin' home?

John wandered away from them, stood staring out through the sparkling, spotless window of the ice-cream parlor into deserted Peacock Alley. He did not like Icey or Walt. They were part of it; they had helped fashion the nightmare. He had known their part in it since the day on the boat. The ice-cream parlor smelled like milk and licorice and burnt almond. All through that hazy spring afternoon he wandered among the wire chairs and tables, gazing with numb, hungerless curiosity at the little trays of candies in the bellied glass cases. Pearl sat in the window by the sleeping tortoise-shell cat and played a little game of house with the doll Jenny. At suppertime John took his place wordlessly at the alien board and ate glumly, answering when spoken to, eyes downcast to the strange plate with its seasoning that was just enough different from his mother's to sicken his heart.

More applesauce, John? smiled Walt Spoon kindly.

No, thank you.

Goodness, boy! You ain't hardly touched your plate. Your sister has licked hers clean twice. You ain't gonna let a girl beat you at eatin' are ye?

I ate some, he said.

By granny, Icey! I think this boy could do with a little sulphur and molasses. Have ye had your spring tonic this spring, boy?

No.

Walt had counted on this frightening the boy into eating but nothing changed him, nothing stirred the sullen lackluster eyes that shone dully with the suffering that none of them could understand. Icey held her peace till after the Italian cream was finished and then she began.

John?

Yes'm.

You've got no cause to act up this way about your mother's marryin' Mr. Powell.

He freed the napkin slowly from his collar.

I declare! I'd think a boy like you would be proud gettin' a fine stepfather like Mr. Powell.

She fixed him with her shrewish and unwavering scrutiny, searching for some effects of these remarks.

Hmmph! I reckon you'd be happy if your ma was goin' to marry Uncle Birdie Steptoe.

He kept his eyes lowered, waiting till she was done, knowing it was part of his lot to endure this, too. Pearl had scrambled down from her chair and dragged the doll Jenny off to the ice-cream parlor again, to the window. The cat followed, meowing softly, thinking she had brought away some scrap of her supper for him to eat. Icey grunted impatiently and snatched up a pile of plates, bound for the sink. John went out on the back porch and sat down on the worn stoop to stare at the moon that had risen and lay in the orchard trees like a rind of golden fruit. He heard a raincrow purling its soft cry down the lane toward the river.

I've put fresh sheets and a fresh bolster case on for you! cried Icey. You'll find it just as comfy as your own bed.

John stood in his nightshirt waiting for Pearl to precede him into bed.

Here, honey, said Icey, marching to Pearl with out-stretched arms. I'll take your doll so's you won't roll on it.

John's mouth flew open, but it was Pearl who spoke.

Oh, no! Miz Jenny always sleeps in the bed with me.

Nonsense! You'll roll on her in your sleep and hurt yourself, honey. Now I'll keep good care of the doll for you till morning—

No, said John in a faraway voice that did not seem to come from him at all. Pearl always sleeps with her doll, Miz Spoon, ma'am.

Icey whirled and glared.

Mind your business, youngster!

He crawled between the cold sheets, his lips the color of death, trembling even after Icey had agreed to let Pearl keep the doll and bent to kiss the little girl's cheek.

Good night, little lamb, she whispered, and she kissed John, too, but said nothing and presently turned out the gas lamp and moved to the door.

Sleep tight, she whispered and closed it, and John lay listening as the old couple moved about in the kitchen beneath the bedroom, talking in low voices and drinking coffee and moving out front from time to time to serve the few customers that came in after the show. The Victrola whirred and whined in the faint distances below and now the corner of the moon gleamed like the prick of a silver knife against the jamb of the window. Pearl stirred, then turned to face him.

John?

Yes.

Where's Mom gone?

Go to sleep, Pearl!

No, John! Tell me where?

To git married.

To Mr. Powell?

Yes.

John?

What, Pearl? What is it?

I'm glad, John. I love Mr. Powell!

You little fool! he whispered but so that she did not really hear, making the words to himself with his lips and clenching his fists in awful desperation.

I love him lots and lots, John!

And John thought: She is with him now—Mom is—and she is on his side and now Pearl is on his side, too, and that makes me alone.

Now Pearl was sitting upright in bed and the doll was sitting up, too, its painted eyes staring into the moon with vacuous and stunned idiocy.

John, if Mr. Powell is Mom's husband then I can tell him about—

His hand with the swiftness of a copperhead flew up and was pressing into her wet, surprised mouth and beneath his strong clasp she struggled, whimpering, and began to squeal softly into his fingers. In a moment he took the hand away, yet held it poised, ready to clamp down again.

You swore, Pearl!

John! Don't!

You swore that day, Pearl! You promised Dad you wouldn't tell!

Oh, I wouldn't never tell, John! You know I wouldn't never tell!

He glared into her face, chalk-white and gasping.

If ever you do, he whispered furiously, I'll get a big, big giant to come and *murder* you!

Oh, John! No!

Yes! Yes! A big giant with a long shiny sticker knife like *he's* got!

I promise, John! Oh, John, I swear!

All right! Just so you remember. Do you *swear?*

Yes! Yes!

Because, John went on, his eyes in the moon now, he'll ask you some day soon.

Mr. Powell?

Yes. He'll come and beg you to tell him.

But I won't tell him, John! I won't tell *ever!* Not even Mr. Powell!

She lay back down, breathing heavily with her thoughts and then: John?

Who has a big sticker knife?

Never mind! Go to sleep!

He lay thinking: Last Wednesday when he was out in the garden helping Walt Spoon spread bone meal he hung his coat on
the doorknob and I poked around in the pocket when he wasn't
looking and there it was only I didn't know what until I pressed
that little silver button and it jumped out and shook my hand.
I tried to get it closed but it wouldn't work and so I just stuck it
back in his coat, open, and run home and I guess he never suspicioned it was me because he never said nothing.

Presently he fell asleep and he was big and strong and he had
a blue gun and he was pointing it at Preacher and Preacher was
not even scared at all and John kept shooting the gun and Preacher
was really dead although he was pretending not to be and then his
mother came in the room and took the gun away from him and said:
John, you bad boy! Look who you went and shot! And he looked
and, Oh, dear God, it wasn't Preacher at all, it was Ben it was Ben
it was his dad Ben and it was too late because Willa took Ben out
and hid him in the mound under the tree where the dark bird sings.

Willa thought: He looks so queer with no coat on, with his narrow shoulders in the white shirt and those suspenders and his
paper collar on the bureau scarf. She felt warm and loving about
him though, because it made her think how like little children
men were underneath; how helpless and unpretending in their
suspenders and no collar. Outside the little hotel a radio was
blaring from an open restaurant down the street. They had taken
a pleasant little room at the Brass House and it was her honeymoon and she kept thinking as she watched him lay Ben's old
watch carefully on the dusty dresser: He is my husband and I
love him. He is not Ben but I will learn to love him even more
because he is a man of God. In a moment she would go down

the hallway to the bathroom by the fire escape and put on her nice muslin nightgown and come back to him. It could not ever be the way it had been with Ben those nights in that old, lost summer with the roller skates thundering faintly out in the darkness at the rolla-drome and the record playing over and over: Lucky Lindy! Lucky Lindy! It could not ever be like the nights of that summer. She would make her mind forget that first hot pulse and gush of Ben's embrace and she would make it something else—something better—between herself and Harry Powell. She lifted the old nightdress from the cardboard suitcase and thought: Because the old clothes don't matter; the cheap, torn Teddy bears and the ragged stockings and the rundown shoes that I've always had to wear. Because I have one nice thing that I gave to Ben and I will give it to him, too—the only nice thing I ever owned: my body. Because it is clean and beautiful and not torn or wore out like the clothes.

Willa, are you going to get ready for bed?

Yes, she said. I was just looking at you, Harry—thinking how handsome and good you are.

Hurry along, my dear! We both need our rest.

Yes! Yes, of course, Harry!

She lifted his coat to hang it up for him and something thick and heavy in the pocket struck against the door of the clothes press. He did not notice when she put her hand in the pocket with a woman's wondering and took the thing out, stared at it curiously for a moment, with a softening of her smile, and then put it quickly back before he should see. She fetched her washcloth and soap and towel and hairbrush and went off to the bathroom with that smile still on her lips but twisted with faint puzzlement now.

It is a kind of a razor, she kept thinking while she waited in the hallway of the little country hotel while a drummer finished in the bathroom and she listened to the thin, rasping voice of the song on the radio down there in the spring street of the river night. A woman laughed in another room and a glass tinkled and a man began singing a coarse parody of the radio tune and the woman laughed louder.

He was in bed asleep when she returned. The lights were out. The ragged window blind flapped like the gray wing of a hurt bird beside the bed and she stared back at her pale sister in the mirror as she stood waiting and wondering if he would call to her.

The only pretty thing I ever did own, she thought. My body. Because even the muslin nightgown was gray from too many washings and the feathers on the slippers had withered and clung to one another since that long-ago night when Ben had won them for her at the shooting gallery at the Upshur County Fair.

Harry? she called softly.

He was snoring lightly. And the window blind flapped.

Fix that window, he said suddenly in a clear, wide-awake voice as if sleep and waking were no different to him; as if he could move swiftly from the world of dreams to the world of waking with no break in the sound track of consciousness; with only a flutter of his thin lids.

She rolled the blind all the way up, thinking: He was pretending to be asleep, he was pretending to snore. That is because he is embarrassed.

She slipped between the sheets, fresh and sweet from some country widow's washline, and lay for a moment listening to the radio down in the town and her own heart thundering and then she turned on her side and stared at the back of his head. She could hear his lips moving in the darkness with a small rapid sound like the feet of mice.

Harry? she breathed.

He stirred impatiently.

I was praying, he said.

Oh, I'm sorry, Harry! I didn't know! I thought maybe—

He turned suddenly and although she could not see his face on the pillow she could feel the anger in it.

You thought, Willa, that the minute you walked in that door I'd start in to pawing and feeling you in the disgusting, abominable way men are supposed to do on their wedding nights! Eh? Ain't that right, now?

No, Harry! I thought—

That's the kind of thing they make jokes about in those filthy burlesque houses downriver at Louisville and Cincinnati! Oh, yes, I've witnessed them with my own eyes! I made myself go, Willa, just so's I could witness with my own eyes the degradation and stink to which mortal men and women can fall!

Her eyes widened in the pitch-darkness of his looming face until they burned and her mouth grew dry as his words lashed her.

I think it's time we got one thing perfectly clear, Willa! Are you listening?

Yes, she moaned.

Marriage to me represents a blending of two spirits in the sight of Almighty God! I reckon it's time I made that clear, Willa!

She shut her eyes, hating herself for the shame and dirtiness and hurt she felt now and she prayed that he would stop but somehow she knew that he had just begun; somehow he seemed to have roused himself to sermon pitch and suddenly he got out of the bed and stood in the yellow light which the window cast into the cheap room: his thin, wiry arms moving stiffly in the sleeves of his nightshirt.

How are they any better, he said, than the Whore of Babylon?

She buried her mouth in the pillow and smothered a moan in the thickness of it between her teeth.

Get out of bed, Willa! he commanded, not violently, but with a dangerous edge of anger still in his voice, while with one arm he pulled the window blind clear to the sill. Now he moved across the room, his dry naked feet whispering on the boards, and snapped the light on. It flooded the room with its uncharitable yellow glare and a faint singing commenced in the golden bulb.

Get out of bed, Willa!

She obeyed.

Harry, what—

Take off your nightdress.

Harry!

Do as I say, Willa!

She obeyed with sick, trembling hands and stood at last, naked and blushing before him.

Now go and look at yourself yonder in that mirror.

Harry, please! Please, I—

Do as I say!

She felt her feet moving, felt the grain of the cold boards under her soles and then the thin, worn nap of the square of carpet by the bureau.

Look at your body in the mirror, Willa!

She made her eyes travel the miles upward and stared into the brown mirror, streaked and stained like the surface of some condemned and poisonous pool. She saw her breasts, still pretty and young and firm and the shoulders that Ben had used to kiss when she wore her bathing suit to the river.

What do you see, girl?

I—

She could see her mouth begin to curl and the vision went blurring then in a burning, yellow wash of tears.

You see the body of a woman! he cried. The temple of creation and motherhood! You see the flesh of Eve that man since Adam has profaned and filthied—has made into a vessel for the corruption and lust of his own rottenness!

He was pacing now, thin and mad and touchingly absurd in the white nightshirt.

Mind you, my girl, I'm not pointing you out as worse than the rest. But that body—*that* body—

He pointed to her shivering loins and the dark feathers of her quivering, convulsed belly.

—that body was meant for begetting children! It was not meant for the whoring lust of whoring men! That's filthiness! I say that's filthiness and the Devil's business, my girl! Do you understand that?

Yes! Yes!

Do you want more children, Willa?

I— No, I—

No! Of course you don't! It is the business of our marriage to mind those two you have now—not to beget more! And if not to beget more—then why should we soil our bodies with sex and rottenness? Ain't that talkin' sense, my girl? Ain't that the way the Lord wants it?

Yes.

He stood staring at her a moment longer, his head cocked a little to one side and that curious remoteness wandering in his eyes again; his face twitching a little as if he were straining to hear, to listen to a faint, far counsel from heaven.

You can get back into your nightdress now and stop shivering, he said.

She felt the gown fall over her hair and shoulders and crawled back into the bed, sick and drained of feeling, while he turned off the light and let the window blind up again. He stood for a moment by the side of the ancient brass bed with the street lights touching his profile of flesh and cheekbone with a thin line of gold.

I'm sorry. She shaped the words soundlessly with her lips, waiting for him to get into the bed, and watched him at last crawl stiffly under the sheets again and turn his back to her again and then listened to the dry, faint breath of his swift, whispered prayer running on as endlessly as a reel of film on an unillumined movie projector.

She lay on her back staring at a dark stain on the ceiling and thought to herself: He is right but just the same it is queer that he would know he is right because he has never had a woman ever in all his life. He is right, though. It is rottenness, all of it, and I'll ask Jesus to help me get cleaned and purified of those thoughts so I can be what Harry wants me to be. He is right: I mustn't never want that again because it is what he says: a sin and an abomination; even when Ben and me did it it was that and maybe God is punishing him and me for it now. Ben. Ben—

And just before she fell asleep she heard another sound and thought: Well, I must be wrong. He wouldn't be doing that!

But it was so. He was crying softly in his sleep like a child and all she could do was lie there in an agony of fear, not able to touch him in any way, not able to reach over into that strange land of dream deaths and save him, not able to do anything at all but soundlessly shape the words against the wrath of God's anger and God's mercy there in the dark room of the little country hotel: Good night, Harry! Good night!

But they were lost beyond recall, beyond answering, borne on the winds above the meadow.

The golden June morning quivered like water in the new leaves of the grape arbor. Pearl squatted with the doll Jenny and the doll was Willa now and the tomato stake with the rag wrapped around it: that was Mister Powell. Pearl stood them side by side against the bricks at the bottom of the arbor and sang a song because Willa and Mr. Powell were married and they had returned from their honeycomb. Now the scissors from the pantry flashed in her fingers as she cut out the green paper faces. These were the two children and she was a patient mother because when the wind blew those mischievous children would try to run away.

Now, Willa! You must make me my supper for I am very hungry.

Yes, Mister Powell! Right away, Mister Powell! And what about our two green children—Pearl and John?

Well, you can make Pearl some supper, Willa, but John is bad. Put John to bed without his supper.

Oh, no! I can't do that, Mister Powell! John is hungry, too!

Well, well, if he promises to be very good and stop being so bad.

Pearl tucked the jagged bits of paper tight between the bricks at the feet of the doll named Willa and the stick named Mister Powell. In the kitchen she could hear her mother rattling pots and plates for suppertime.

Now! cried Pearl, when she had fed her family. Now it's bedtime! Off you go, children!

But suddenly the errant wind swept fitfully through the vines. John and Pearl fluttered away from the child's helpless fingers, sailed, and drifted high over the buttercups, into the sky, over the sun.

Come back, you bad children! wailed Pearl. Come back!

We shall bow our heads in grace.

John waited till Pearl's eyes were closed and then he lowered his shaggy head over his plate of ham and hominy and shut his eyes. The light shone distant and red through the quivering lids and he waited, mouth watering, as the rich incense of a dish of watermelon preserve tickled his nose. Preacher's grace rolled on in interminable catalog. At last his voice rose to conclusion.

—Though we live under the curse of Cain, Almighty God, we turn our backs against the temptations of this mortal flesh. Bless this good food, Oh, Lordamighty, and let it build up our stren'th to fight the Devil's fiendish persuasions and the temptations of sex and gold and lust amen pass the bread please, boy.

Willa kept her eyes on her plate throughout most of the meal. She ate very little. Perhaps more than any of them, John saw the change that had come over her since Preacher had entered the family. Her eyes bore dark shadows and her mouth was thinner—paler—and her flesh itself seemed to have capitulated to the urgent moral protocols of her marriage until the very roundness of her sweet figure had turned epicene and sour in that lean season. Still, in a curious way, she seemed happier in her strange union with Preacher than she had ever been with Ben Harper. Something new had come into her life. Willa had discovered Sin. It seemed somehow that this discovery was something that she had sought and hungered after all her life. She talked about Sin constantly to John and although Pearl understood only that Sin was being bad she was pleased to sit and hear Willa out when the sermonizing mood was upon her. Willa kept after them ceaselessly each night to be sure that each prayed long and well, on their knees, on the cold, naked floor by the bed. Preacher's spring revival meeting in a tent down the river at Welcome had brought them enough money to live on through the summer. These meetings had been highlighted by Willa's own impassioned testimony, and her shrill, fevered voice had risen above the cries of the most penitent sinners in the valley.

You have all suffered! she cried out one night, her eyes burning in the torchlight, her face blanched and bloodless with the thrill of her vision. And you have all sinned! But which one of you can say as I can say: I drove a good man to lust and murder and robbery because I kept a-hounding him and a-pestering him night and day for pretty clothes and per-fumes and face paint and do you know why I wanted them things? I wanted them so's he would lust after my body more and more and more!—instead of thinkin' about the salvation of his soul and the souls of them two little kids down yonder! And finally he couldn't stand it no more and he went out and took a gun and *slew!*—yes, slew two human beings and stole their money and come home with it to give it to me and say: Here! Here! *Here*, Whore of Babylon! Take this money that is tainted with the blood of Abel and go to the store and buy your pretty dresses and per-fumes and paint! But, brethren!—ah, that's where the Lord stepped in! That's where Je-e-esus stepped in!

Yes! cried Preacher, rolling his head gently till the paper collar bit into his neck. Ye-e-es!

Yes! panted Willa, her voice rising to hoarseness, to a scream. The Lord come down out of the sky and stood by the smoke-house that day and told that man that the money would just drive his poor weak whore of a wife to hell headlong!—*headlong!*

Yes! Yes! panted the sinners and the saved under the tent, under the torches.

—and them two kids would git dragged along to hell, too! *Headlong!* Yes! Yes!

—and their almighty souls would bu-urn in hellfire, too! Yes!

—and the Lord told that poor bloody-handed man to take that rotten money—that Devil's money—that bloody gold of greed and murder—

Yes! Yes!

—that money that dri-i-pped with the blood of a murdered man!—of *two* murdered men!—

Yes!

—The Lord said, Take it and throw it in the river yonder, brother! Wrap it 'round a stone and *throw* it in the old Ohio River and let it get washed clean down into the Mississippi! For it is better that it be your neck with that stone tied on it and throwed to the bottom of the river than to lead one of my little ones astray!

Yes! Yes! Hallelujah!

—Throw that money in the river! *In the river!*—

Amen!

—and let it wash out into the ocean where the fish can look at it! Because a fish has got more sense sometimes than a man!

(Laughter.) Yes! Oh, yes, Sister Powell! Praise God!

—and then the Lord told that man to give himself into the hands of the Law and let justice be done—!

Amen! Yes!

—and after justice had been done to Ben Harper the Lord made me suffer alone like Moses suffered in the Wilderness!

Praise God!

—and then he led Brother Powell to me and said, *Salvation cometh!*

Amen! *Amen!*

And the Lord bent down and said to me: Marry this man and go forth with him and preach the Word!

Amen! Amen!

And then someone began to lead them in singing "When the Mists Have Rolled Away" and they sang for nearly half an hour until the whole bottomlands echoed with their voices and under the headlights of Ben Harper's old Model T that night Preacher counted out the collection and told Willa it had been one of their best. It was close to thirty-five dollars, two bushels of Winesaps, and a half-gallon jug of maple sirup.

Somewhere—somehow Preacher always managed to find John alone in the house after supper. Now he stood beside him at the cellar door and because Preacher was standing in the way it was impossible to walk down the hallway to the stairs and go up to bed. Willa had gone to Cresap's Landing to visit after supper with Icey and Walt. Pearl was still playing with her doll family under the grape arbor.

Because, Preacher was saying, and his manner had long since stopped being wheedling and pleasant. Because sooner or later I will find out where it's hid, boy. It's just a matter of time.

I don't know! I don't know nothing about it!

Yes. Yes, you know!

No, said the boy, impudently. I don't.

I could thrash you for contradicting me, boy. That's back talk.

John thought: I would rather have the thrashing than the questions because the thrashing hurts quick and then it's over but the questions keep on forever and ever amen.

Well, boy?

No, he thought. No.

Where is it hid, boy?

He thought: And even she is changed now—my mother. If I go to her and tell her that he asks me the question all the time she says I am lying, that he is a man of God, that I am making it up because I hate him and because I am sick with Sin and because I am trying to turn her against him.

Preacher read his thoughts.

Your mother says you tattled on me, boy. She says you told her that I asked you where the money was hid. Isn't that so, boy?

Yes. Yes.

That wasn't very nice of you, John. Have a heart, boy.

It don't matter, the boy murmured.

No. That's right. It don't matter. Because it's your word against mine. And it's *me* she believes!

Yes, he thought. Because you have made her be crazy.

She thinks that money's in the river, smiled Preacher.

John listened to the tick of a death watch somewhere hidden in the ancient, dark wood of the old house.

But you and me—we know better! Don't we, boy? John pressed his lips tight, listening to the far-off chant of Pearl, making her little home under the grape arbor.

Don't we, boy! Goddamn you! Answer me! Answer, you little son of a bitch!

I don't know nothin', he said dully and thought: Now he will shut up and go away from me for a while. After he shouts at me he goes away. He takes the knife out of his pocket like he is doing now and he presses the button and the sharp thing flicks out and he looks at me for a minute and then he starts paring the big, blue thumbnail on the finger without a name and then he goes away.

No matter, Preacher said in an even voice, and the knife dropped back in his pocket. Sooner or later, boy, you'll tell. The summer is young yet, little lad.

He loomed above the boy, a vast dark hulk against the light behind him on the hall table: the lamp with the stained-glass shade and the silver chain pull that Ben Harper had given his wife one Christmas.

Now go and fetch your sister and put her to bed!

The big figure did not move aside for the boy to pass, making him flatten against the damp wallpaper of the passageway to get through. John ran to the kitchen and strained his eyes into the golden river dusk. The grape arbor was luminous in that twilight; its luxuriant leaves possessed strangely of their own rich light at this evening moment.

Pearl?

He could hear her voice, intimate and whispering as she scolded the doll named Willa and the stick named Mister Powell.

Pearl!

What, John?

Bedtime!

In a minute.

No—now, Pearl! I'll tell Ma!

All right.

He moved down across the grass, already wet with evening dew, toward the shape of Pearl's light pinafore: like a tiny moth within the green, dark cavern of the cool grape leaves.

Come on now, Pearl!

He could see her face turned up to him now, moonround and pallid with the big eyes like dark pansies above the tiny mouth.

You'll get mad, John, she whimpered.

I ain't mad, Pearl. Only git on up to bed. It's—

You'll get awful mad, John. I done a Sin.

You what?

He could hear her frantic movements at some task on the damp bricks at his feet; he could hear the crisp rustle of paper in her frightened hands.

Pearl! You ain't—

John, don't be mad! Don't be mad! I was just playing with it! I didn't *tell* no one!

His legs turned to water at the thought; the flesh of his neck gathered in quick, choking horror.

It's all here, she whispered placatingly and the furious movements continued.

Now the white moon of early summer appeared suddenly from the hill beyond the meadow and a vast aura of pale, clear light illumined the sight before the boy's eyes: the bricks beneath his feet littered with the green fortune in hundred-dollar bank notes that the little girl was frantically gathering together again.

Pearl! Oh, *Pearl!*

Now she was stuffing them back where they had been all along; pushing them through the rent in the cloth body of the doll Jenny that was held closed with a safety pin beneath the shabby toy dress. John fell to his knees and sank his hands into the pile of certificates that had slipped through Pearl's frightened hands. And then the soft footfall in the wet grass at the other end of the grape arbor told him that the hunter had returned.

John?

Oh—yes?

Preacher: standing in the blue mists of the moon, shading his eyes with his hands to see what the children were about.

What are you doing, boy?

Getting Pearl to bed. I—

What's taking you so long about it?

It—she—

What's that you're playing with, boy?

Pearl's junk, he said, magnificently. Mom gits mad when she plays out here and don't clean up afterward.

And then he stuffed the last of the bills into the soft cotton body and fumbled the safety pin back into the tear again. Preacher had not stirred. But John could sense that he was alert, suspicious, sniffing.

Come on, boy. It's chilly out here tonight.

Yes.

And now he arose and held out the doll to Pearl and then turned, facing the long, the interminable distances to the end of the green arbor where the dark one waited: giving the doll into the frightened hands of his sister and taking one of those hands then he began to lead her, to walk slowly and ever so cautiously toward the shape of the man against the blue smoke of the moonlight and all the while praying awkwardly and badly because the only prayer he knew was about Sin and this was a prayer about escaping.

Preacher cracked his dry palms together in a whip crack of impatience.

Hurry, children!

How many miles to Babylon? Three score miles and ten, John heard his riotous, foolish brain recite softly. Can I get there by candlelight?

He could see the gleam now of Preacher's watch chain against the death-gray vest and thought: He ain't guessed yet. He don't know.

A thousand miles to Babylon, ten thousand miles to walk yet to the end of a moonlit grape arbor where a dark man stands and he walked carefully, slowly, putting one foot before the other cautiously and holding Pearl's hand and thinking with growing nausea: But he heard me talk about cleaning up. Won't he think: Cleaning up what? Where's the paper I heard rustling? Where are the paper dolls?

And now he stood directly before him, the watch chain gleamed like fire before John's eyes and he did not breathe, did not move, waiting.

Now, said Preacher, up to bed with the both of you!

And now he was walking slowly up through the yard toward the lamp in the kitchen window and Preacher was following along behind and the boy fought back the flood of hysterical laughter that struggled and welled in his throat. He choked it back and led Pearl up the porch steps and into the kitchen.

Up! Up! scolded Preacher. Hurry!

On the steps he thought with a child's strange and wondrous irrelevance: There is a moon tonight. Maybe it won't rain. Maybe Uncle Birdie will take me fishin' in Dad's skiff tomorrow.

Within half an hour Willa returned home from the Spoons' and John listened to her voice and the voice of Preacher below the bedroom in the kitchen and presently her footsteps creaked on the back stairs and the door opened a crack.

John?

Yes, Mom, he whispered, because Pearl was asleep.

Are you in bed?

Yes.

And Pearl, too?

Yes, Mom.

He thought: Then he seen it after all. He guessed and he has let her be the one to come up and take the doll downstairs and cut it open with the knife and find the money.

Did you pray?

I forgot— Mom, I—

Get out of bed. Get Pearl up, too.

He shook his sister's arm, awoke her, whining and yawning

with sleep, and together they knelt and he felt the cold, rough boards on his knees under the little nightshirt and opening one eye he saw the moon like a dandelion through his eyelashes and listened while Willa's shrill, angry voice talked for a while about Sin and Salvation. When they were back in bed again, she stood by the bed for an instant, her tired hands, grown old too soon, folded before her waist.

Were you impudent to Mister Powell again tonight, John?

Mom, I—I didn't mean—

What were you impudent about?

He asked me about the money again, Mom!

You know that's not so, John! You always make up that lie. You're always saying that Mister Powell asks you about the money. There's no money, John. Can't you seem to get that through your head?

Yes'm. I told him—

You think you can turn me against him, don't you, John? she whispered. Don't you know he's a man of God?

He said nothing and heard a whippoorwill swoop and cry in the meadows where the river mists shone like lamb's wool beneath the moon.

You sinned, boy, she said. Ask God to forgive you for making up that lie about Mister Powell.

What's a Sin? said Pearl suddenly, rising with the doll in her arms.

Hush, Pearl! Did you hear me, John?

Yes.

Ask God to forgive you. Ask him, John.

Forgive me, he said. God.

And she closed the door and the tired footsteps stole away down the back stairs to the kitchen again and presently Pearl spoke, dreadfully worried.

John?

What?

John, I done another Sin tonight. I cut up two of them—only *two*, John. I cut them out with the scissors—the faces—

He thought: So I will be God. Then I won't be so scared of Him.

I forgive you, he said. But don't never do that again, Pearl. And don't never take them out again. You hear me, Pearl?

Yes. Yes, John. I swear!

And she fell asleep again, face to the summer moon, dreaming.

Come back! Come back, you naughty children! she cried in the dark nest of sleep. But the paper children spun away into the summer wind: beyond recall, beyond heeding, whirling and dancing over the buttercups, into the sun.

It is a night for dreams. John sleeps and once again he is playing in the grass beside the smokehouse with Pearl in that late afternoon of Indian summer.

There comes Dad yonder! he cried, jumping to his feet, and Pearl stood up, too, with the doll named Miz Jenny in her arms.

Where, John? Where?

See! There comes the car down yonder! You can see it through the apple trees!

When Ben Harper's Model T rounded the bend in the lane below Jason Lindsay's orchard the loud racket of its pounding engine always drifted clear and sharp toward the house. Now the old car bounced and rattled up the ruts into the yard below the grape arbor. Ben fell through the door and came staggering up toward the house.

Dad! Hey, Dad!

John ran down the yard toward him, thinking: I'll bet he has brought me and Pearl a present from the five-and-ten because he is acting funny and when he plays jokes on me like this there is always a little poke in his coat pocket with a cap pistol or a toy lead streetcar or something in it.

Dad! Hey, Dad!

Ben whirled and staggered, squinting his stunned and blood-shot eyes toward the direction of the voice and wiped his hand across his face as if to tear away a veil that had fallen there.

Hey, Dad! You bring me a present?

He could hear Pearl stumbling along behind him on her short legs, wailing for him to wait and then he was looking up at his father, seeing the eyes, seeing the torn shirt sleeve, the dark, spreading stain.

Dad! What's wrong?

Where's Willa? Where—

She ain't here. She's gone to Cresap's Landing to buy some calico. Dad, what's wrong. You're bleeding, Dad.

Ain't nothin'. Now listen to me, boy—

Dad! Dad! You're hurt bad!

Boy! Listen to me! There ain't much time! John, listen!

And the boy listened for a moment and then saw the gun in Ben's left hand and the thick roll of bank notes in the other. Then he began to scream; the world was gone mad. And Ben Harper stuck the pistol in his heavy motorcycle belt with the big glass studs and slapped the boy smartly across the face.

Listen to me, John! For God's sake, listen!

Pearl put her finger in her wet mouth and watched with grave eyes.

I done something in Moundsville, Ben whispered, wincing and swaying a little as if against the wind. They're comin' to take me, boy.

Dad! Dad!

Hush! Hush, boy! This money here—

Dad!

—I stole it, John. Yes. I stole all this money.

John did not know what stole meant but he knew it was all right because it was Ben.

They mustn't get it, whispered Ben, his eyes gone crazy now. None of them! Not even Willa! Do you understand me, boy? Not even your mom!

Dad, you're bleeding! he wailed.

Hush, John! Just listen—

John thought: I mustn't go to screaming again because then he will think I am a coward the way I was that day the moccasin bit me down among the cattails while we were fishing for blue-gills.

We've got to hide it. Now think, boy. Where? We've got to hide the money before they come to take me.

John thought: But why not give them back the money and then they won't be mad anymore: the men who are coming?

There's close to ten thousand dollars here, boy. And it's yours. Yours and little Pearl's.

He thought: I don't want the money, Dad, because already some of the red has dripped off onto the green numbers and if I touch the money it will get on my hands and Mom will think I been fighting.

Think, boy! Think! Where? Behind a stone in the smoke-house. Yes, that's it. Ah! No! Under a brick under the grape arbor. No! They'd dig for it.

Pearl knew it was all a game her dad and John were playing and she sat down suddenly in the daisies and threw Miss Jenny high above her head, falling back into the ironweed and Queen Anne's lace, kicking her legs at the sun.

I just can't clear my head! Ben was crying, shaking his shoulders like a wounded dog. What's happened? God a'mighty, what was I thinking? Because she ain't strong enough for it—in her hands it would be just like a gun—she'd drag them all to hell headlong. No! I remember now! It's for *them!* Yes, that's why I done it. Sure, that's it. Them kids! That Pearl and John! That's the way it was!

John looked at the trees and the hills behind and the black hood of the smoking Model T and each thing in the world had a tiny fringe of red around it and he felt the sour bile of fear well against his back tongue and he swallowed hard and clenched his fists like small, hard apples and thought: When the moccasin bit me down in the cattails I was ashamed because I was scared and I screamed when Dad taken his gutting knife and cut the place to make it bleed so's I wouldn't die!

Now Ben's mad eyes opened and squinted and opened wide again and focused on the doll in Pearl's arms and he smiled as if under the impact of a fresh and wonderful revelation.

Why, sure! Sure! In the doll! Sure! That's where!

There was a torn place in the doll's cloth back and it had a safety pin keeping it closed and now Ben fell to his knees and scrambled through the grass toward her and lifted the doll from her hands.

No! No! Miz Jenny!

Wait! Wait, now, honey! I won't hurt her none. Pearl, baby! Wait, now!

But Pearl wailed in anguish when Ben plucked the safety pin loose and the rent place fell open and he reached in and tore out a great wad of cotton stuffing from the doll body and then stuffed the thick roll of green bills inside.

Now, then! Now let them look! Now, then!

And then the pin was back and the cheap little toy dress had fallen and the doll was back in Pearl's hands and she had stopped crying and squatted cross-legged in the grass, snuffling angrily and glaring at her father.

You hurt her!

Ah, no! She ain't hurt, baby. That little spot of blood on her dress. That ain't doll's blood, Pearl honey. It's mine! No, she's all right!

And he struggled to his feet again, swaying and passing the back of his hand over his sick eyes, his face drawn and lean like the face of the Christ in passion.

Listen, John! Listen to me now! You must swear, boy! *Swear*, boy!

What? I—

Swear means promise, John. You must promise that you will take good care of Pearl yonder. That's the first thing, boy. Promise? Swear?

Yes! Yes, I—

With your life, boy!

Yes, Dad!

And then swear you'll keep the secret.

About—

—about the money. No matter who asks. Never tell. Never let them know, boy! Not even Willa! Not even your mom!

Yes, Dad!

Swear!

Yes! I swear!

—and when you grow up—you and Pearl—it'll be yours. Do you understand that, John? Do you swear? Say it, boy—say, I swear I'll guard Pearl with my life and I won't never tell about the money—

John repeated it with thick, fumbling tongue.

And *you*, Pearl! You swear, too!

She did not know what the game was about but she laughed and said yes and then fell to pouting again, hugging the wounded Jenny to her with fresh anger at what he had done to her baby. They heard the whine of motors and the two touring cars appeared in the bend in the lane at the corner of Jason Lindsay's orchard.

Here they come! They're comin' yonder, boy! Mind, now!

Where you goin' to, Dad?

Away, John! Away!

You're bleedin', Dad!

It's nothin', boy. Just a scratched shoulder.

But there's blood, Dad.

Hush, John! Mind what I told you!

Yes, Dad.

And you, too, Pearl. You *swore!*

And now the blue men were coming closer and she thought: This is part of the game, too, and she watched them move cautiously through the tall grass, the tanned, grim faces white around the lips. There are guns in the hands and one of the men spits a dark jet of amber into the daisies every three or four steps he takes.

Drop the gun, Harper!

They circle now, two of them fanning out below the smokehouse; two of them in the grape arbor; another standing up tall and fearless among the black-eyed Susans with the blue gun ready in his hand.

We've got you, Harper! Better give it up! We don't want them kids hurt!

I'm going now, John! Good-by!

The boy's lip convulses once but the line of steadiness comes back and he knows that Ben does not hear the tiny whimper in his throat.

Just mind what you swore, John!

Yes!

And take good care of Pearl. Guard her with your life, John!

Dad! Who's them blue men yonder?

Never mind them! They come and I'm goin' away with them, John. That don't matter, boy. Just mind what you swore! Mind, boy!

Yes!

Now the child leaps and awakens sweating and quivering under the sheet. He is lying in bed and the cold summer moon is a silver coin stuck to the windowpane and Pearl is breathing softly in the bed beside him. He is wide awake now and he knows where he is and that it is Now instead of Then and yet he thinks: Just because I am awake don't mean that the dream isn't still going on out there. Now the blue men are moving up through the grass below the smokehouse again; now they are hitting him with the shiny wooden sticks and the blue guns and they are dragging him away to the big cars and there is a dream me watching it happen and when they are gone I will see it again in the grass, under the Queen Anne's lace, where it fell out of his coat pocket when they were hitting him: the little brown paper poke with the jew's-harp in it for me and the toy baby bottle with the real rubber nipple for Pearl's doll. Because he never come home of a Friday once without bringing us a present from the five-and-ten. Not even once.

Yes, it is a night for dreams. Willa has prayed for nearly half an hour on her knees before crawling into the ancient brass bed beside the sleeping body of the man and even after she is in bed she begins praying again, automatically, and she has fallen asleep in the middle of a phrase and finds herself thinking how strange it is that spring is gone and here it is suddenly winter and the window has grown thick with hoar and the gas is a flickering forest of blue and yellow in the asbestos of the bedroom fireplace and it is Ben beside her in the bed. Why, it had none of it ever happened and they had only been married two months and here they are in the big house her uncle had left her.

You asleep, hon? Huh-uh.

Gee, but I love you, Willa. Me, too, Ben.

Sometimes I think it's just too blamed wonderful to be real and one minute I'm so happy I could dance and the next minute I'm sad. Sad, honey?

Yes, sad like when they die in the show and I keep thinkin': Well, it just can't last—you and me, Willa.

It'll last, she said, and he embraced her then and she had closed her eyes and thought about their wedding night at the tourist cabin, their honeymoon, and outside the window that tune playing over and over again. She had worn the only pretty thing she had, her green wool skirt and the jacket to her old suit and the lace dickey that was still good, and she didn't have a single new thing but it didn't matter because she knew she was going to make him happy. When he looked across the room at her hanging her clothes on the chair the record started playing again: Lucky Lindy up in the air—Lucky Lindy flew over there! and he had stared at her with his gentle, burning eyes and said how beautiful her breasts were. It was the first time he had seen her naked. Why, sure they are! she laughed, blushing, eyes flashing, running to him, still giddy from the whisky they had drunk. Why, sure! It's the only pretty thing I own—my pretty figure.

A dream within a dream; lying there in the bed with him and thinking about the short time they had been married and all the Wonderful Time to be.

What'll it be, honey? he whispered afterward. A boy? Maybe a girl?

A boy first! Then a girl—

What next? More boys?

Heck no, honey! Two will be enough.

He fell silent, brooding and far away from her as it often was with him.

What's wrong, Ben?

Aw, nothing.

Yes! What is it?

She had reached out her fingers and pulled his stubbly chin around so she could look into his eyes and find the trouble.

What is it, Ben honey?

I just keep thinkin' that I don't want any kids of mine ever knowin' the hard times I had!

They won't, honey! We'll be rich some day!

Rich! Sellin' rakes and hoes and onion sets in a hardware store?

No, honey! You'll get something better. Maybe you'll start a store of your own some day.

Maybe. Maybe.

You will, Ben. I know it.

He sighed long and deep and she could sense that his desperate eyes stared into the flickering gas of the fireplace; searching there among the guttering blue-and-gold phantoms for the visions of the Big Tomorrows.

It don't matter so much about you and me, he said. We'll always get along no matter how rough it gets. I don't get the awful feeling when I think about you wantin'—me wantin'. But I'll never let a kid of mine want. It don't matter how I git it—no youngin of mine will ever want for nothin'.

I know. I know, honey, she whispered, soothing his brow, his quivering eyelids, with her loving, gentle hands—her fingers bright with the pretty dime-store ring he had wed her with.

But now she woke and caught her breath, knowing it had not been real, that it had been a dream, and she felt ashamed and commenced to pray again because it had been adultery, thinking it was Ben Harper in the bed there with her and dreaming that he had embraced her in the way that Preacher had helped her see was the Devil's way. The moon rode high in the pale, unblemished sky above the river. Willa's eyes shone and her gray lips moved soundlessly in the darkness, in the shadow of the body of the man beside her.

Praise the Lord! she whispered fiercely. Praise the Lord!

And in another part of that same night Icey and Walt prepared for bed. After Icey had turned out the gas lamp in the hallway she went back into the bedroom and removed her teeth and put them in the fresh tumbler of water by the bedside. Walt rolled over to face her and rose on his elbow.

You sure all them lights is out downstairs, Mother?

Yes. I'm sure.

It always irritated her: to have him make her talk in the bed after she had put her teeth in the water glass. Yet Walt was in a mood for talk.

Icey, I'm worried about Willa.

Icey grunted and pressed her face deeper into the feather bolster but Walt's words interested her so much that she could not think of sleep. She sat up and fetched her dripping dentures from the drinking glass and fitted them into her mouth again with a faint sucking click.

How do you mean, Walt?

He was silent for a moment until she nudged him impatiently with a fat elbow.

I'm figurin', he said, how I can say it so's you won't get mad.

Say what? Walt Spoon, you can be the most—

There's somethin', he interrupted, something wrong about it, Mother. Somethin' I can't name—somethin' I feel in my bones.

About what? About—

About him. About Mr. Powell! *All* of it!

Walt!

Now, Mother! A body can't help their feelin's.

But she was out of the bed now, standing there in the dark, and he heard her fumble for a match to light the lamp. She stood now in the pale light, glowering at him furiously.

May the Lord have mercy on you, Walt Spoon!

Mother, I—

That man of God! Offerin' that widow the only salvation left to her and them fatherless kids!

He sighed and closed his eyes, pretending to be trying to sleep again. But he opened them again, submitting to her lashing stare.

You're no better than that boy, she said.

He said nothing; sorry already that he had spoken; seeing a night of arguing ahead of him because of his foolish candor.

—Thinking evil! she said. Making up tales on that poor man!

Mother, I only—

Lying tales! snapped Icey, rousing herself now to fresh wrath. Willa has told me all of it. How that boy accuses Mister Powell of talkin' about the money all the time—sayin' he says the boy has it hid somewheres. Such lies as would shame Ananias. And now *you*, Walt Spoon! How you could *dare*—

Well, I was wrong, he sighed. Now that I think about it—

Yes, you were, she said, but stood a moment longer to glare at him before she huffed out the light and crawled back into the bed beside him.

Yes, he said, after a spell of consideration. I was wrong. Sometimes we misjudge them most that serves the Lord best.

He heard her sniff and knew that she had forgiven him, that she had retired into herself in triumph and that now he might rest. Yet presently he roused from a half-sleep to feel her shake lightly with laughter.

What's eatin' you, ol' woman?

Oh, shoot, Walt! Just thinkin'!

Well, what?

About all that money, she said.

Yes, he said. All that money—just layin' there molderin' on the river bed. Ain't it enough to make a body ponder?

Lordy, yes! I swear sometimes I get an awful itch to rent a skiff and go draggin' for it!

Shucks, you'd never hook it. Not in a million years. Walt Spoon, shame on you! I was just jokin'! Pshaw, I wouldn't touch that filthy, bloody stuff for nothin'! Shame on you!

Her hand rose to her mouth then, the lips gasped suddenly, and presently the teeth settled gently, grinning, in the glass of spring water, while Icey turned her back on them and fell into the healthy sleep of a fat, innocent child. Yet Walt Spoon lay awake. It was something he had learned to do in their marriage: hammering his thoughts into the shape she wanted. It was a price of peace, of sleep itself. Whatever unframed and as yet unshaped suspicions he had had of Preacher were soon gone—stamped and trodden into the soil of domestic orthodoxy.

It's true, he thought. He's a man of God. Yes, anyone can tell that.

And he slept then, his snores soon mingling in rough counterpoint to those of the old woman. Only the teeth in the glass maintained their ironic vigilance: smiling reflectively above the heads of the innocent sleepers.

BOOK THREE

THE RIVER

"Not cleverness, child, but only thought.
A little thought in life is like salt upon rice,
as the boatmen say. . . ."

—KIPLING, *The Undertakers*

The dangerous shadow was no more than a faint dappling of darkness among the sun-speckled shallows. Uncle Birdie hunched in the skiff and pointed a crooked finger.

Yonder, boy! See! Right yonder! That's him—there by the big root!

John bent suddenly to the skiff's stern and the shadow was gone. It had not moved, it had not fled; it had simply dissolved suddenly from the deep tobacco-dark water and then there was nothing but the sun dapples again.

Meanest, orneriest, sneakinest son of a bitch in the whole damn river, boy! A gar! Did you see him?

Yep. And he stole your bait, Uncle Birdie?

You seen me plunk that there crawdad on the hook, boy. Then you seen me cast—and when I pulled her in the bait was gone. Ain't no tobacco box can do that, Cap. Ain't no little sunfish can swipe bait like that. It was that sneakin', egg-suckin' son of a bitch.

Uncle Birdie blew his nose against one scarred, horny finger and cocked a wise blue eye sidelong at the boy in the boat.

Your ma don't know I cuss—does she, boy?

Shucks, sighed John. She don't even know I'm here half the time.

Well, you ain't opposed are ye?—to cussin', I mean?

No.

Tell you why I ask, boy—your step-pa bein' a preacher and all that I—

John's lips grew thin as string and the old shadow flickered back behind his eyes again: the dark gar in the river of his mind.

Birdie stuffed his cheek full of fresh Mail Pouch and stared off into the shore willows, draped softly out over the still shallows clean to the bend below the orchard.

Never was much of a one for preachers myself, said the old man, with another sidelong glance, quick as a robin's eye. But then I reckon there is all sorts.

John swallowed quickly and his wide eyes were lost in the river. Now Uncle Birdie reached out a scaly, hook-scarred finger and turned the child's face to meet his eyes.

Stepped on your toes that time, didn't I, boy? Well, no matter. I don't know what's wrong up at your place and I don't figure to ask. But just you remember one thing, Cap—if ever you need help you jus' holler out or come a-runnin'. Ol' Uncle Birdie's your friend. Now reach me that can of hooks yonder and I'll show you how to catch Mister Gar as neat as snappin' a tick off a redbone's ear.

John relaxed and his face shone as he handed the old man the hooks. They understood one another that day because of a great many things that neither of them could say and because, for some wonderful and ancient reason, when two men are alone in a boat on a river it is nigh impossible for them not to understand one another, no matter if no word is said at all.

Better pick out a big un, Uncle Birdie.

Big un, hell! I'll pick the littlest one of the lot! The one thing you got to understand about old Mister Gar is this, boy—he is a crafty sort. Why, there hain't nary hook in the land smart enough to hook Mister Gar. What a feller needs is—

He tugged his greasy hat from his shaggy white head and sought among the motley flies and hooks and lures and presently plucked a long gray hair from the greasy, frayed band.

—is mother wit—and a horsehair.

A horsehair!

You heard me, Cap. A horsehair. A horse *tail* hair, mind ye—a good long one like this here. Now watch! First you loop your old horsehair and make a little lasso. See there?—And then you hang your baited hook right down in the middle of it—like so!—See?

John followed the old man's swift hands with brooding, enchanted eyes.

Like this. Now fetch me that piece of crawdad there, Cap. That's a lad! Now! There we are!

Won't he bust it, Uncle Birdie? Won't the gar bust the horsehair when he gits lassoed?

Shoot! A horsehair'll hold a whale, Cap. You jest watch now. You see old Mister Gar comes along and sneaks up on the bait and when he gits his head right smack-dab in the middle of the noose we snap him up. Watch now!

Uncle Birdie lowered his line cautiously into the placid shallows, dark as old mahogany under the golden tessellation of the willow trees and sky. John's eyes peered into the water until they ached, and every submerged can and leaf seemed the dark shadow for which they waited, every cloud or bird that passed above them in the afternoon cast its image in the mirroring river and seemed to the boy to be the black hunter. He thought: Like him. Like his ways. Sneaking around after the bait, only he ain't as smart as a gar—he don't know where the bait is so he can't steal it. Time ticked on and the old man's eyes glared shrewdly into the depths and then suddenly, without warning, Uncle

Birdie thrust his arms upward and the boat rocked like a cradle and the air was full of sparkling pearls of water.

There! There! There, you slimy, snag-toothed son of a bitch!

And John wiped the water from his face and saw the ugly, thrashing creature in the skiff bottom.

Don't git your fingers in the way, boy! cried Uncle Birdie, snatching off his mud-crusted shoe. He grasped it by the toe and flogged the thrashing nine-inch fish flat into the floor boards with the heel.

Meanest, suck-egg, bait-stealin' bastard between here 'n' Cairo! roared Uncle Birdie in a proper riverman's rage. Presently he peered, with John, at the broken body of the dark, slim knife-jawed fish in the skiff bottom among the cans and bilge.

There now, boy! He's done!

Can we eat him, Uncle Birdie? Can we cook him?

Shoot! If you've got an appetite for bones and bitterness you can. That's what makes a body so derned mad about a gar. They ain't fit for nothin' after you go to the trouble to catch 'em.

Birdie fetched the creature up gingerly by the tail and threw it far out into the river and watched with angry eyes as it floated away on the quickening current near the channel. Then Birdie spit in the water and went to baiting his line for sunfish again. They had a panful already and the sun was standing close to the crown of the mine tipple across the river on the Ohio shore.

Queen City's due past tonight, said Uncle Birdie softly. She don't put in at Cresap's Landing no more but she still blows as she passes!

John had seen this last of the great Ohio River packets once or twice in his life; glimpsed it from a distance, through trees, or from the window of his bedroom, a great mountain of decks and white paint and proud stacks spilling black smoke all down the sky. And like all river folk he had heard the sweet enchantment of her whistle on many's the lonely night: that hoarse, sweet chord that seemed the voice of all the great, dark river's past: the brooding spirit of that rich and feral stream and the ghosts of the men of long past times and the good and evil that they made upon her: the Harper and Mason and the Devil Girty and God's own Johnny with his poke of appleseeds.

And so they rowed back to the landing and tied the skiff again under the willows and wallowed up the shore again to the wharfboat.

John had grown restless again with the coming of night. He watched Birdie cleaning the little fish while the skillet began to sizzle on the fire in the stove.

I reckon I better be goin', Uncle Birdie.

What! You mean you caught all these here fish and then you hain't stayin' to taste 'em? Aw, shucks, no, Cap. You can't do thataway.

Mom will be wonderin', Uncle Birdie. It's sundown.

Well, boy, I reckon maybe you're right.

You done a good job with Dad's skiff, Uncle Birdie.

Nothin' at all, boy. She's your skiff now. But say! I reckon I could have your permission to take her out once in a while on my own?

Shucks, yes, Uncle Birdie. You're practically a part owner. You fixed her up.

Well now, boy, it'd be just grand if I could take her out ever' day for a little mess of catfish or tobacky boxes. Besides—a boat needs usin' to keep her trim.

I don't mind, Uncle Birdie.

By granny's, I'll take her down to the deep place first thing tomorrow and catch me some tobacky boxes. That's where they're thick. That deep place down by Jason Lindsay's pasture— there by the west fence.

Restlessly John turned his eyes to the window of the wharfboat and stared out into the peaceful river night. The sun had gone down behind the mine tipple now and dusk gathered like smoke upon the land.

Mind, now, Cap! cried the old man and the little fish cried out as he flipped them one by one into the hot grease.

What, Uncle Birdie?

Mind what I told you! Mind what I said—if you ever git in a crack—just give a holler—just come a-runnin'!

John made no reply but scrambled up the plank and up the bricks of the landing and off down Peacock Alley toward the river road. But the old man knew that he had heard: saw that the scared shoulders were a little braver now.

He sat alone by his bedroom window, watching the moon rise on the hills. The raincrow fluted its soft, grieving notes down in the meadow. And then a soft step sounded on the threshold behind him. John?

He leaped and whirled, gaping and livid with fright but saw that it was only Pearl.

Ain't you hungry, John?

No. He turned his eyes to the hills again, to the impassive and impartial moon in whose far, vast, mottled face he had found, upon so many nights, a solace.

Mom sure was mad, prattled Pearl, not entirely displeased with John's punishment. She sent you to bed without no supper when she found your shoes was wet.

He sighed, letting the silly female chatter roll off his weary head. But then the rich, maddening scent of fried chicken brushed against his senses and he turned just as she fetched it up from under her little calico skirt and held it to him: the thick drumstick from her own plate.

Here, she said, full of ancient, motherly solicitude. Eat it, John.

You swiped it?

Well, I wasn't really very hungry, John. I kept it off my plate.

He would have died for her then and took it from her hand and ate ravenously, like an animal, hunched out of the moon's light, beneath the window sill. She watched him eat and sighed, warmed with something years beyond her, a need that moved her heart often when she pressed the doll against it in the dark.

You feel better now, John? she said, cocking her head.

Yep.

Did it taste good?

Sure. Thanks, Pearl.

One time, she sighed, Mom sent me to bed without no supper and I got so hungry it was just awful, John.

Thanks, he said finally, wishing the subject to be closed and she sensed that and moved away and sat down on the salt box carpet stool by the dresser and regarded him with grim maternalism.

But just the same, John—you really shouldn't associate with that filthy old man.

At the window now he was watching Willa's stooped, nervous figure hurry down the tanbark walk toward the lane on her way to spend another evening at Cresap's Landing gossiping with Walt and Icey. He watched the light fade slowly from her figure as it moved away from the gold circle of the eternal gas lamp beneath the oak tree and when she was out of sight he thought: Now we are alone again in the house with him. He will come upstairs directly and it will start again: the questions and the being scared. In a minute he will be standing there in the doorway and we won't even have heard his shoes on the stairway because he moves that way. This house at night is like the river shallows under the skiff, under the willows where it is shady and dark, and that makes it so he can move without anyone knowing it, without anyone seeing him: like the dark shadow of the gar. Only there is nowhere in the world a hook small enough, a horsehair strong enough.

Woolgathering, children?

And he had been there all along, God only knows how long, standing in the doorway watching them, thinking maybe they would let slip some little clue, some little crumb of bait and then he could move quickly like the gar and snatch it into his evil maw.

There's my little Pearl!

She cried out happily and ran to him and threw her arms around him and the doll Jenny fell forgotten by his shoe toes. John knew that he could not win this battle; the little girl was drawn irresistibly to the stepfather.

Ah, such a sweet little soul, crooned Preacher, stroking her curls with his big, branded fingers. We're not talking to John tonight—are we, Pearl? John's been bad.

Pearl's moon face turned slowly in the gloom and her finger rose to her pouting lips.

No, she said softly. John's been bad.

John was sent to bed without his supper, wasn't he, Pearl?

And John knows that if he disobeys again he'll get a taste of the strap—doesn't he, Pearl?

Yes, said Pearl, pressing herself closer to Preacher, farther from bad John. The strap! You better be good, John!

Ah! Ah! We mustn't even speak to John, little sweetheart. John don't like to be spoken to. We'll just have a little talk between the two of us—how'll that be?

Pearl raised her arms so that he could lift her. He smelled like the cellar, like iron, like old leaves in autumn under the grape arbor.

John is a feller, said Preacher softly, who likes to keep *secrets*.

Pearl fell silent now; something had begun to tug: a wind blew from the east and one from the west and she could not tell which to hark to.

John is a great one for secrets, Preacher continued softly. Especially about *hiding things*.

John hid his eyes in the window and thought: That is the moon. I can grab her doll in my hand and go through the window and grab the moon and climb up and he cannot get me there and it will be safe after all.

But *you and me!* cried Preacher softly, intimately. We don't keep secrets—do we?

No, whispered Pearl, doubtfully, and plucked at her lip with her finger.

Especially, secrets about—money!

Now the finger popped into her mouth and her eyes moved gravely from the face of the hunter to the pale moon of John's face by the window.

For instance, Preacher said, cunningly, I'll tell *you* a little secret!

Pearl listened now. She loved secrets; all of them, that is, but the money secret and that secret scared her because it made John mad.

Would you like that, sweetheart? Would you like to hear a secret?

Yes!

Good! The secret is this—I knowed your daddy.

Pearl frowned.

The blue men, she said solemnly. They come one day and took him away—

Who?

The blue men!

Ah, yes. The blue men, of course. And you know what they did with him? Eh?

No.

Why, they brought him right to me. I'll bet you didn't know that, now, did you?

Where's Dad?

Never mind about that just yet, said Preacher. All things in due time, little bird. First just let me tell you what your daddy said to me. He said: *Tell my little girl Pearl that there's to be no secrets between her and you.*

Where's Dad? she whined again.

Tut! Tut! I'm a-gettin' to that part. But first you've got to understand that other part—the thing I just told you—what your Daddy said about *secrets.* Did you understand that, now?

Yes!

No secrets between you and me. None at all. Did ye understand that?

Yes.

John's back arched slowly like a bent elm stick. A single droplet of sweat crept down his shoulder blades like an ant and his eyes fell irresistibly to the sprawled cloth body of the doll by Preacher's shoes. And the darkness softly breathed while Preacher whispered the next question.

Where's the money hid?

John had learned to throw during the summer that Ben had taught him to play ball in the meadow below Jander's Livery Stable. That is why the heavy hairbrush struck Preacher and not Pearl. He heard the black wood ring on the bone of cheek and forehead and heard the soft intake of breath and could not be sure for a moment if it had been Pearl's or Preacher's.

You swore you wouldn't tell! he screamed, stamping his feet and beating the air with his fits. You swore! You swore! You swore!

And then he fell silent and Preacher said nothing but Pearl said: You're bad, John! You hit Daddy with the hairbrush!

And he lay against the window sill with the night at his back and thought: Why don't he say nothing? Maybe it didn't hit him after all. Don't he *feel* things? Why don't he put her down and come over and kill me or something instead of just standing there because even in the dark I can tell: he is smiling about it, smiling because it hurt, because I hit him, smiling because of what he knows he will do to me later to get even. But Pearl didn't tell. Anyway she didn't tell!

So you see? Preacher chuckled presently, his voice as if nothing had happened. We can't have anything to do with John—can we, little sweetheart? John's just plumb bad through and through.

Yes. John's plumb bad!

He thought: So he has won again. So now I know why he didn't get mad. It's because he was glad I hit him with the hairbrush because that way he can make her think I'm bad and she will tell him the secret.

And so, Preacher said cheerfully, you and me will just lock poor, bad old John in the room, little bird—

And watching them move toward the door he thought: But the doll is on the floor. So there is a chance. Because maybe she will forget about it when he takes her downstairs to talk.

—and you and me will just go on downstairs to the parlor and have a nice little chat, Preacher finished. Would you like that, Pearl?

Yes, said Pearl. Yes, and we won't let plumb-bad John come, will we?

Oh, gracious, no! John *throws* things. We'll punish him later, of course—but first we'll go and have a talk about all kinds of secrets!

And as he moved to the door she twisted suddenly in his grasp and stretched her twinkling fingers.

Miz Jenny! Miz Jenny!

And Preacher stooped with a chuckle and caught up the flopping cloth body.

Just you and me and Miz Jenny, he said.

We'll all have a nice little talk, Pearl cried happily and the door closed and the brass key turned and John watched the line of golden light in the crack above the threshold as their shadows split it and then moved softly away toward the stairs.

Willa smiled.

I bear my cross with pride, Icey, she said. I bear it graciously as He meant me to.

I know. I know that, honey. But there ain't a bit of sense in lettin' that youngster break up the happiness He meant for you and Mister Powell to have together.

The Lord has His own ways!

Well, sometimes the Lord needs a little help, said Walt. And I don't reckon a little switchin' around the legs is no sin.

John favors his father, said Willa. He's got that streak of Harper, you know.

Yes. Yes. Stubborn and mulish as a sheep.

I don't know what to do with him, Icey. Whippin' won't change him—always suspicionin' and lyin' against that man of God. It is my cross, Icey. I must bear it with pride.

Well, sighed the old woman. It's a pity. It's a shame. I hope he never grows up to have children of his own serve him that way.

Willa's face shone with the strange, sweet radiance of one possessed. She rose now and bade them good night.

Good night, honey! And watch your step on the road. Want Walt to walk you?

No! No, thank you! I'll manage fine, Icey.

At the threshold the old woman caught the girl's thin face between her fat palms and kissed her quickly.

Willa! Willa! Walt and me couldn't care about you more if you was our own.

I know, Icey! I know!

And plan on stayin' longer next time. 'Deed you hardly get settled till you're frettin' to git home again.

Willa sighed and smiled, loving the cross she bore.

I'm needed, she said. To keep peace and harmony between them. It's my burden and I am proud of it, Icey!

God bless ye. God bless ye, signed the old woman and closed the screen door and stood with old Walt watching as she left: the hearts of them both full of blind and troubled concern.

Willa walked down the dust of the lonely lane, into the tranquillity of the summer night. A thick mist had crept in from the river and now the moon illumined it to a glowing meadow of white beyond her in the rolling bottoms. Off in the distance the single flame of gas blossomed in the yard lamp beneath the oak, and Willa hurried toward it, yearning for the solace and comfort of her bed; there was so much praying to be done this night. The pearly flute of the raincrow drifted through the darkness to her and upriver—beyond the hills—the faint, soft voice of the old river queen sounded for the bend. Willa moved through the open gate and up the tanbark walk. More than ever this night her heart was full of the curious and nudging sadness that had come over her since that strange and wonderful night in the hotel room: her honeymoon, the turning point in her life; the eve of Salvation. But now something stayed her at the bottom step of the porch and she stood in the darkness with the fireflies drifting past her and heard Preacher's voice within the house and the prattle of the little girl in bright counterpoint to it and Willa thought: She, at least, loves him. John will never love him because he is full of the old evil of the father but my little Pearl loves him. They are together now in the parlor, she thought warmly. And Harry is telling her a dear old Bible story. But still she paused, womanlike, curious, listening to their voices and the thump and feathery scramble of a June bug against the screen.

John is bad, Pearl said. We won't let him be with us, will we?

No indeed! boomed Preacher softly. We'll have our own talk—just you and me.

About secrets, said Pearl. Tell me a secret, please.

Aw, have a heart! exclaimed Preacher. That ain't fair. I told you *my* secret—all about knowin' your dad. Now it's your turn.

All right, then! What secret shall I tell?

Well—you might start in by tellin' me how old you are!

That's no secret! I'm five—going on six!

Well, sure, now! That's no secret, is it? Then how about this. What's your name?

Pearl chuckled outrageously.

You're just fooling, she said. That's no secret, either. My name's Pearl!

Tut! Tut! cried Preacher, in mock dismay. Then I reckon I'll have to try again—

Tell me another secret! cried Pearl. About my dad!

Aw, no. Now it's your turn. You have to tell me a secret now.

All right. Then will you tell me another one?

Yes! I will! I will!

He paused a moment and Willa stood, smiling, listening happily. The night wind drifted slowly through the house and she could hear the cold tinkle of the Chinese wind chimes far off in the pantry.

Where's the money hid?

But now Pearl grew still again, biting her finger, thinking of plumb-bad John locked in the room like an evil prince, behind the black door, with the chicken bone in his hand.

John's bad, she said softly.

Yes! Yes! Never mind about John now. *Where's the money hid?* said Preacher, and the voice was choking a little, the madness so very close now to the dark pool's surface, the gar circling wildly in the sun-dappled shadows of the shoals.

But John made me swear, she breathed.

And now he could contain it no more. The game was played out; the toys swept up and dumped in the box and the lid clamped down and the children's hour was done. The gar darted up from the green depths and now the ripples broke. His voice was as swift and solid in the evening silence as the thump of a butcher's cleaver in the block.

Where's the money! Tell me, you little bitch, or I'll tear your arm off!

Willa's mind swung back into focus and she smiled and thought: I am standing here in the darkness and I am dreaming. It is a silly dream I am dreaming and directly I will wake up and I will pray again. Praise the Lord! Bless his Holy Name!

Tell me!

Pearl flung the doll to the carpet and tore loose from him and fled screaming through the golden lamplight just as Willa moved smiling across the threshold. Preacher caught himself against the hall tree and the face he turned to her seemed stunned: the head shook as if in disbelief at this miscalculation and then as swiftly as the drawing of a blind the face fell again to a mask of utter and timeless composure.

Willa! I didn't expect you home so soon!

I was worried. The kids—What's the matter with Pearl?

He shrugged and passed the fingers named Love wearily across his brow.

It's that boy, he sighed with a patient smile. He's been talking to her again about that—money. I locked him in his room, my dear. He's scared that poor little girl half out of her wits. Willa, what in time are we goin' to do with that boy?

I don't know, she breathed, moving past him toward the muffled voice of weeping in a closet somewhere, hoping that he would not touch her nor follow, moving now with some old, undamaged instinct toward her child.

Amen! she whispered at last, and he had lain there in the dark listening to her praying throughout that solid hour of whispering: of the pained and tortured catalog of her own transgressions and those of her children.

Are you through? he said clearly.

What?

Through praying, he said. Because—

Yes, I'm through, Harry.

—because I want to know something—and you'd better tell me the truth!

What?

The truth! What did she tell you in there?—in the bedroom when you seen her to bed and heard her prayers? What did she—

Who? I don't—

Pearl. You know who. What did she say I done to her?

Willa lay still for a while, smiling still, because it was not real.

What did she tell you?

You know what, Harry.

And you were listening outside the parlor window so you knew it all anyway. Weren't you? What did you hear, Willa?

You know—

Yes, I know. I want you to say it. What did you hear? What did she tell you I done to her? Why did she say she was crying?

It's not in the river is it, Harry? It's somewhere here amongst us—still tainting us with its stink—

Answer me!

The fingers were around the soft flesh of her thin arm, naked under the prim, old woman's nightdress: his grip banding her arm bone like a ring of thin, cold steel.

And Ben never told you he throwed it in the river? Did he? She said.

Then she thought: Why is my lip bleeding? Why can I taste the blood running back into my teeth and tongue? And then she remembered that he had struck her with the dry, shiny flat of his hand and it had happened only a second before though it seemed like a long time.

—then the children know where it's hid? she said. John knows? Is that it?

And the dark gar wheeled patiently in his pool again, the long sentry of circling dusk and shadow, of wisdom and darkness under the sun-dappled pool. He had risen from the bed now and stood silhouetted against the square of moonlit window and his head was cocked a little toward the light as if harking to a whisper late in coming, and she thought: Why, he is so little. He is only a child. He looks like a little boy in his nightshirt. It was Ben who was the grown-up, dirty man.

Then it is still here, she went on. Somewhere amongst us?

The child did not move yet, the whisper had not come.

So you must have known it all along, Harry, she said, and heard the great boat blow in the channel again, closer now, feeling its way through the darkness and the fog.

But that ain't why you married me, Harry. I know that much. It couldn't be that because the Lord just wouldn't let it. He is a God of Love! He made you marry me so's you could show me the Way and the Life and the Salvation of my soul! Ain't that so, Harry?

But he did not hear because now the night was filled with Whispers and they were for him. And she knew suddenly that he was not going to ever say anything more to her as long as she lived; that whatever was going to happen next would be not words but a doing. But still she kept on.

—so you might say it was the money that brung us together, she chanted softly to the ceiling, not looking to see whatever it was he was fumbling after among his clothes on the back of the rocking chair. The rest of it don't matter, Harry—all the common, dirty old ways I used to lead with Ben! I got shed of them, Harry, like a body would take off a dirty old dress. Because that night in the hotel at Sistersville you showed me the way—

She paused, listening to him and then thinking: But it still ain't enough. I must suffer some more and that's what he is making ready for me now: the last and total penance, and then I will be clean.

Praise God! she cried as he pulled down the window blind and the pagan moon was gone and something clicked and switched softly open and she heard the swift rushing whisper of his bare feet on the floor as he moved through the darkness toward the bed and she thought: It is some kind of razor he shaves with. I knowed what it was the first night!

John stirred in the valley of his pillow and opened his eyes. Something had moved in the dark and secret world of night: something like the quick soft break and gasp of a sudden blowing flame in a coal grate in the dead of a winter's night. And even as he listened, the house stirred. For old houses move in their sleep like the dreaming, remembering limbs of very old people. Boards whisper, steps cry out softly to the whispering remembrance of footfalls long gone to earth. Mantelpieces strain gently in the darkness beneath the ghosts of old Christmas stockings. Joists and beams and rafters hunch lightly like the brittle ribs of old women in their sleep: the heart recalling, the worn carpet slippers whispering down the halls again. But now there was another sound and John lifted his face from the damp pillow because his breath against the cloth might have been the sound after all. But the noise continued and then he knew well what it was and he slipped from his bed and crept to the window. It was the whinny-and-catch, the whinny-and-catch that the old Model T made when someone was cranking it. This was the sound among the other night sounds: beyond the fog, beyond the grape arbor and the smokehouse, beyond seeing. Behind the night of white mists he could hear the faint, vivid voices of the shantyboat people in skiffs along the shore, gigging for frogs under the willows, and someone was playing a mouth harp behind the moon. But the other sound came clearer than the rest: clear and unmistakable: the whinny-and-catch, the whinny-and-catch and then the cough and the pause and then beginning again and now the hoarse chatter as the motor caught, and after a bit the sound racketed off into the stillness and the night slid back again. John lay in the bed now thinking: What is it? Has he given it all up and stolen Dad's old car and gone away? Has he decided he won't never find that money and so he has quit and settled for the car and gone away forever?

And so he fell asleep, his hand on the face of the doll whose painted eyes, staring between his fingers, kept a blind yet faithful vigilance against the night.

Walt Spoon was out in their garden, hoeing the second planting of beans, when Icey came to the door and called him. He rested the hoe against the white picket fence and wiped his face on his bandanna.

Walt! Come quick! she cried again.

I'm coming, Mother.

Walt hurried down the rows toward the kitchen porch.

What's wrong, Mother?

She leaned against the threshold and with one trembling, freckled hand tugged him inside.

What's—

Shhhhhh! Whisper, Walt! He's out there at one of the tables. I don't want him to hear me. Keep your voice down.

What's the matter? Who—

It's Mister Powell, she whispered. He just come a-runnin' from the house. Somethin' awful has happened, Walt!

Well Lordamighty, woman, will ye tell me what?

Willa has run away!

No!

Willa's run away! she repeated, a little louder now.

I'll be switched!

Walt, when that man told me the story I thought I'd faint. I didn't know what to *say*. Why, I thought when I heard him come in it was the butter-and-egg man.

Well, didn't she say nothin'—didn't she leave no word?

A note, said Icey, pressing her lips together and squinting one eye. 'Course I never asked him what it said. She took out of the bed sometime during the night—there was right smart of a fog so no one seen her go—and taken the old Model T—you remember—Ben's jalopy.

Now, then, I'd never have thought that of Willa Bailey, said Walt, softly, sitting suddenly in a straight-backed chair by the sink. I declare, Icey, I never would have thought it!

Walt, I just didn't know what to say.

To *him?* Well, I reckon you didn't, now!

He stood there in the doorway when I come out to see who it was and I asked him what was the matter and he told me and, Walt, I just couldn't believe my ears so I made him tell me again.

Is he hit pretty bad by it?

Icey motioned toward the ice-cream parlor with her head.

Just hear him! He went all to pieces after he'd told me— throwed himself down at one of the tables and put his head down in his arms and went to prayin' and cryin' all at the same time! That's when I come a-runnin' for you, Walt.

Walt turned his eyes sadly toward the door, toward the sound of weeping.

There's a little peach brandy, he said, rising and moving toward the spice cabinet. Maybe a little sip of that—

Walt! A man of the cloth!

Walt's hand hesitated but he fetched the bottle down anyway

and poured an inch of the liquor into the tin cup by the pump. He tossed it down and bent, coughing into his sleeve.

Walt Spoon, that's for sickness in the house.

Well, I'll be blamed if news like that don't make a body sick, Mother.

He turned his eyes toward the door, toward the sound of faint, thick weeping in the other room.

What can we do, Mother?

Well, she said, I thought if you went and talked to him. Another man.

What—what does a person say?

Well, shoot, Walt, I don't know! Maybe if we was to get some idea where she could have run to—some hint she might have dropped. I mind last night she *did* seem upset when she left here. Didn't you mind that? The way she kept staring and biting her lip and she hadn't hardly set down till she was up again—wantin' to go?

Yes. I mind that. She left around ten it was.

Now the weeping beyond the door eased and there was no sound but the measured ticking of the hall clock.

There, said Walt. Sounds like he's got ahold of himself! You better wait out here, Mother. I'll go see if there's anything we can do.

But Icey followed just the same, through the door into the ice-cream parlor, and peered around her husband's shoulder at Preacher at the table by the window. He was sitting up now, his back to them, and he had the little pocket Scripture he always carried and he was reading silently, his dry, thin mouth working faintly as two fingers traced the crabbed tiny script.

Mister Powell?

Walt stood awkward and helpless before the grief of another man. Preacher did not stir, gave no sign that he knew they were there. Then Icey touched him gently on the shoulder.

Mister Powell? Me and Walt thought maybe—

And as if a loose wire in a loud-speaker had suddenly been

jarred into contact again, the whispering rose to a full booming voice as he read:

—for a whore is a deep ditch! And a strange woman is a narrow pit!

Amen! whispered Icey. Amen!

She also lieth in wait as for a prey. And increaseth the transgressors among men.

Now suddenly he folded the little book and turned to them and they were touched beyond words at his reddened eyes and the little smile of courage that flickered at the corners of his lips.

My dear, dear friends! Whatever would I do without you?

Mister Powell! wailed Icey.

In the fear of the Lord is strong confidence. And His children shall have a place of refuge.

Walt said: Is there anything?—anything?

Preacher stuffed the Bible into the pocket of his coat and smiled.

It is my shame—my crown of thorns. And I must wear it bravely, my friends.

What could have *possessed* that girl? snuffled Icey.

Satan, said Preacher, simply, as if it were all cut and dried. It was him that possessed her.

Outside in Peacock Alley the air trembled and glistened like cold spring water and the wind flowed clean and steady from the shore. It was a fresh morning in late July—a young girl of a morning when the land was a bosom of milk and honey and the night mists long gone.

Didn't she—didn't she leave no word—no explanation? said Walt.

Yes. If you could call it that. A note. I tore it up and burned it.

Didn't you have no inkling? said Walt, sitting across from him at the table.

Preacher smiled bravely and blew his nose and then tucked his handkerchief away before he spoke.

Yes, said Preacher. From the first night.

The first night?

Our honeymoon. The night we was married in Sistersville and stayed at the Brass House.

How's that? said Walt.

Why, she turned me out of the bed.

No! gasped Icey, while Walt blushed and fumbled in his pocket for his pipe.

Yes! said Preacher. I reckon having had what she was used to from a man like Ben Harper—she wouldn't want nothin' from a man of God.

Yes! said Icey. Ben was lusty and ornery, I'll grant. And you think that's why she run off?

She still longed for the old life, said Preacher softly. Carousin' of a night and beer drinkin'—and that other, I reckon. I couldn't give her that kind of life. I wouldn't if I could, dear hearts. I taken one look at them little ones of hers and I said to myself: Better that a millstone should be fastened around my neck—

Icey was weeping again now, sobbing in swift, fat little gasps, her lawn handkerchief balled tight against her lips.

And what do you figure to do, Mister Powell? said Walt, puffing on his old pipe.

Do? Why, what would any man of God do? cried Preacher, standing up. Stay and take care of them little kids in the way Jesus would want them to be brought up! Maybe He meant all this to happen this way, my friends. Maybe He never meant for a woman like Willa to taint their young lives and so He sent me—

Praise God! choked Icey.

That's mighty fine of you, Reverend, said Walt, snorting and dabbing at a moistness in the corner of his eye. Mighty brave, I'd say!

I reckon maybe it has been ordained this way, Brother Spoon. The Lord has set my task before me. Those little lambs—

Icey, control abandoned now, shook and snuffled in unabated emotion. Walt scratched his cheek with his pipe-stem and shook his head.

I just wouldn't never have thought that of Willa Bailey, he said softly. Runnin' off that way and leavin' a husband and them two kids.

He paused, puffing silently.

And she left a note?

A scrawl, said Preacher. On a piece of notepaper on the bureau. Something about how she had failed as a mother and a wife and she wasn't no account at heart nohow and she might as well run off somewheres where people was as bad as she was.

He held out the fingers of his hand and stared at them in disgust and then wiped his palm dramatically on the sleeve of his other arm.

I burned it, he whispered. I tore it up and burned it—it stank so strong of hellfire!

Amen!

The pitcher, said Preacher, has went to the well once too often, my friends.

And you plan to raise them kids up yourself? said Walt. Providin', of course, Willa don't come draggin' her tail back home?

Preacher smiled and shook his head.

She'll not be back. I reckon I'd be safe in promisin' you that.

Walt puffed in silence a moment longer, reflecting.

Her conscience might git the better of her, he said. And she'd come a-runnin'.

She has no conscience. She was weak.

Or maybe she's just run off on a spree.

No!

Well, there's no harm in hopin', Reverend.

There ain't no sense in it, neither, said Preacher. I knowed she was goin'—I figured something like this was brewin' when she went to bed last evenin'.

How?

Because she tarried around the kitchen for a good half hour after I'd gone up, smiled Preacher, twining the fingers of his hands together. And when the clock struck eleven-thirty I went downstairs to see what was wrong.

And what—

She'd found a fruit jar full of dandelion wine that the husband—Harper—had hid away somewhere in the cellar.

You mean she—

Preacher nodded.

She was drinking, he said.

Icey stopped weeping and stared, scandalized.

Her flesh, smiled Preacher, was just too full of it for it not to git the upper hand, dear friends—too full of Pride and Sin and Self-indulgence! I tried to save her—

I know you did, Reverend! cried Icey. Oh, I know how you tried!

But it was too late, said Preacher, cracking his knuckles together as the fingers began to twist. The devil got there first! You see?

And he held up the locked hands and twisted them some more and Icey and Walt stared transfixed at the writhing fingers with the blue letters of Love and Hate warring together in mid-air. At last the fingers of the left hand closed over the fingers of the right and Preacher brought both hands down with a mighty crash to the table top.

The devil wins sometimes! he whispered in a hoarse, choking voice. But can't nobody say I didn't do my best to save her!

The afternoon was hot: the morning coolness from the river was gone and the air lay like a shimmering yellow sea over the bottomlands. Still, in the dark cellar of the old house it was cold and dank, with a smell in the air of a perpetual autumn: of apples and spider webs and winter coal. Pearl shivered and hugged her doll.

John, why do we have to hide?

It was dark behind the shelves of Mason jars, behind the barrel of stale winter apples and the bench with its boxes of onions and turnips and potatoes. Yet she could see the white shape of John's face clearly, and the dark eyes burning in it.

John, why?

Hush up!

Yes, but, John, why?

Because! he whispered furiously, thinking: Isn't it enough that I have to save her from him? Do I have to put up with the rest of it, too: the questions, the whys?

John, where's Mom?

He thought: Mom is dead. Because she wouldn't go away and leave *him* that way. She might leave us but she wouldn't leave him and so she must be dead somewhere.

John?

What? Pearl, hush up!

But where's Mom?

So he lied: She's gone to Moundsville.

And he thought about the sound of the car in the night and he thought that maybe that might not be a lie after all, that maybe she had seen him at last for what he was and fled for her life and that scared him worse than the thought of her dead so he stopped thinking it.

To see Dad? Pearl was saying.

What?

Did Mom go to Moundsville to see Dad?

I don't know. Yes, I reckon that's it. Now will you hush?

Why, John? I want to see Daddy Powell.

He shuddered, thinking: It's too much for me: hearing her

call him that while I am trying to save us both from him and all the time her trying to stop me, to get to him anyway, even though he would kill her for what's hid in the doll.

Someone, he said, is after us, Pearl!

He thought: If I scare her too bad then she will start crying and he will hear it and come find us. But maybe if I scare her a little bit she will shut up.

Why is someone after us, John?

Never mind about that. Just be still, Pearl!

I want to go upstairs, she said. It's cold and spidery down here. I'm hungry, John.

He turned in the darkness and grasped her firmly by the shoulders, feeling her tremble under his fingers because now she could feel his own fright flowing through his fingers into her arms.

Now listen to me, Pearl, he whispered. You and me is runnin' off tonight.

What's runnin' off?

Runnin' away, he continued, and brushed some crawling creature from his leg. If we stay here somethin' awful will happen to us.

Won't Daddy take care of us?

No, he said. That's just it! No!

Where are we goin', John?

I don't know yet. Somewheres, Pearl. When it gets dark and he quits huntin' for us and goes up to bed—

Who? Who's goin' to bed?

The man, he said carefully. The man who's hunting us. When it's night—then we can tiptoe up to the kitchen and—and steal somethin' to eat—

Oh, no, John! Mom will punish us. That's spoiling our supper.

No, he said. It don't matter about that now. Just do like I tell you, Pearl.

All right, John. I will. I promise.

And she was still for a moment at least.

John, is Mom running away, too?

No.

So she fell silent again and they waited, listening to the far, faint sounds of the distant daylight: so remote that they might have been from another world. There was a single barred cellar window in the stone wall beneath the joists above the coal bin. And they fastened their eyes to that single square of world, watching as it faded to gray and then, as twilight fell, winked shut like the lid of an eye, and they could hear him moving about in the dark house above them as he had throughout all that dark day, singing to himself and then stopping a spell to listen, to poke and search, and then call their names again in that tight, shivering voice of outrage. Then he would commence his singing again.

Leaning, leaning! Safe and secure from all alarms!

Leaning, leaning! Leaning on the everlasting arms!

And when Pearl fell asleep against him John crouched listening alone in the roaring darkness, and the footsteps padded back and forth and the closet doors squeaked open one by one and then he would call again and after a spell he would begin to sing again and then after a bit they heard him cry out softly to himself as if he had thought of something and the footsteps moved along the hall and directly the cellar door opened far away in the distance and Pearl knew by the cold, tightening fingers on her arm that John meant for her to be still.

Children? he whispered.

John?

Hush!

And suddenly and with astonishing loudness a cricket commenced chirping in the apple barrel and John, gasping with fright, imagined somehow that this might lead the hunter to their hiding place.

Pearl? called the voice softly from the stairs.

And then a portion of the whitewashed wall sprang suddenly into light as he moved down the steps with the candle in his hand and stopped halfway, straining his angry eyes into the shadows.

I know you're here, children, he said, not shouting, not angry-sounding at all. So you'd better come out before I come find you myself. I can feel myself gettin' awful mad, children.

John? she whined faintly. He said—

John's hand clapped quickly to her mouth and his fingers pressed into the warm cheek. He could feel her fluttering, frightened eyelashes on the heel of his palm.

I hear you whisperin', children. So I know you're down there.

John listened to the cricket among the Winesaps and thought: If we was crickets we could hide under the cool apples, deep in the dark barrel, and he would never find us; never ever find us.

Very well! My patience has run out, children. I'm comin' to find you now.

And his footsteps were quick and angry on the creaking steps and now the whole cellar was alive with new shadows and stretching light from the moving candle in his fingers. John peered between two half-gallon jars of candied apples and he could see him: his back to them, the black of one shoulder and the corner of his head as he stood by the furnace and held the candle high.

This is your last chance, my dears. I'm just gettin' played out. I'm just gettin' so mad I won't be responsible!

Now the whole web of light and dark tore loose and stretched itself and danced again as he moved toward the coal bin and bent to peer inside.

Children!

And then they all heard the voice calling from the kitchen and John thought for one moment of salvation: It's Mom come back! It's her upstairs in the kitchen! Nothin' has happened to her after all!

Yoohoo! Mister Powell!

They could hear him shuffling back across the stone toward the steps and John counted them as the footsteps mounted to the door to the kitchen.

Gracious, Mister Powell! You frightened me!

It was Icey Spoon, and Preacher closed the cellar door and they could hear him greeting her in that coaxing, warm voice he could put on when he wanted.

Here! Icey was saying. It's just a little hot supper I fixed for you and the children. Walt and me got to thinkin' about you lonely and helpless over here without a woman in the house and it seemed the least we could do.

Then it was his voice again, fawning over the basket of supper she had brought and then his voice fell and John knew what it was he would be saying.

Because directly Icey cried out: They what? Oh, no! They haven't!

And now his voice again: whining and trembling with pious concern and bewilderment.

Yes! Yes! he cried. They're down there playing in the cellar and they won't mind me when I call them and I just don't know what to do. It just seems a little too much with everything else on my mind today—Willa and all. Would you mind trying?

The door flew open again and now it was Icey's voice, clear and commanding.

John! Pearl!

It's as if I didn't have enough on my mind, Preacher was whimpering. The grief and burden of what the mother has done—

Icey's voice crackled with authority now and John knew that the jig was up; the business of disobeying a woman was somehow too much for him.

John! Pearl! You get up out of that cellar this very minute! Icey clapped her hands sharply.

Come on! Shake a leg! I won't have you worryin' poor Mister Powell another minute. Hurry!

John appeared, blinking, and moved into the gaslit kitchen and Pearl followed, hugging the doll sheepishly before her shamed eyes.

Now just look at you! cried Icey, brushing the cobwebs from the little one's curls. Dust and filth from head to toe! If that ain't a poor way to serve Mister Powell on a sad day like this!

She turned to Preacher and raised her eyebrows.

Want me to take them up and wash 'em good?

Thank you, no. Thank you, dear Icey. No, I'll tend to them. Thank you.

Well, smiled Icey, folding her hands beneath her apron before she departed. At least you'll all have a good hot meal tonight.

She turned and patted John's shaggy head, bowed now in dreadful and stunned defeat beside his sister.

Don't be too hard on them, Reverend, she whispered. Like as not they've took it hard—the mother runnin' off that way. Poor lambs! Poor motherless children!

Preacher chuckled and reached out his hand and ran the fingers named Love through Pearl's tumbling, dusty locks.

I've been thinking, he said, of something that might ease the pain.

Yes? said Icey.

I thought I might take them away for a week or two, he said. To my sister's—down at Marietta.

Well, now!

The change might help, he sighed. A different scene. Good country food for a while. A kindly Christian woman to tend them.

Well, now! Hear that, children? Don't that sound nice?

Yes, said Preacher. I think I may do that. It would give me time to—help mend things.

That's a grand, sensible plan, Mister Powell. Just grand!

She gave Pearl's head a final pat and pinched John's cold, livid cheek and moved out onto the porch with Preacher.

And remember, now, Mister Powell. If you need anything—any time of night or day—don't be afraid to call on us. Mind now! Good night!

Good night, Miz Spoon. Thank you. The Lord will watch over us all.

And in a breath her fat round figure was a small shape, bobbing away into the green dusk under an early moon. Preacher came back into the kitchen and smiled at the children by the pump.

Weren't you afraid, my lambs? he said softly. Down there in all that dark?

For a moment the kerosene lamp teetered and rocked on the littered table but then the old hands darted out and caught it and steadied it before it fell. Uncle Birdie snatched his bottle from under the rocker and filled the tin cup half full again. Then he began shaking worse than ever, teeth chattering like an angry groundhog, and Uncle Birdie knew suddenly that whisky wasn't going to help him that night: it would take more than that to exorcise the day's phantoms. And yet he drank it swiftly and choked once and settled back again, rocking and moaning softly to himself and sucking the liquor from his dripping mustaches. Earlier he had considered lighting his lantern and taking Ben Harper's skiff back down along the shore to the deep place to see if it was really there: what he had seen that morning. But he thought that seeing it again would drive him crazy with fear and he would fall out of the boat and drown. And so he sat a

moment longer, rocking with that measured beat of children and
the very old, hugging his tough, scrawny arms around his chest
like a frightened old woman, and then he labored to his feet and
steadied himself on his way across the wharfboat cabin wall to
the hair chest by the stove. Bess would understand why he was
so powerfully and brutally drunk this night. Bess would forgive
him his intemperance once he told her what he had seen that
morning in the deep place below Jason Lindsay's west fence. He
fell thickly to his knees and fumbled at the green brass hasp to
the chest and got the lid up at last and fetched out the faded
cardboard photograph in the cheapjack tin frame he had bought
from a country peddler thirty-five years before, and when he had
stumbled back to his rocker again he propped the little picture
against the lamp and fell back into his cushions.

Now, Bess! Don't go preachin' at me again. I'm drunk as a
lord and I know it but hear me out, woman. Hear me out and
you'll understand. Now, Bess! Don't scold!

And he turned his face away from the proud black eyes of
the handsome country girl in the picture. And still not looking
at her he commenced rocking swiftly now and considered how
he should shape the tale, how he could tell his long-dead wife
why he had been driven again to the awful drunkenness that
had been the plague and sorrow of their marriage. Something
dripped with the soft rhythm of blood on the floor boards beside
him and he saw that he had upset the bottle and the soft whisper
of the falling drops made him shake all the worse and for a while
there was no sound but that and the cry of the rockers and at last
he dragged his eyes back to the stern cardboard face. Because she
was waiting to hear his excuse and Bess got angry when she had
to wait for things.

This mornin'! he choked. I borried Ben Harper's skiff and
went down in the deep place along the shore there below Jas'
Lindsay's west fence. I 'lowed to catch me a few cats for supper,

Bess. Now hold on, woman. Wait! The boy didn't mind me borrын' the skiff. I figgered to take her out every day like that for a little fishin'. He said I could!

Yet the eyes seemed to mock him: burning with scorn under the unfailing gleam of the lamp.

Hear me! Hear me out, woman! Hold on now, 'fore you go to preachin' me!

Now he leaned toward the picture with starting eyes and jaws agape and his hands clamped to the table's edge like the prisoner's on a bar of justice.

Christ God Almighty! he breathed. If you'd a-seen it, Bess! Swee' Jesus, if you'd a-seen it down there in the deep place!

Then he shut his eyes against the scorn of the dusty face and fell back in the rocker again and the faint, wooden tread of the rockers resumed like the pace of a damned sentry and he could hear her voice again: vibrant and rich with disdain as it had been in those decades long gone to earth: Drunken sot! You worthless, drunken fool!

Bess, don't go 'way! Don't leave me, Bess! Wait! Wait now till I tell ye—

And the hands thudded back to the table and the old face was back to the picture again, his nose fairly brushing it.

Under—the—stern, he grated. That's whar I seen it! It was water black as No Bottom but I jedge it was ten foot down. Christ God Almighty, Bess, my heart like to bust inside me then—

He shut his eyes and slavered for a moment with the sheer horror of it and then he shook his head and lifted his eyes to the yellow lamp chimney.

—And like as not they'll think it was me that done it, Bess. Like as not Jake Arbogast and them deppities'll come and drag me off to Moundsville and slip me the noose, Bess. Oh, swee' Jesus save us all!

And he could hear her voice now as plain as the voice of

the man downshore in the houseboat laughing and joshing his sweetheart under the summer moon. And so he knew he would have to tell it all to her, from the beginning: what it was that he had seen. And so he gulped and licked his lips and turned his face away from hers before he began, mouthing the tale with his thick, drunken tongue.

About ten this mornin' it was. I mind that, Bess, 'cause the nine-thirty eastbound was long gone. I taken Ben Harper's skiff. John said I could! And I was down there fishing for cats over the deep place below Jason Lindsay's west fence and directly I felt my hook catch on somethin' and I bent over the stern—Swee' Jesus, I can see it yet!—Swee' Jesus save poor old Uncle Birdie! 'Deed, Bess, I thought first it was a snag or a tree root and I leaned over the stern—Bess, you know how clear the water is down there except in flood stage. Well, that's right where it was, Bess, where the kids used to swim—where the water's way over a man's head.

Now he leaned closer across the table and his eyes burned back at the stern stare of the paper woman in the cheap tin frame. His fingernails bit into the table wood as he spoke.

—'Twas there I seen it, Bess. Down there in all that water. Ben Harper's old Model T and her in it!—Jesus save me!—Her in it, Bess—just a-sittin' there in a white gown and her eyes looking at me and a great long slit under her chin just as clean as a catfish gill!—Oh, Godamighty!—and her hair wavin' lazy and soft around her like meadow grass under flood waters. Willa Harper, Bess! That's who! Down there in the deep place in that old Model T with her eyes starin' and that slit in her throat just like she had an extry mouth. You hear me, Bess? You listenin', woman? Swee' Jesus save us all!

He paused, choking and gasping with fresh terror, and snatched up the bottle and greedily sucked from it the few drops that had not spilled, and then whirling as if at the footfall of an enemy hurled the bottle crashing through the wharfboat window.

And there hain't a mortal human, he whispered, not just to her but to the night now, to whatever ears might be harking at the shattered window through which the breath of the mist already curled. There hain't a mortal human I can tell but you, Bess. For if I go to the Law they'll hang it onto me.

He staggered sobbing to his feet and wallowing his way to the door like a listing boat, steadied himself against the jamb and stared off wildly into the darkness toward the shore to southward: where the tiny lamps of the shantyboats gleamed in the dark.

One of them, he whispered, slobbering into the stubble of his chin. It was one of them shantyboat trash done it. But they'll think it was me. Christ God Almighty, they'll think it was old Uncle Birdie!

And he stumbled back into the tangled blankets of his cot and fell to snoring, rousing up from time to time to quarrel with his dreams, while the eyes of the woman stared through the unwavering and golden lamplight: eyes unforgiving, dark with scorn and outrage now fifty years lost in the dust of the Ravens Rock churchyard.

I'm hungry, John. Let's go downstairs and eat supper. The door's locked!

Why did Daddy lock us in our rooms? Were you bad again, John?

Hush up! I'm thinkin', Pearl.

What about?

About gettin' away. Listen to me, Pearl. You've got to mind me tonight.

All right, John.

They huddled in the bedroom, hearing Preacher below in the kitchen eating the hot supper Icey had brought and taking his time about it because they would be there as long as he wanted them there and because presently he would climb the stairs and have the first real privacy he had ever known when he asked them the question again.

No matter what he says! whispered John. No matter what he does, Pearl—remember what you swore!

Yes.

But he thought: But there are ways. He will take her on his lap again and start in again about the secrets and she will commence to giggle directly because she loves him because she is too dumb to know what he really wants.

Preacher had finished his supper now and was singing while he rinsed the dishes and stacked them by the pump. And when the house grew still again John thought: You never hear him coming up steps because his feet are like leaves falling, like shadows in the moonlight. He is coming up them stairs right this very minute, I bet, and directly he'll unlock the door and we will hardly hear the key.

Hello there, children! Guess what? I saved you some supper. Have we got good appetites tonight, my lambs?

I'm hungry, said Pearl.

Why, sure you're hungry. And guess what's waitin' for you. There's fried chicken and candied sweets and cornsticks and apple cobbler!

Can I have my supper please?

Well, sure. Naturally. I'll go warm it up for you directly. But first—

Can I have milk, too?

Yes, little bird. To be sure! he cried, gathering her gently into his arms. But first of all we'll have a little talk.

Pearl frowned and put her finger in her mouth, remembering the night he twisted her arm.

—About our secrets! he said softly.

No, whispered Pearl.

No? And why, pray tell?

Because John said I mustn't!

Ah, but we both know what a bad, bad boy John is. In fact, I think we had better punish John tonight for the way he's been carryin' on lately. But we'll attend to John later, won't we, my lamb? Now let's just you and me talk. We'll have a nice little chat and we won't even let John open his mouth.

Pearl scowled at John.

You're bad, John! We'll have a chat and we won't let you open your mouth!

The moon had come up: a sickly wisp of silver in the last phase, hanging like a harvester's sickle in the apple tree below the grape arbor.

Do you have any secrets you'd like to tell me, Pearl?

Yes, she whispered, torn by those strange winds of yes and no.
What is it?

She was still, her eyes moving gravely back and forth between the two of them.

The money, she said softly and darted a glance at John.

Ah, of course! The money. And where is the money, little darling?

She began to sob.

John said—she choked softly.

Preacher slapped his knee and his eyes crackled dangerously.
Never—mind—what—John—said!

He thrust her to the floor and towered above them, radiant with fresh fury.

I've told you once, my girl, that John ain't even here as far as you and me is concerned. John don't matter! Can you understand that? Eh?

Yes.

John is a meddler! Do you understand that? John is a nasty, sneaking, mean little—! *Stop sniveling!* Looky here a minute! In my hand—here!

He shot his left hand into the alpaca coat and brought out the knife and bounced it twice in his palm: the blade still secret in the bone helve, awaiting the cunning button's touch.

See this, now? Know what it is?

Yes. I know.

Looky! What do you see now? What is it, Pearl?

I don't know.

Well then don't say, I know, if you don't. That's lying. This is a knife! Want to see something cute? Looky now!

He clasped the bone handle in his palm and, closing it, touched the button lightly with the finger named H and now the six-inch silver blade, honed to paper-keenness, flicked out like the clever bright wing of a toy bird. Pearl smiled.

How about that, now! he cried, proud as a child, but then his face snapped back into a mask of blanched leather and his lips curled angrily.

This, said Preacher, is what I use on meddlers, my lamb! Get me? *For meddlers!*

He laid the knife open on the bright calico of the quilt on the bed and lifted his eyes to the boy.

John, he said, might be a meddler, mightn't he? Or mebbe he's got better sense, eh, little lamb? John would be sorry he meddled! In fact, if John so much as breathes a word—*if he so much as opens his mouth—*

Pearl ran over and reached a hand to take the cunning bright toy.

No! No, my lamb! Don't touch it! Now, don't touch my knife! That makes me mad! Very, very mad!

So she hugged the doll, humbled by this new sharpness in his voice, but then his face fell into softer lines as he smiled and laid the hand named Love on her soft, dark curls.

Just tell me now, he said. Where's it hid?

Pearl turned her eyes to nasty, bad John, stunned and frozen beside the white water pitcher on the washstand.

—the money! whispered Preacher, bending a little now, and flicking his tongue across his quivering lips. Think, baby! Think of all the nice things we can buy with it! A new dress for dolly and a new pair of shoes for you!

Where's Mom?

Ah, that's a secret, too, little bird. And I can't tell you my secrets till you've told me yours.

Can John have a present, too?

Well, I reckon so. We'll even buy a present for nasty, naughty John.

Pearl sighed and turned her awful eyes to the boy.

But I swore, she breathed. I promised John I wouldn't tell!

John—doesn't—matter! he cried, leaping to his feet. Can't I get that through your head, you poor, silly, disgusting little wretch!

Pearl's mouth quivered and a large tear brimmed suddenly in each eye.

There now! See what you went and made me do? You made me lose my temper! I'm sorry! I'm real sorry! Sometimes the old Devil gets the upper hand and I just go all to pieces! Sometimes that old left hand named Hate gits stronger than his brother.

Pearl snuffled and wiped her eyes with her free fist.

Now! said Preacher, knowing that she was broken at last. Where's it hid?

John thought: Now there's nothing more for me to do but to do the bad thing. It is a terrible, awful thing but I must do it because there's nothing left to do. I must make a Sin. I must tell a lie.

I'll tell! he cried out.

Preacher did not reach for the knife; only his eyes swung dully and fixed the boy with a steady stare.

I thought I told you to keep your mouth shut.

No! said John. It ain't fair to make Pearl tell when she swore she wouldn't! That's a Sin! *I'll tell!*

Preacher's eyes crinkled and then he turned to Pearl and smiled brightly.

Well, I declare! he chuckled. Sometimes I think poor John will make it to heaven yet! Did ye hear that, little lamb? With all his carryin' on—John's going to be the one to tell us after all.

And now his eyes snapped back to John like a whip and the voice meant business.

All right, boy! Where's the money?

In the cellar! cried John. Buried in the floor behind the big stone jar of pickled peaches!

Preacher picked up the knife and pressed it closed in the palm of his hand, never taking his twinkling eyes from John's face for an instant.

It'll go hard, boy, he said, if I find out you're lyin' to me!

I ain't lyin'! cried John valiantly, while he prayed that Pearl would hold her peace throughout this crucial ruse. Go look for yourself! It's all there! All that money—buried under a stone in the cellar! Right where Dad stuck it that day!

All right. Come along.

What?

Come along with me—the both of you—to the cellar! You don't reckon I'd leave you—

Don't you believe me?

Why, sure, boy. Sure. But just the same—come along. I'll risk no tricks.

He made them walk ahead of him down the stairway to

the kitchen and they waited by the pump while he fetched a candle from the china closet and a match from the stove and John thought: Pearl, hush! Pearl don't say nothin'! Please, Pearl! Please, God! And he took his sister's hand and led the way down the steps into the cellar while Preacher followed, holding the candle high in his hand and John could feel the dripping hot tallow soaking through his shirt, while before them their long shadows darted and stretched across the floor among the apple barrels and the old trunks.

Now where, boy? And mind now—no tricks; I can't abide liars!

Yonder! John pointed, and the shadow pointed, too, among the bright, rich-gleaming rows of Mason jars on the shelves: the winter's provender of years gone: candied apples and parched corn and long, crisp pickle strips behind the shining glass bellies.

Where?

Right yonder behind that big, tall shelf there! Behind that stone jar! Under the stone in the floor!

Preacher was panting with excitement as he spilled tallow on the lip of the great stone jar and set the candle in it, holding it till the wax set and held it; then he fell to his knees and brushed the dust away with shaking fingers.

Why, this ain't no stone floor, boy. It's concrete! There hain't no stone here for nothin' to be buried under!

Now Pearl could hold herself in no longer.

John made a Sin, she said softly. John told a lie.

Preacher got to his feet slowly, his face gone as yellow as the flesh of a pawpaw before the frost. The hand slid slowly into the coat pocket and when it came out again the boy saw the striped tan and black of the bone hasp and the dull shine of the button.

Yes, Pearl. John told a lie. John just never stopped to think that the Lord ain't the only one that hates a liar.

John watched, thinking: It's so quick you can't see it: the silver blade is as quick as the tongue of the blacksnake me and Uncle Birdie seen on the big millstone that day. His thumb moves and the silver tongue licks out and there is just a little click.

I'm listening. And the Lord is talkin' to me now, he said, moving toward them a little. And He's a-sayin': Not yet, brother! Stay thy hand a while! Give these lambs one more chance!

John did not move: not even when the knife was touching him: the blade pricking the soft flesh beneath the ear and Preacher's hand was closing around the nape of his neck with his free fingers.

The Lord's a-talkin' to me just as plain, John! Can't you hear Him? No.

Well He is! He's a-sayin': A liar is an abomination before mine eyes! But the Lord is a God of Mercy, boy! He's a sayin': Give Brother Ananias another chance. Now speak, boy! Speak! Where's it hid? Speak before I cut your throat and leave you to drip like a hog hung up in butcherin' time!

Pearl commenced sobbing with terror and Preacher whirled on her, smiling.

You could save him, little bird. You could save John if you was to tell.

John! John!

Pearl, shut up! Pearl, you swore!

Shut up, you little bastard, let her speak! Where, Pearl? Where!

Inside my doll! Inside my doll! she screamed, and Preacher withdrew, his jaw sagging, and then he threw back his head and roared out a single, hoarse cry of laughter.

In the doll! Why, sure! Sure! By God, what a clever one Brother Harper was! The last place anyone would look! In the doll! Why, sure, now!

And he went for Pearl just as John moved, ducking under

Preacher's sleeve, moving more surely than he had ever moved in his life; thrusting out his hand to the solitary flame and knocking the candle into the peaches and then feeling for Pearl in the blackness and grabbing her little damp hand; dragging her screaming away into the darkness toward the steps. Preacher's shrill bleat of anger filled the cellar with shattering echoes and they heard the stone jar of fruit go crashing and slopping over among the rakes and hoes against the shelves and then a cascade of bursting Mason jars as Preacher stumbled, groping, and thrust his hand among them. And John thought: Because I know the cellar like I know my own room: the way among the boxes and the barrels, the way across the dank, broad floor to the steps, and he don't know the way and he will fall among the rakes and hoes and the apple baskets and trunks and if only I can get Pearl and me and the doll up them steps and lock him down here there will be a chance. They were halfway up the steps now and the door to the kitchen was ajar before their eyes, a bright bar of lamplight and safety in that hell of blackness, and behind them they could hear Preacher go down cursing again in another welter of crashing jars and Pearl was screaming in a high, keening wail. John slipped on the very top step at the landing and almost carried them both backward down the steps and into the hunter's arms and in that dreadful instant they heard the scramble and slap of his feet on the steps behind them and then they were through the threshold and John slammed the door behind him with all his might. Preacher screamed in anguish and John felt the evil fingers crush between the door and the jamb and so he drew back and slammed again and pushed the door tight and before Preacher could rally the iron bolt flew home. John sank, gasping, against the wallpaper and listened to him, crouched at the top of the steps like a trapped fox, his mouth pressed against the crack of the door, breathing hoarsely, sobbing faintly, thinking, scheming.

Children?

Cajoling and gentle: the voice now.

Children? Listen here, now!

John thought: the river. That is the only where. The warm, dark mother river running in the summer night and the only friend in that whole, swarming vast and terrible darkness: Uncle Birdie Steptoe. Yes, the river now. Quick! Quick!

Children, won't you listen to me for a minute? It was all just a joke. Aw, have a heart now. Children, can't you see? The only reason I wanted that money is so's you could have it. That's right! See? It ain't a-doin' no one no good sewed up in that doll baby. I wanted to make you see that, children.

John was still too exhausted to move; still fought to find his breath again while Pearl sobbed and hugged the doll Jenny by the pump.

Listen, little Pearl! You'll listen to me, won't ye now? Won't you, little bird? Little lamb? Listen. I'll make a bargain with you both. That's what I'll do. The Lord just spoke to me, children.

The Lord just come out plain and loud and he rebuked me for my meddlin'. Yessir, if you'll let me out I promise I'll go away tonight and never come back. Pearl? You listenin', little lamb? Want your mommy back, lamb? Want me to go get her right now?

John!

Hush, Pearl! Come on!

Children! Children! Are you listenin' to me? Open the door! Answer me, you spawn of the Devil's own whore!

And now there came a sudden rain of hammering fists against the door and the old hinges strained and squealed as he set his shoulder to the panels again and again, stumbling and slipping on the steps, and then lunging again against the old wood. Pearl screamed again as John snatched her hand and dragged her toward the kitchen door and into the night. The moon cast a little shine: a thin, sickle moon that stood now in the last phase before the dark. Behind him in that stricken house John could hear the thundering shocks on the failing cellar door: a rhythm and a clamor no louder than the thunder of his pulses as he and the girl, clutching her doll, fled pell-mell down the lane to Cresap's Landing, to the wharfboat, to the river, to Uncle Birdie Steptoe and the last asylum against apocalypse.

The landing was stone-silent except for the drowsy chirp of a shantyboat guitar down in the mists below the willows. John spied the ruddy, dusty glow of Uncle Birdie's smoking lamp in the window and led Pearl stumbling down the bricks to the wharfboat. He could not call out: his breath was gone and he dared not call out lest behind him in the sweet, untroubled streets of the summer night the hunter might be listening. Indeed, he could scarcely be sure just then from whom he fled: the blue men of that half-forgotten nightmare-day or the smiling eyes of the mad evangelist. In the doorway to the wharfboat he stared at the sprawled figure of the old riverman on the cot.

Uncle Birdie! Uncle Birdie!

An eyelid flickered, rolled back, closed again, and the old face writhed in a sick grimace of remembrance.

Bess!

Uncle Birdie! It's me—John Harper! And Pearl! You said to come a-runnin' if we needed you!

The boy's hands tugged at the old man's bony shoulders beneath the worn blue shirt.

Bess! Don't, Bess! Bess, I—

Uncle Birdie!

John slipped to his knees now, weeping unashamedly and Pearl stood against the hair trunk, clutching the doll and watching.

Uncle—Birdie! Oh—please! *Please wake up!*

Something roused in the old man then and he lifted himself on one elbow and wiped the slaver from his chin and stared at the pair with starting, unblinking eyes, pondering who they were, what they wanted, whether theirs were faces of this world or another.

Johnny! he gasped and fell face down again in the flour sack of cornhusks that served as his pillow.

But the boy beat him now with his fists, pummeling his back and wailing softly and now the face lifted again and the man sat upright with enormous effort and hung swaying there like a precariously balanced cadaver, glaring wildly at the children who had come to plague him for the thing he hadn't done.

—Never done it, boy! Chris' God, never done such a terr'ble, terr'ble thing! Shantyboat trash, Cap—done it! Shantyboat trash!

Hide us, whispered John. He's comin' after us, Uncle Birdie. Listen to me! Please, Uncle Birdie! It's him that's after us—Mister Powell!

Uncle Birdie scowled and deep beneath the troubled fogs a faint lamp of comprehension gleamed for an instant on the dark river of his consciousness and now, licking his lips, he frowned again. Who, boy?

Mister Powell! Hide us, Uncle Birdie! He's a-comin' with his knife!

But now the lantern blew out behind the eyes and the old fear swept back like night mists and Uncle Birdie shrank against the wall, warding off John's wild stare as if it were a blow, and shaking till the tin shaving mirror chattered above his basin.

But I never done it, boy! Swee' Jesus, I never done it! I'll swear on the Book to it, boy! I never done it! I never!

John got to his feet, knowing suddenly how lost it all was: what a world had failed him, how deep a night when the last lamp of all went flickering down the darkness. Uncle Birdie swung his shivering, knobby legs to the floor and crooked an old finger toward the picture beneath the lamp.

Go yonder now, boy! Just go ask Bess! Bess knows it t'warn't me. Bess'll tell you boy.

John turned his eyes now to the black door, into the darkness from which he knew would appear in a matter of seconds the face of Salvation with a knife in his lettered fist.

Swee' Jesus, Bess, I'm drunk! Swee' Jesus, I don't know what's goin' on aroun' my own boat now. Who done it? Who's a-comin' after us all? The Devil, Bess? Is it Jedgment Day? Is that it, Bess? Lord save poor old Uncle Birdie Steptoe that never hurt a fly!

John thought: There is still the river. Dad's skiff is down there under the willows. There is always the river.

He took Pearl's hand and led her out into the night again while behind them in the wharfboat cabin the old man had fallen again in a welter of shame and grief and sickness and was snoring loudly in the rags of his cot. Above them the street bricks gleamed in the circle of lamplight beside the shop where the great wood key creaked and squawled on winter nights. Now it hung dumb and the street, leafy with summer night, was dreaming, while the pleasant tinkle of lemonade glasses drifted down Peacock Alley from the kitchens of the nice houses: the sound and picture of tranquil and provincial innocence, while beneath that smiling, drowsy face such a horror raged. For now the very bricks of the street seemed waiting, already vibrating to the swift and raging footsteps of the hunter. As an ear pressed to a steel rail can sometimes catch the thunder of a far-off train, John's whole flesh sensed Preacher's imminent approach. And even as he caught Pearl's hand again and dragged her into the sumac and pokeberry bushes toward the place of the skiff, the shadow of the man broke suddenly into the lamplight by the locksmith's.

Pearl, be quiet! Oh, please, Pearl!

John, where are we—

Hush!

His feet slipped and sucked in the mud and the weeds tore at his legs as he led her stumbling on toward the boat but Preacher had heard them and now his sweet, tenor voice called after them.

Hurry, Pearl! Oh, Godamighty, please hurry, Pearl!

You said a cuss word, John. That's a Sin.

He thought desperately, staring into a great patch of mists: Maybe the skiff is gone. Maybe one of them shantyboat trash borrowed it tonight.

John, where—

Hush! Hush! Hurry, Pearl!

Then he spied it, the bow jutting sharply in the blanketing white and Pearl, yawning now in a perfect picture of a child bored with a stupid game, hugged the doll Jenny and fought her way wearily through the ooze to the skiff.

Children! *Children!*

They could hear him above them, thrashing down through the high brush filth, fighting his way toward them.

Get in the skiff, Pearl! Oh, Godamighty, hurry!

Children!

John! she cried out, pausing. That's *Daddy* calling us!

He uttered a sob of despair and thrust her brutally over the skiff side and down among the bait cans and fish heads in the bottom. Now they heard Preacher hacking at a vine that had entangled him and John knew well what it was he hacked with and in an instant he was free again, thrashing down through the brush not ten feet away. But they were in the boat now and John's hand grappled for the oar the way poor old Uncle Birdie had shown him that day and the way he had watched men do it since the first time he had seen the river. But they moved not an inch in the muck so tightly was the skiff grounded.

Ah, my lambs! So there you are!

John thrust and strained against the oar until the flesh of his hands tore under the wood's ragged grain and the boat moved and he bore down again, straining with every ounce of flesh and bone, and it moved again. But now Preacher had cleared the brush filth and was stepping swiftly through the mud toward them. John gave a final thrust that nigh burst his heart and the skiff swung suddenly into the gentle current.

Wait! Wait, you little bastards! Wait! *Wait!* wait!

Even in that faint show of moonlight, even with the mists wisping and curling against the land, they could see the livid, twisted, raging oval of his face: the mouth gaping and sick with hatred. Now he wallowed rapidly toward them through the shallows, the bright, open blade winking in his fist, and then he staggered and slipped and fell, floundering in the water for a moment and then rising again, splashed after them. John bore back on the oar in the lock and the blade skimmed the water ineffectually and he thought: Why can't I do it when I know how to do it! Please, let me do it! Please! And he bore back again and the oar blade bit hard into the stream and the boat swung erratically like a leaf.

Wait! *Wait!* wait! Damn you to hell!

And now some errant current in the vast, dark river caught them upon its warm wing and the boat began moving, blessedly moving, spinning at first like a mad October leaf and then heading into the channel while still they could hear Preacher: every sound drifting clean and sharp across the flat water: he was back on shore now where he could follow better, clawing his way down the brush filth through sumac and pokeberry, cursing and shouting amid that wiry jungle of the river shore, but now they were moving beyond him, they were free.

John? gasped Pearl.

He dragged his eyes to her, not answering, collapsing face down upon the crook of his arm upon the stern: spent and exhausted even in the face of this near miraculous exodus.

We forgot to take Daddy, she said.

Yes. Yes, Pearl, he murmured, too tired to explain, and then suddenly feeling his flesh seized with a shivering like the ague or some dreaded river fever because of what he had just managed and because he would never quite believe again in all his life that he had been able to do it at all. Preacher stood now, thigh-deep in the shallows under the willows a dozen yards above the row of shantyboats, and opening his mouth began a steady, rhythmical, animal scream of outrage and loss. And the shantyboat people ceased their sleeping, their love-making, their singing of old sweet tunes and harkened: hearing something as old and dark as the things on the river's bed, old as evil itself, a pulsing, ragged bawling that came down the water to them in hideous rhythm. It might have been the ghost of old Mason himself or Macijah Harpe or the renegade Girty for all the hellishness in it. And those river folk fell silent, waiting for it to stop, waiting for the flowing river night to wash it into the darkness again and leave the hour to the sounds a night should have: the scritch of green frogs, the sudden leaping of a fish, the squeal of a buck hare up in the orchard before the ravening weasel's leap. Even when the skiff had floated far away down the dark and silent river the children could hear the faint, distant drift of that hoarse and terrible chant.

John? Pearl whispered.

But he was beyond answering.

John?

But he was asleep. And so it was to the doll that she spoke. And since the game she and John and Daddy had been playing was finished she began another one. And in the silence of the great brooding river night she whispered to the doll Jenny a little story about a pretty fly she had seen one day in the green, sweet leaves of the grape arbor. He had a wife, this pretty fly, and one day she flew away and he was very sad. And then one night

his two pretty fly children flew away, too, into the sky—into the
moon. But it was a story without an end because presently she
was sleeping, too.

Walt! Oh, Walt! Look here what the mailman brought this
morning!

He took it from her hand: the cheap, colored postal card
with the inevitable courthouse and the courthouse yard with the
brass cannon and the two nameless and immemorial town loafers
lounging against the old soldiers' monument.

Now see, Walt! I told you all your frettin' was for naught!

Walt turned the card over and commenced reading aloud:

Dear Walt and Icey: I bet you been worried and give us up
for lost. Took the kids down here with me for a visit to my sister
Elsie's farm. Thot it would do us all a world of good after so much
trubble and heartache. A little change of senery—

Ah, the poor, poor soul!

—a little change of senery will do us good for a month or so.
At least the kids will git a plenty of good home cooking and some
meat on their bonns and ther is a fine revival going on down here
and they ask me to preach next Wensday. God be with you till
we meet again from yr. devoted Harry Powell.

Now ain't you relieved, Walt?

Well, sure I am. But don't forget—you was worried, too,
Mother. Him takin' off with the kids like he done that night and
never a word of good-by.

But that would be like him, she said. Feelin' he'd already been
burden enough in his time of need.

Well, I reckon! Walt lied, half remembering his old suspicions of Preacher. I just got to worryin' for fear some of them
gypsies might have busted in the house one night and done off
with all three of them.

Shucks, Walt, them gypsies has been gone a week.

Yes, but not before one of them knifed a farmer down on Ben's Run the other forenoon and stole his best field horse.

I read that in the *Echo*. Was he bad hurt?

He'll live. But they never caught the gypsies nor the horse neither. I tell you, Mother, a body ain't safe in his own parlor these nights.

Icey snuffled and scurried off to the kitchen, glowing with happiness and relief.

Sometimes when I think of the courage of that great soul, she cried, above her pot of fudge, it makes me ashamed of myself that I ever complained, Walt!

He came to the kitchen and stood beside her.

It wouldn't surprise me none, she went on, if he was to come back next month and put the house and lot up for sale. And it might be the best thing. So many, many memories there!

Walt went out in front to the ice-cream bins and, leaning his bare elbows on the frosty lids, scowled at the card. Something itched and worried behind his eyes, far back in his mind, and yet he said nothing, thought nothing. Icey came out of the kitchen then, her eyes sparkling.

Walt Spoon, I think I know why Mister Powell took them kids and left the other night.

He looked at her, saying nothing.

Walt, I bet Willa's run aground somewhere and sent for him to fish her out again.

Yes. Well, maybe—

It would be like him, she said, to go and lift her up and forgive.

Yes, I reckon it would—

The ninety and nine, Walt! Mind the old hymn. Where the one sheep run off and the ninety and nine was left and the shepherd never rested till he'd found that wanderin' one.

Walt grunted and lighted his pipe and, squinting one eye, stared into the fair morning beneath the trees of Peacock Alley.

The ninety and nine, crooned Icey softly, thinking of the wonderful thing that Preacher was doing, and stuck the pretty postcard in the frame of the big mirror over the shelf behind the counter, above the gleaming jars of licorice and gumdrops and frosty mints.

That man of God, she said softly and stared at the bright penny postcard alongside the faded carnival photo of the sheepish, laughing girl that had once been Willa Harper.

The people saw him that August in a dozen little towns along the river: the quiet, brooding man on the horse. He would ride in town early in the morning and they could tell by his clothes and the stubble of beard that he had spent the night in some farmer's hayloft and fed his horse on some farmer's corn. They paid him no particular never mind because it was a depression year—a time of wanderers on the land. He would tell them he was an evangelist and hitch his horse to a fence post and fetch a dusty Scripture from the pocket of his ragged coat and then preach a hell-raising half-hour sermon in the shadow of a country store or under the trees of a courthouse square and no sheriff ever bothered him because it was a depression year and everybody was a little bit scared of God just then. Sometimes he would get a few coins in his old hat or maybe a sandwich from a board-front restaurant with no other sign over it but *Good Eats—No Credit* or maybe a storekeeper would give him a loaf of last week's bread and a jar of old preserves. He preached often about children: about how an ungrateful child is an abomination before the eyes of God and about how the world was fast going to damnation because of impudent and disobedient youngsters flying in the face of Age.

Preacher, how many kids you got?

He turned and glared at the man, shading his squinting eyes under the hand that was grown so dark with sunburn and wind that the blue letters of Love were nearly gone.

I had two, brother. But the Lord seen fit to take them away.

Well, meanin' no smartness, Preacher, but if you had the five I've got to put up with and feed six or eight times a day you'd know how true them words you just preached really was.

Thank you, brother!

And on top of that, cried the other one, spurting a brown stream of amber into the dust among the sleeping dogs in the shadow of an old Chevrolet, my ol' woman wanted to take in them two wild savages Gailey Flowers chased out of his tomato garden last week!

The which? Say that again, brother. Two, you say?

Two little kids. Orphans, I reckon. Old Gailey Flowers has that piece of land down at the forks in the road below Hannibal Station and he catched them kids stealin' tomatoes there the other mornin' about sunup.

When was that? When, brother? When did you say?

Is them kids yourn, Preacher?

When? When was they seen last?

He had hold of the man's arm now and the fingers of his dark left hand pressed into the farmer's tough wrist.

It was a Wednesday morning! called an old man from the crowd. My woman seen 'em, too. They come up to the house a-beggin' for bread and bacon. Shucks, we hain't had bacon on our table since '31.

There was something now that they all sensed about Preacher that seemed hungry and unclean. His lips quivered, his eyes were too bright, his fingers too pleading as he went around to each of them, laying hands upon their arms, begging for more details about the children. It was a year of depression. It was no strange sight in the land in that lean and fallow time: children running the woodlands and the fields without parents, without food, without love. Families were shattered and broken asunder in that black decade and the children were driven to fend for themselves like the whelps of random litters: in the lanes of the back counties, roaming the big highways, sleeping in barn lofts or in old abandoned car bodies on town junk heaps; stealing food where they could or accepting it from the hands of some kind farm woman who could see within their ravaged and disenchanted faces a vision of herself or of her own kind or of some dark portent of what yet might come to pass upon herself or to her own. But these men, who had seen and understood this loving-kindness and mercy in the faces and voices of their good wives, saw none of this in the face of Preacher; saw instead the dry-toothed cunning of the hound on the hunt. They moved away from him. The dusty congregation dispersed and went back to whittling, to waiting at the post office doorway for the posting of the WPA jobs or the passing out of relief commodities or perhaps merely homeward to loaf in sullen and broiling discontent and stare at their empty, impotent hands.

And so the dusty stranger moved on from town to town: sniffing, nosing under scrap heaps of corner gossip for a word, for a clue; eavesdropping on feedstore porches, idling with a ready ear by crossroad post offices and short-line depots or in the lobbies of the country hotels where the drummers drink and tell ornery stories and listen for the midnight train to go wailing off into the velvet, star-sweet night.

He worked a week here and a week there, picking peaches or working in the late corn harvest: earning a meal or a night's lodging or a few pennies, moving on through the river counties, his nose and eyes ever to windward, moving with an implacable and unceasing revenge after the ones who had cheated him of that which the Lord had said was his own.

Sometime, he knew that he would come suddenly upon a farmhouse, lazy and golden in the dusk under the pin oaks in the lambent light of Indian summer. And there—perhaps playing in the dust beside a cistern or squatting on the freshly scrubbed stone porch of that solid bottom-lands farmhouse he would see them at last: a little girl with an old doll and a little boy with no toy at all, their haunted faces like moonflowers in the dusk.

To have seen the children in that troubled time one might have supposed them to be fallen angels, or dusty woodland elves suddenly banished from the Court of the Gods of Moonlight and of faery meadows. They blew along like brown leaves on the wind. All the long hot day after their escape they had drifted upon the swift river channel and then the river night dropped abruptly upon them and there were no lights but the stars and the shanty-boat lamps along the shore and the drifting dust of fireflies against the black, looming hills above the narrows. They fell asleep, hungry and discouraged and frightened, and the old river night had seemed to set about them the sentries of her own history: fiddling keelboatmen and the blue-eyed old captains of the Louisville trade.

In the morning John awakened with a sprig of willow leaves tickling his face. He opened his eyes and saw that Ben Harper's skiff, those ten feet of ark that had borne them safely above the black flood of Preacher's malevolence, had providently run aground on a sand bar near the mouth of a creek. The sun stood high in the brush pines on the hill above them and there was a fine, cracking wind from the river. They were ravenously hungry. John shrewdly dragged the boat onto the bar as far as he could and gathering broken branches from the drift against the banks covered the boat so that they could safely leave it and forage for their breakfast among the bottom farms. They were an unkempt and raggle-taggle pair those two—foul with the smell of fish tails from the skiffs bilge and smirched with tar from Uncle Birdie's generous calking of the old boat's seams. John spied an orchard far up beyond a bluff above the river road and told Pearl to wait while he went to fetch them a shirtful of fruit for their morning meal. So Pearl squatted beneath the nodding tops of the snowy Queen Anne's lace that covered the meadow like an old woman's Sunday tablecloth and chatted and sang to the doll while John was gone. Presently he appeared, running toward her again and there were cries behind him among the little peach trees and he beckoned her to follow him and they fled again down the pasture to the shore. The farmer did not pursue them there and they sat on a large, flat rock, disconsolate and hungrier than ever, chewing on blades of sour grass, and glumly surveyed the gray expanse of morning river.

John, when are we going home?

Just wait, now, Pearl!

But if we went home, John, she reasoned stubbornly, Daddy would fix us our breakfast. And Mom is terribly worried, John.

But he knew better than that. Scraps and tatters of old Uncle Birdie's sodden mumblings had stayed with him since that terrible moment in the wharfboat when all of heaven's unreasoning judgment seemed to rise against them. John knew that his mother was gone. She was as blurred now in his hopes—even in his memory—as the misty, half-forgotten figure of the hanging man on the red bricks of the wall. Preacher had done away with her in some dreadful and final way. Preacher and the blue men had finished her. It was a world that hunted the children now.

He caught a hellgrammite in a muddy, stagnant pond up on the bar and Pearl screamed at the dreadful, crawly, squirming thing as he speared it on a hook he had found in a rusty snuffbox in the skiff. He weighted a short length of line with a pebble and dropped it in the shallows, hoping that there might be in that bare foot of depth a hungry catfish. But it seemed useless after a bit and he retired to his stone again to stare bitterly at Pearl and think that somehow she was to blame for all of it. It was not easy: keeping always before him the realization of what it was he was fighting to protect. For it was more than his life and hers; it was that solemn child's oath that he had taken that day in the tall grass by the feet of his doomed and bleeding father. He ran to Pearl and snatched the doll from her clinging hands and looked to see if the safety pin still held closed the gap in the soft cloth body and, poking a finger through, felt the crisp bills of the dead man's plunder. Yes, it was really there: it was not a dark dream. Yes, he had sworn to save it and he felt his throat tighten, remembering suddenly how important and dreadful and irrevocable it is to swear to a thing.

By noon hunger had emboldened them to seek a farmhouse kitchen for a meal. The fat wife stopped her churning in the cool of the casaba vines along the stone porch and stared at them there on the stone stoop worn curved with time. She wiped her itching nose on a freckled forearm.

Hungry are ye? Well, where's your folks?

We ain't got none, said John truthfully, and hearing the words in his own ears gave a sudden, dreadful substantiation to the fact.

Well, sit down there and don't come trackin' up my porch with your muddy feet. I'll see if there's any potato soup left. Gracious, such times when youngins run the roads!

She waddled off to the kitchen, quarreling with life, and returned presently with big thick bowls of hot potato soup and three thick slices of homemade bread spread over with cinnamon-sweet apple butter. They finished in a breath and came and stood with wide, grave eyes, holding up the empty bowls, waiting for her to notice them again. She grumbled and took their bowls away and filled them again only this time there were no bread and apple butter. When they were finished John sensed that it would be wise to leave. The woman stood kneading her butter in a wooden bowl, squeezing out the sour buttermilk with a flat paddle with which she scored the sweet, golden pat when she was done.

Git ye filled up?

Yes'm.

Well, what do ye say? If ye was born ye must have had a ma and she should have learnt ye to say thanks for things.

Thank you, ma'am.

Thank you, said Pearl, making a feeble little try at the curtsy Willa had taught her at Christmas time two years before.

Go away! the fat woman's eyes seemed to say. Go away because you remind me of something dreadful in the land just now: some pattern that is breaking up: something going that is as basic and old as the wheeling of the winter stars. Go away! Don't remind me that it's Hard Times and there's children on the roads of the land!

And so they went back to the river and sat by the skiff until the wild, Indian paintbox colors of a river sunset swarmed against the west and the day shut like a door in their faces and they were alone with a cool breeze soughing in from the silent, flowing stream. Yet John was reluctant to embark again in the skiff. He felt a physical need to spend a night on land, with floor boards and earth beneath. The river was too beguiling and treacherous in her female moods of gently passing shadows and strange voices floating crystal-sharp across the ripples and lights passing like fallen stars among the dark, distant trees. Pearl yawned and suddenly the moon rose round and full across the river in the bluffs.

Come on, Pearl, he sighed, rising and reaching for her hand.

Are we going home, John?

He remembered a barn he had seen in another farm up the river road: a gray frame building set back three hundred yards from the home of its owner, under the green umbrella of an

enormous sycamore. Down in the farmhouse someone was playing a mouth harp and a girl was singing and the lamp in the
kitchen window was a dusty orange glow and John yearned, for
an instant, for the kindness of a room and the sound of a voice
that was loving kin.

Are we going to stay in that big house, John?

Shhhhh! Hush, Pearl! Yes!

That's a funny house.

It ain't a house, Pearl. It's a barn.

Pearl's nose itched and burned at the smell of the big house.
Inside it she heard the gentle nudge and stamp of the cows and
turned to John aghast and quaking.

John! There's big dogs!

Them's cows, he said gently. They won't hurt.

He found the ladder to the hayloft and showed Pearl how
to climb it and presently they were settled in a great, prickling
bed of sweet, fresh timothy with a fine broad window that surveyed the vast and silent bottomlands for miles on either side
and beyond it the dark river. The moon swung high above the
valley, lighting it almost to the brightness of dusk, making the
river a shining ribbon of black glass and touching the spreading
night meadows with the dust of its illumination.

Now, Pearl, warned John sternly, don't go near that big door
yonder. That's where they put the hay in. If you was to fall out of
there you'd kill yourself sure.

At his warning she shrank back and hugged him and they fell
asleep thus, among the aromatic hay, while down in the meadows a whippoorwill cried and whooped its liquid laments and
country yard dogs barked and quarreled in the faraway stillnesses.
John had not been sleeping more than an instant until he heard
it—faint yet distinct on the barely stirring air. He opened his
eyes. The moon had not moved: it stood where it had been when
his eyes had closed: half obscured by the beam and pulley which

jutted over the aperture. Pearl had not heard, did not stir, asleep
in untroubled conscience with her thumb between her pouting
lips and the doll cuddled sweetly in the cradle of her arms. John
half rose and stared off into the moonlit valley. Nothing moved,
nothing stirred upon the ruts and dung clusters of the deserted
barnyard, nor upon the far moonlit arena of the valley as far as
his eyes could see. Yet as plain and clear as the song of the now-
stilled field bird had been he had heard the faint, sweet rise of
that unforgettable voice.

Leaning, leaning! Safe and secure from all alarms!

Leaning, leaning! Leaning on the everlasting arms!

John held his breath, harking, and then breathed it out quickly
and breathed in again, holding it so that he could listen again, his
eyes burning and straining through the dust of moonlight, ready
to pick out the tiniest motion anywhere upon the vast, spreading
tableland between the barn and the river. It was as clear and distinct now as if the tiny voice were in the mountain of hay at his
elbow, and then suddenly in the distance John saw him on the
road, emerging suddenly from behind a tall growth of redbud half
a mile away: a man on a huge field horse, moving slowly and yet
with a dreadful plodding deliberation up the feathery dust of the
river road. The figure of the man and horse were as tiny as toys in
that perspective and yet, even in those diminished proportions,
John could make out each dreadful and evil line of those familiar
shoulders. Now in a dozen farms on both sides of the river the
hound dogs had come out to bark at the sound of the singing, and
a tan beagle bitch emerged suddenly from beneath the porch of
the farmhouse just below the barn and raced braying to the gate
to herald the singer's passing. But the singing did not stop and
the figure, moving still in that infinitely sinister slowness, passed
directly below the house and was obscured again by a tall growth
of pawpaws and still the voice continued unabated while John
huddled in the hay with thundering heart. And even long after

he had passed, faded down the road, lost in the moonbeams of the lower farms, John could still hear the faint, sweet voice and he thought: Don't he never sleep? Don't he never find a barn and climb up in the hay and shut his eyes like other mortals do at night or does he just keep on hunting me and Pearl to the end of the world?

In the hour that followed the dogs fell silent and the moon moved an inch. The whippoorwill began his argument again, but more softly now, as if his own voice had been humbled and affrighted by a thing that had passed in the night, a darkness that had brushed his wings like the mower's scythe.

At daybreak the children awoke and stole down to the barn door and when John had brushed all the straw from Pearl's skirt he made her put on her brightest morning smile so that they might present themselves at the farmer's kitchen for a bit of hot breakfast or at least a crust of biscuit and a dipper of cool water from the cistern. The gaunt young farmer's wife cried and prayed over them until they were sticky and smothered with her ministrations and had, indeed, fled presently before she could begin to ply them with questions. She had set such a poor breakfast table that it was scarcely surprising that she had not asked them to stay for lunch. For it was Hard Times in the land and larders held precious little extra for roadside wanderers. And so with the edge gone from their hunger and with unaccountably cheerful hearts the children returned to the river and set off again in Ben Harper's skiff. Pearl sat in the skiff's stern chuckling and playing with the doll Jenny while John whistled and fooled around with some lengths of leader, trying to unsnarl them and fastening them to some of Uncle Birdie's old hooks in the hope of catching a catfish or two. At Marietta they rolled grandly past the bustling little landing and not a soul noticed them. The showboat *Humpty Dumpty* was docked there that day and the cheerful piping of the calliope skipped across the live water like bright, flat pebbles of sound. John stood up in the skiff like a pirate and admired the grand sight from afar and Pearl lifted dancing eyes from the scolding of her doll. Farther downstream after the river had turned and straightened again they drifted in silence past a panorama of unrolling shoreline, of sleepy farms and drowsing woodlands and the swelling bosom of rich bottomlands in the full cry of summer's last harvest. The hay hands stood in the rippling grass and waved and hollered but in a moment their voices were gone and the unceasing river carried the children on into the sweet silences of the early morning. Still hungry, they had eaten the pork sandwiches in the greasy little paper poke the kindly farm woman had given them and now they dreamed, longing again for the home and solace that, to John at least, seemed never to have existed at all. On both sides of them the land unfolded like the leafing pages of a book and when John turned his eyes to the West Virginia shore he thought: I will be glad when it is dark because he is somewhere over on that shore, in one of those towns, along that winding road somewhere, and when it is dark he can't see us. Because he is still hunting and there is only the river between us and those hands. And as the warmth of the morning sun filled the air he fell asleep again and Pearl slept, too, cradling the doll, and John dreamed that he was home in his old bed again and Ben Harper was down in the parlor playing his favorite roll on the Pianola and Willa was clapping her hands and humming because she did not know the words and it was a thousand years ago.

When he opened his eyes again all motion was gone. The sun stood high overhead at noon and there were trees between it and his blinking eyes and on a root that jutted from the crumbling riverbank a redbird shrilled and scolded at him. A turtle, dusty and parched from the fields, labored scratching down the mudbank to the water, craning his wrinkled turkey neck toward the running stream. John thought: They make turtle soup but I'll be derned if I know how and besides I wouldn't know how to go about getting him open.

Pearl, awake before him, had wandered up into the grasses above the willows on the steep cliff that jutted from the meadow plateau and was gathering a bouquet of daisies. Each saw the woman at the fence at the same moment. Pearl's hand froze with the nodding daisies in her fisted fingers and John scrambled the length of the skiff and lifted the heavy paddle threateningly.

You two youngsters git up here to me this instant!

John's mouth, at the authority in this voice, fell agape and Pearl turned a frightened face to his.

Mind me now! I'll fetch a willow switch and bring you up *here jumpin'* directly!

John—half of a mind to run for Pearl and try to make it back to the skiff—merely stared. The woman was in her middle sixties, staunch and ruddy-faced and big-boned. She wore a man's old hat on her head and a shapeless gray wool sweater hung over her shoulders.

Now she snorted like a fieldhand and came over the fence a-straddling and snatched a switch of willow as she came, scrambling down the bank with the alacrity of a boy. John could not make himself move. The woman had caught Pearl up in her stout embrace now and was making for John, her big shoes squishing through the mud, the switch rising to catch his calves when they were handy.

Now git on up there.

Pearl, opening her mouth, began to wail; her face wrinkling and scarlet with outrage.

Don't you hurt her! cried John, quivering and standing his ground in the skiff bottom.

Hurt her nothin'! cried the old woman. *Wash* her is more like it! And you, too, mister! Now git on up there to my house and don't set a foot inside till I've fetched the washtub for the both of ye.

And she herded them grimly before her up through the meadow like angry little lambs and when she was within earshot of the gray frame house she began to shout to its inhabitants.

Ruby! Mary! Clary!

Above the rows of tomato plants, over the top rail of her neat, white fence, three children's faces appeared, bright as morning hollyhocks.

Yes, Miz Cooper! they cried in chorus.

Ruby—run fetch the washtub and fill it. Mary! Clary! Fetch a bar of laundry soap from the washhouse and the scrub brush, too.

And the faces disappeared and Miz Cooper shoved John and Pearl through her gate and then turned to survey them again, her lips pursed and working with anger.

Gracious! If you hain't a sight to beat all! Where you from?

John could not find his tongue.

Where's your folks? Speak up now.

He stared at the big, man's shoes on her feet, crusted and heavy with garden mud.

Gracious! So I've got two more mouths to feed! All right. Git them clothes off now and throw 'em yonder in the grass. Ruby'll wash 'em.

Neither child moved.

Mind me now! Mind!

John slowly began unbuttoning his little shirt and the old woman stooped and began tugging at Pearl's knotted shoelaces. The oldest girl, Ruby, moved from the kitchen doorway, grinning with a flash of white teeth. She bore a washtub to the grass beside the pump and began filling it with gushing cold water.

The strange children stood staring as John and Pearl took their clothes off. John listened to the sharp, nasal chant of the pump handle and stared at the washtub. He shivered at the prospect. And yet his heart was curiously warm within him with the unreasonable illusion that he had come home.

BOOK FOUR

A STRONG TREE WITH MANY BIRDS

"Oh, the gold! The precious, precious gold!
The green miser'll horde ye soon! Hish! Hish!
God goes 'mong the worlds blackberrying!"

—MELVILLE, *Moby-Dick*

She was old and yet she was ageless—in the manner of such staunch country widows. Gaunt, plain-spoken, and hard of arm, she could stand up to three of the toughest, shrewdest cattle dealers in Pleasants County and get every penny she thought her hog was worth. Or if pork was off that year she would butcher and can her own sausage and smoke her own hams and have enough left over to present the preacher's family with a nice meal of spareribs. In the summer she sent the children into the woodlands and brush filth with buckets for berries, and it was her old, wise hands that taught their young fingers how to pick them and schooled their eyes in the ways of berry-finding. She had a cow and she churned her own butter and sold it at New Economy wrapped in cool, damp swaths of immaculate muslin. She had chickens and their eggs went to market, too, in a bright yellow basket spread across with a napkin. From the fat of her butchered hog she made soap, standing in a drenching March rain beside her brawling iron kettle in the back yard till the task was done. Fifteen miles downriver at Parkersburg a waitress had short-changed her and that was a quarter of a century before and she had never gone to that town again.

Widowed a full forty years before, she had raised a son and

seen him off into the world but she had soon grown lonely in the haunted stillness of the old home and so there had never been a time in the quarter of a century since that her house had not sheltered a child. And children were easy to come by in the river lands. Many a dark-haired farm girl lost her wits to an August moon and the mouth of a cunning lover and found herself, after he had gone away to work in Pittsburgh or Detroit, with the fruit of their ecstasy squalling and unwelcome in her poor mother's kitchen. Once the child was weaned and toddling it was to Rachel Cooper's door that he was carried, like as not, and there was never the bad word uttered for what he was: poor little wood's colt. On Sundays his mother might come for a visit and a walk with him in the fields and at sundown he would be returned to Rachel's bed and board, unprotesting. She fed her children till they were rosy and full, scrubbed them till they were red and squalling, spanked them when there was cause, and taught them the Lord's tales on Sabbath mornings. That very summer she had packed her ugly cardboard suitcase and gone to Chillicothe to visit her own boy Ralph, who was forty-three now and doing well in real estate and married with a nice wife and four grown girls of his own. But the years had improved Ralph. Prosperity had given him a taste for Oriental rugs and expensive modernistic furniture and a big new Victrola and, truth to tell, he and his wife Clarice had been embarrassed by the old woman's visit. She was really no one you would want to show off: that tough, ruddy old woman with the country smell still strong in her shawl and her hands all broken and red from laundry lye. She had stayed with them three days and fretted and growled at them for having so many forks at each place at supper and she chased the little Negro maid away from her bedroom each morning and made her bed herself. And when Ralph's boss and his wife came to dinner unexpectedly that night she had sat afterward on a straight chair in the farthest corner and laughed at the wrong times and picked nervously at her fingers and acted such a perfect fool that she could have killed herself with self-reproach. She took the noon bus for home next day and had ridden out of the strange town furiously angry at something or someone in the world that had made her feel so coarse and out-of-date. Clarice had not liked the stone pitcher of maple sirup she had brought in her basket of gifts for them; nor the Mason jar of cucumber pickles, nor the green-tomato relish. Rachel felt certain that they had thrown these things away after she got on the Greyhound bus and rode away, waving her little handkerchief at them (the fancy one that she never used and always kept in her bureau drawer under the little cloth bag of dried rose petals)—mincing and smiling at them from the bus window; trying to act like a lady Ralph would be proud of calling his mother and then grumbling and quarreling with herself all the way home because she had even cared, because she had even tried to put on a show. And then when the big bus hissed to a stop at the crossroads she got out and thanked the driver and stood alone in the river wind, in that country silence, and smelled her house down the road, smelled her little orchard and smelled her good black land, and that was when she felt the grand, old surge of comeback in her heart. Ralph was gone from her house—gone from her thoughts—and that was the way Life meant it to be, and then she heard the three little girls come screaming and shouting toward her across the field and she thought: Why, shoot! It don't matter. I got a new harvest coming on. A new crop. I'm good for something in this old world and I know it, too.

They had a wild happy supper together that night. She sent home the neighbor woman who had stayed with the children in her absence and then she got busy fixing the things she knew they all liked. She even opened a jar of watermelon preserves, and the children knew that this was indeed special: this treat never appeared except at Thanksgiving or Christmastide. She had brought them each small presents from the Chillicothe five-and-ten and after supper everyone opened her gift and screamed and squealed with joy and kissed the old woman until her lips began to purse and pout with impatience and she shoved them gruffly away and shook her shoulders angrily lest they discover in her face all the love that was there.

There were three, the children: Mary, the youngest, child of a half-breed Cherokee harvest hand from Paden City and a waitress in the Empire Eats at New Economy. Mary was four, with raven-black hair as straight as a mare's tail and eyes like dark little pools of stump water. Clara, eleven and thin as a rail, with the smile of one who had not been smiling long—a thin, aimless child with freckles like bits of butter floating in the churn, with crooked teeth and foolish rag-doll eyes. Ruby, thirteen and big and shapeless and stooped from being with the other smaller ones so much and trying always to be down there sharing their world with them, not missing a trick. Ruby was Rachel's problem girl. She broke the Mason jars when Rachel set her to scalding them at canning time; she broke the warm, brown eggs when her big, wooden fingers gathered them from their cool, secret hiding places about the yard; she tripped on milk pails full and sent them splashing. And yet when her hands touched a little child she was transformed and her eyes shone until, like lamps, they illumined the pale, ugly flesh of her face. And so when old Rachel would go to prayer meetings on Wednesday she left the girl with the other two—little Mary and Clary. And when she returned she would find those two on the floor at the red, naked feet of the strange girl: reciting little bits of Psalms Rachel had taught them all by winter lamplight or playing cat's cradle with a length of butcher's twine.

And this was the house of Rachel Cooper—a strong tree with branches for many birds. And so the coming of two more did not make much of a difference. They were children and they were hungry and they needed love and a bath and a spanking and sometimes Rachel would think when she looked at them, any of them: 'Deed to God, sometimes I feel like I'm playin' a big joke on the Lord. Why, when He comes looking for old folks He won't even see me—He'll see them kids and maybe He'll just pass on by and say: Why, shoot! That there's a *mother!* I can't take her!

At night when they were in bed she would come down and stand in the kitchen for a spell and think: It's my last harvest. My gathering of summer's best and last sowing.

To John she was a perfect and agonizing enigma: an unfathomable mixture of female authority and tenderest motherliness. He loathed her those first few days and spoke not one single word of answer, or request, or denial to her in all that time. Sullenly, stubbornly, tragically the boy submitted to her disquieting scrub brush, her fierce, unflagging ministrations to his long-untended hair, her spankings when it came his turn to receive them. When she gathered the children about her once a week, on the grave, sweet Sunday dusks with the harvest moon hung full-blown as a chilled, fresh melon on the hills above the river; arrayed them on little square carpet stools about her in a semicircle and read them a story from the Scripture, John remembered only the voice of Salvation that he had left screaming and frothing among the cattails on the river shore upon that dreadful night of their exodus.

John, you hain't heard a word I said.

He did not lower his eyes from the lamp, did not move his hands from his knees. He might have been carved from pine, for all his movement. And then she knew it would be wise to let him be and not try to speak to him too much or to make him answer, knowing in her wisdom that the dark, frightened bird that crouched shivering and hurt in the deep forest of his mind would one day poke its bright eye through the leaves and presently (if she paid no special notice) it might hop out onto a limb and then they would all hear it singing brightly and boldly some afternoon and only then would they turn and pretend to be surprised and welcome it to their picnic cloth.

Pearl, in that autumn, was so hungry for love that she would have turned and taken suck from an old ewe. And soon she had edged little Mary over just a mite to share in the old woman's most favorite and tender partiality. Pearl adored Rachel and it was a devotion scarcely less than that she felt toward the girl Ruby. Ruby took complete charge the night the strange new children first slept under Rachel's roof. John rebelled when she attempted to undress him for bed and Rachel intervened, but it was Ruby who held Pearl in her arms until she was asleep and could be laid trusting and smiling, thumb tucked between her pouting, sweet lips, beneath the cool, fresh sheets of the old spool bed in Rachel's attic room. John lay awake beside his sister that night in a perfect agony of misgivings. He had not felt such rejection of his fortunes even in the darkest days when Preacher had put in his first appearance at Cresap's Landing. It was not that he believed old Rachel might be in league with the blue men who had dragged off his father or even with the insane evangelist. This was curiously worse: it was as if in some unutterable and beguiling way Rachel schemed against the very identity of him. John had grown so accustomed to the climate of flight and danger and to the clear definition of Life's mortal enemies that somehow Rachel's goodness seemed more darkly perilous than any of the others. And yet in the time to come, as the days stretched into weeks and the weeks wound like country lanes among the shaking, burning leaves of Indian summer and the end of harvest was upon the land, it seemed to John that what he had felt that morning on the sandbar when old Rachel had come upon them there, that sense of coming home, might be true. He found that his chafed spirit rankled less and less beneath the stern, wholesome regimen of Rachel's household.

One night they were all at the black stove making seafoam

candy: old Rachel and the girls prattling and carrying on over the buttered tins where the candy pieces were to be spread to cool. He sat apart from them, alone on the back stoop in the crisp air, under the moon in the black walnut tree beyond the washhouse. He had almost thought for a moment that he would like to go indoors and stand close to them, not to say anything because he could not speak yet, but just to stand, to be one of them, perhaps to touch the old woman with his hand, to let her know that the broken bird in the dark tree stirred its wings and tried them and already thought of the morning when it would venture upon those outer limbs and try its voice upon the stillness.

On the night when Rachel read to them from the Bible about Moses he had been moved even more.

Now, old Pharoah—he was the King of Egyptland! she cried, spreading her hard old hands across the tissue-thin pages of the Scripture. And he had a daughter and once upon a time she was walkin' along the river and she seen something bumpin' and scrapin' along down on a bar under the willows, back in the cat-tails where the devil's darnin' needles was flashin' in the mornin' sun. And do you know what it was, children?

No! gasped Ruby and Clary and Little Mary and, hearing them, Pearl cried out, too.

Well now, it was a skiff washed up on the bar, whispered the old woman, her black eyes twinkling in the light of the kitchen lamp. And who do you reckon was in it?

Pearl and John! cried poor, big Ruby.

Not this time! cried Rachel. It was just one youngin—a little boy babe. And do you know who he was, children?

No! cried Ruby and Clary and Little Mary and Pearl in a single voice.

It was Moses!—a king of men, Moses, children, that was to grow up to lead his people out of the wilderness—to save them all from death and pestilence and plague.

John heard it and came to them that night, drawn irresistibly by this tale that was so completely his own, and sat boldly in the circle, beside Ruby's carpet stool, and listened some more, and the old woman wisely paid him no mind.

The river brought the time of gold into the valley. Up in the woods the hickory nuts rained their dry patter throughout the still afternoons and there was smoke in the air and the ghosts of Cornstalk and his young martyred Princes stalked the land again and the hunters' guns boomed and racketed in the hollows and soon the frost would come to blacken the yellow pawpaws. John had come home. The bird was freed and had flown into the sun to return each dusk to its nest. All the love of that house had been too much for him: it was in the butter, in the smell of the clean clothes that Rachel patched and sewed each night where they had torn them, in the odor of fresh bread on fall afternoons and in the nasal, hearty crackle of her impatient voice when she hailed them in for supper. And yet despite this capitulation John kept his eyes on the river road, and guarded the doll in his sister's arms with unremitting vigilance; harking ever for the clop of that strange horse on the windy, midnight highway, for the creak upon the threshold, the whisper of the hunter's steel. Not through any logic, but through a grim and pragmatic cynicism of instinct, John knew within his heart, within his flesh, that the idyll would be broken in the end: that upon one day before the snow fell again he would hear that sweet and fateful voice drifting clear and dreadful through the affrighted autumn dusk.

One night, sensing that he might want to talk, Rachel sent the other children off to bed but kept John with her in the kitchen. She bent her head, squinting through her poor, taped-up, crazed spectacles at the darning of their tattered stockings under the golden circle of lamplight.

Git ye an apple from the cellar, boy. And git me one, too.

He obeyed, pounding down into the cellar, happy that she

had kept him up after the others to make this a special time for him alone, to set him upon a chore whose fruits they would share. He clambered up the side of the great barrel and stretched his fingers deep inside among the chilly, clustered heaps of last year's McIntoshes. And when he had found two without rot or blemish he scampered back to the kitchen, washed them at the pump, and gave one to Rachel. Now she set her darning-gourd abruptly aside, bit crisply into the fruit, and glared at him with that tart, twinkling grimness that he had come to recognize as all the world's safety.

John, where's your folks? she said suddenly.

He lifted his eyes to her and said the word plainly, knowing its awful truth.

Dead.

Dead, she nodded with finality and let that matter be. And where you from?

Upriver, he said. A ways.

Well, I know that, John! I didn't figger you'd rowed that John boat up from Parkersburg! Have you any kin?

He shrugged.

Kin, she repeated. No aunts, no uncles, no grandfolks?

I don't know, he said.

Far up in the dark, above the house, above the world, the vast locust voices began their insensate, rackety skirl. And suddenly, and with a tenderness that nigh broke the old woman's heart, John reached out his hand and laid his fingers on her old knuckles.

Tell me that story agin.

Story, honey? Why, what story?

About them kings, he said. That the queen found down on the sandbar in the skiff that time.

Kings! she scolded. Why, honey, there was only one.

Oh, no, he said. I mind you said there was two.

Well, shoot! Maybe there was! Yes, come to think of it—there was two, John.

And she fetched the old Bible and read him the tale again, in a soft, gruff voice because she did not dare let him see how she felt just then, and changed the story around so that there were really two in the bulrushes, in the basket, in that lost and ancient time.

Git to bed now! she cried at last, rising with angry, moist eyes and smacked his bottom smartly before her as he fled up the kitchen steps. Git to bed now and no nonsense. Gracious, it's nigh eight o'clock and we've all got to be up tomorrow bright and early to fetch them eggs and butter to town.

He lay in bed that night, hearing a strange steamboat blow softly down somewhere under the lower stars, and he thought for the first time: Well, maybe he won't come at all now and maybe it wasn't none of it real and maybe there wasn't even any Mom and Dad or none of it and I am a lost king and Pearl is a lost king, too.

The trip to New Economy with the week's butter and eggs was the great event toward which each of the seven other days moved. Upon this day Rachel dressed each of them in his best and together they went to the river landing where the old ferryboat made its dozen daily trips to the Ohio side. At this ferry landing there stood an ancient locust tree upon which, hung on a leather thong nailed into the bark, was a battered brass bugle. More times than not, the ferry captain dozed with a Western magazine over his face up in the cabin of the rickety little gasoline boat and it was the custom of travelers on the other side to wake him with the bugle to come and fetch them across. Rachel always carried a bit of the fresh, clean muslin she used for straining jelly so that she could wipe off the brass mouthpiece of the bugle that was not uncommonly crusted and bitter with the tobacco juice of its previous user.

Dirtiest critters under God's blue sky!—Men! she would scold and then lift the horn to her mouth to blow a lusty, impatient trump across the glassy, silent stream.

In New Economy they had a good restaurant meal at the Empire Eats and when the day's trading was done and if their produce had brought a good price, Rachel would take them to Ev Roberts's pharmacy and treat them all to an enormous, communal sack of licorice drops and sometimes ice-cream sodas. Then it was back to the ferry again with empty baskets and high spirits and roaring appetites for supper. Folks turned on the streets to stare after Rachel Cooper and her brood. Every woman with children of her own envied the proper, obedient way the children followed the old woman's polka-dot skirts. Men, respectful of Rachel's hard, shrewd bargaining sense at the cattle auctions, bowed to her, tipped their hats, spoke words of greeting. When they passed Ev Roberts's bench out in front of the drugstore on their way to the street again the late-afternoon loafers and whittlers had suddenly gathered.

Hi, Miz Cooper.

Howdy, Gene.

Got two more peeps in yore brood, I see.

Yes, and ornerier than the rest! she cried. Don't kids just beat the Dutch now! Just look at them two little ones—Pearl and Mary. I'll swear I scrubbed them two till they was raw 'fore I come over here this mornin'.

Where'd ye git them new ones, Miz Cooper?

Driftwood! she cried. Just plain driftwood warshed up on a bar!

And then she could have cut her tongue out for saying that: for letting those loose-jawed scalawags know anything about those two. Nine chances out of ten that boy John had fibbed to her about having no folks and next thing she knew some WPA family would come rattling and banging up the yard in a busted-down fruit truck and claim their two lost biddies and light into Rachel for kidnaping them in the first place. Rachel bit her tongue angrily and hurried the children toward the ferry. Sure as sin, some father would show his face in town and those gossips would tell. And sure as sin he would come a-hunting his kids.

As a matter of fact, it was not three days later that the stranger with the funny hands bought Ruby an ice-cream soda and a movie magazine in Ev Roberts's pharmacy and told her what pretty eyes she had.

That summer Rachel had arranged for Ruby to learn sewing from Granny Blankensop—an aged, widowed seamstress who lived with her daughter across the river at New Economy. Each Thursday evening Rachel tied up a fifty-cent piece in the girl's handkerchief and gave her two dozen eggs' tuition in a yellow basket. Then she took her to the ferry landing and saw her safely on board the little boat which was to be met on the Ohio side by Granny Blankensop's middle-aged and unmarried daughter Nevada. At nine Rachel would come back to the landing to meet the girl. It seemed to her that nothing in this procedure could permit the disastrous encounter between Ruby and any of the ornery farm boys and evening loafers who lounged on the bench in front of Ev Roberts's drugstore.

Yet, the first night Nevada Blankensop was to meet Ruby at the New Economy landing she was, in fact, overcome in her bedroom after two tumblers of her mother's dandelion wine. And so Ruby had stood in bewilderment on the alien bricks and pondered what she was supposed to do next, what the purpose and meaning of her mission there might be. It was something Rachel wanted her to do. It was something she was supposed to learn that would make her a better girl. Through the branches of the chestnut trees along Water Street she saw the bright lights of New Economy. She heard the drifting, random sounds of men's easy voices and the music of a radio and the noise of an occasional flivver. Now as she moved into the glitter of Pike Street things began happening. The night above her was filled with golden, winding wires of light and stars that winked off and on like enormous, sweet fireflies. The men on the evening bench saw her then: the whittlers and the tale tellers and the watch traders and the killers of time. And Ruby had found the world.

Rachel never knew. The eggs and the basket were often forgotten in that sweet, breathless scuffle down on the road berm under the pawpaw leaves and when Ruby got off at the West Virginia landing she would be empty-handed and Rachel would think: Well now, if Granny Blankensop don't have her nerve—keeping my very best egg basket.

Ruby lived for those Thursdays. She had found a wonderful thing that she could do well: something that never went wrong like gathering eggs did, like washing jars did, because there was nothing to drop, to break, to spill, to forget. And on the dozen occasions that Nevada Blankensop had actually been there to meet her and take her up to the house, fusty and thick with the smell of old women's sleep, Ruby had squirmed and twitched her buttocks on the split-bottom chair the whole time of the sewing lesson: heeding not a smidgen of it; learning not so much as a single, twinkling stitch. One night she had lain in her bed in a perfect trance of yearning and thought desperately: I just can't wait till Thursday! Because that's five sleeps away! I'll steal the money from Rachel's sugar bowl and go there tonight—to the river—

But she had been afraid to do that and waited anyway and that Thursday night Nevada had the vapors and was not there to meet her and she had fairly run to that place in the street in front of the drugstore where the eyes of the evening loafers awaited her.

That's her right yonder! whispered Macijah Blake to the stranger, nudging him and pointing to the girl moving down the street. That's Ruby and I reckon she'd be able to tell you what you want to know about them two new ones Rachel took in here a while back!

The stranger had appeared in New Economy that afternoon and hitched his horse to the iron courthouse fence and wandered away while the mare munched and tore at the untended grass. At dusk he had sought out the evening loafers and told them the story that he had repeated in a hundred dusty crossroad gatherings until he could say it now by rote: how he was a preacher of the Gospel looking for his no-account wife who had run off with a drummer and how his two blessed children had gotten lost in the scuffle. He told them how he had gone a-hunting and a-wandering through the bottomlands all that summer and how he had tracked down a dozen lost lambs and none of them his. A little boy and a girl with a doll? Yes, thought Macijah Blake, that was them. But *she* would know for sure—that bad girl Ruby—and it was Thursday and chances were she'd come over to town tonight. The others moved away from him with that disgust he seemed to arouse everywhere now. All but Macijah Blake and he stayed to point Ruby out as she came to stand before the assemblage of them: waiting in the dust of Pike Street with her big shoes close together and her fingers locked around the basket handle.

You're Ruby—ain't you, my child?

He had come right over to her, had not sidled up as the others always did, sneaky as sheep-killing dogs. This itched her curiosity. He was older than them, too, and stronger somehow and his eyes were strange: handsome and old and cruel as Herod.

Ruby, I'd like to talk to you, my dear.

Yes, she said. Yes, I will if you'll buy me a chocolate soda.

What? You'll what?

And the evening loafers were all laughing and catcalling again and she knew suddenly that she would do it for him for nothing because he was so wonderful.

Watch out, Preacher! She'll drag ye down in the dust right there in the middle of Pike Street if ye don't watch her.

He turned and glared at them.

Shet your dirty mouths! he boomed across the stillness. Shet 'em!

So she waited, smiling at him, loving his grand, manly sternness; basking happily in his anger and the violence she could feel like the warmth of a radiant stove against her body.

I want to ask you a question, girl. And if you'll answer me God's truth I'll buy you whatever it was you said.

A chocolate soda, she repeated, and he took her into the drugstore and Ev Roberts's nephew waited on them and while Preacher watched her, seething with impatience, she began to eat.

Now it's time for you to keep your share of the bargain, he said. Will you tell me——

But without answering she slid from the wire chair at the table and wandered off with wanton, swaying hips to the magazine rack and stood with the basket still heavy against her thigh and leafed through a new movie magazine and thought how beautiful she must be.

Will you tell me?

Buy me this? she smiled, her small eyes shrewd and bargaining, and he cried: All right! All right! and went to lay the money on the marble and came back to her side, waiting, glaring with choking impatience into the pale-pink gums of her wanton mouth.

Ain't I purty? she said suddenly.

And he smiled and relaxed then, knowing how he could get her.

Why, you're the purtiest gal I've seen in all my wandering! 'Deed, I never seen such purty eyes in all my born days! Didn't no one never tell you that, Ruby?

No, she breathed hoarsely. No one never did.

And then she danced over to the big brown mirror over the soda fountain and grimaced coquettishly at the image behind it. He came and brought her back to the table and made her sit and finish the soda while he told her some more about her pretty eyes, and when the soda was gone, the last of the sweetness sucked through the gurgling straws, he made her give him the movie magazine until she had kept her share of the bargain.

Two little youngins, he said. There's two new ones over at your place, ain't there, Ruby?

She nodded dumbly.

What's their names? he whispered, bending closer.

Pearl and John.

Ahhh! And when did they come to live at your house?

She frowned, recollecting.

This summer?

She nodded again.

And is there—a doll? Is there a doll anywhere that either of them—

Pearl, she said. She has a doll. Only she won't never let me play with it. She won't let none of us kids play with it and Miz Cooper says us to leave her doll alone because it's hers.

Ahhh! Yes!

Pearl and John, she said again pointlessly and belched softly and tasted the soda again and stared longingly at the movie magazine he held away from her.

Ruby?

Yes, sir.

Not a word about this little powwow to Miz Cooper, eh? That's part of the bargain. Eh?

And she smiled and nodded and he gave her the movie magazine again. And when he said good night and began to walk away she sprang to her feet and followed him and when he felt her fingers on his shoulder his face turned, already writhing with disgust and fury.

What do you want now?

She lifted her mouth and whispered it in his ear.

What?

Don't you want to? she mumbled. You can if you want to—

Get away from me!

He thrust her heavily away and walked rapidly out into the street, past the evening loafers, striding furiously through the dust toward his horse, choking and cursing, his mouth gaping with nausea.

In the doorway she stood for a moment, watching his receding figure. The golden neon caught the color of paper flowers above her face and she thought: He is not like them.

She moved past the men on the evening bench, hurrying toward the river with the basket of eggs swinging on her arm, not turning at their catcalls and whistles.

He is not like them! she kept on thinking and the ferryboat lamp shone like a piece of moon through the elms and she knew that the night was gone but she hugged the movie magazine against her breasts thinking: He is not like them. He is different and next time I am with him I will make him want to and I won't even ask him to buy me the ice-cream soda or the movie magazine again.

After Rachel found the movie magazine under Ruby's skirts that night she took it from her. Ruby sat on the straight-backed chair by the kitchen door and wept soundlessly into her big fingers. After a while she took her hands away from her face and let the great tears squeeze slowly from her quivering lids. Rachel sat opposite her on the canning bench, scowling at the girl in troubled speculation and massaging the yellow soles of her bare feet. She was sure now: Ruby had been with a man. It was a swift, country knowing: a realization that swept over the old woman in choking dismay.

Ruby, stop your weepin' and look me square in the eye and answer me.

The puffed red lids opened and stared.

Ruby?

Yes'm.

Ruby, you didn't have no money to buy that movie book did ye?

No'm. But I never took nothin' from your sugar bowl. Miz Cooper, you just know I wouldn't steal nothin' of yours.

Now, I know you wouldn't, child. I'm not accusin' you of nothin'. Just tell me and tell me the truth. Where'd you git the money to git that there book?

You'll whip me!

Shoot! When did I ever? You been spanked by me and you may be again but you never got a whippin' after the day you walked over my threshold. Just tell me, Ruby. There hain't nothin' to fear.

He give it to me, she babbled. He said—

Who?

That man down at the drugstore!

I see. You was at the drugstore. And this here man—

He was a nice man, said the girl. He said my eyes was the purtiest things.

Pshaw, now! And who ever said they warn't! You're a beautiful young girl, Ruby, and that's the very reason I don't want nothin' happenin' to you.

Now the old woman, roused and fidgety with anger at the world's trifling men, fetched her tiny can of brown snuff from the table, shook a smidgen into the lid, and dropped it daintily into her lower lip, beneath the gums.

Miz Cooper, said Ruby, snuffling and bending forward, her face aglow now with the new ecstasy of confession. I been bad!

How, Ruby?

Miz Cooper, the girl continued, her face illumined. I never went to ol' Miz Blankensop's all them times.

Where did you go, child?

Miz Cooper, I done it with men! Yes, ma'am, I done what they asked me to!

Dear God, child! With *men?* Was there more than one? And that loosed it and the girl told it all in a spilling babble: about the Thursday nights when she had not been at the seamstress's house at all, about the boys that had taken her down the river road in fruit trucks, in family jalopies, and afoot. She told how at first she thought it was what Rachel had sent her to do and when she finally found out that it was bad and that she was supposed to be doing something else it was too late to stop. And then she burst out crying again and Rachel joined her, hugging her and rocking gently with her in the lamplight, and they both enjoyed a good, female cry together for a spell and then Ruby told Rachel about Preacher.

But he warn't like them, whispered the girl, like one who has seen a vision. He just bought me the sody and the book and he said my eyes was the purtiest—

But he must have wanted something, Ruby. A man don't waste his time on a girl unless he gits something. What—

He asked about John—and Pearl.

And Rachel thought: And so it has come as it has come before. Sooner or later they come back for them and take them away and it's just like they was to take and cut a piece off me.

Is he their pap?

Ruby shrugged.

Well, girl, didn't he say?

No'm. He just said was them kids Pearl and John livin' here.

He said that, eh?

Yes'm.

Rachel arose, livid with anger, biting her tongue with it. She stomped across to the pump, splashed the dipper full and, rinsing the snuff from her gums, spat it out through the open screen door.

Then I'd just like to know why he never come right up to the house today and showed hisself! she cried. Just come right up like ever'one else does in broad daylight and said, Them's my youngins! Much obliged, madam! Hand 'em over! Shoot! I just plainly can't abide a sneak!

He was nice, observed Ruby. He said my eyes—

Hush, child! What else did you tell him?

I said they come to live with us last summer Pearl and John did.

All right. And then what did he say?

Ruby squinted and stuck her tongue out with a pathetic try at shrewdness; trying to remember how it had been.

I forgit, she said, scratching her head slowly.

Rachel glared out the open window into the black night of autumn.

He'll come a-callin' soon enough, she mumbled, hugging her withered breasts and rocking gently and thinking: All the love and worry and fretting like they was my own. I just wonder to God if they know when they come calling to claim them again after they've had their fill of sporting and carrying on and leaving me to mind their kids: to pray over them and wash their bottoms and pick school lice out of their heads and keep their britches patched—I just wonder if they know what a chunk they're cutting out of me when they come for them at last.

Fool! she scolded out loud. Derned old fool!

And then she fetched a candle and shooed Ruby before her up the kitchen stairs to bed. Rachel despised all womankind that night, including herself.

It was Ruby who saw the man on the horse first and dropped two brown eggs splattering on the flagstones by the stable. He rode slowly up the path through the meadow from the river road and Ruby scampered off to the basement where Rachel was setting up the fresh quart jars of apple butter she had canned that week.

It's him!

Who?

The man! The man!

Well, shoot! Don't take on like it was the Second Coming, Ruby. Git on up to the kitchen and put your shoes on. I'll be up and talk with him directly. Gracious sakes alive, girl, don't act so simple!

He tethered his horse to a fence post and walked across the yard toward the back porch, his head cocked slightly, his eyes creased in cautious greeting.

Mornin', ladies.

Ruby sat suddenly in the rope swing under the apple tree. Rachel stood behind the screen door, her hands folded under her apron in the timeless pose of country women greeting strangers.

How'do!

He stood for a moment staring at them: at the old woman and then the girl and then back to the old woman with a bow.

You're Miz Cooper, I take it.

I am.

Then you're who I'm lookin' for all right, ma'am.

Rachel stepped boldly onto the stoop and approached him across the grass. She had forgotten her shoes and yet her feet, even at her age, were strong and graceful among the plantain and buttercups.

It's about them two kids I took in, she said. That John and that Pearl?

Ah, then it's true. You have them.

Yes. I have them.

His face twitched with emotion then and his voice broke in great, thankful sobs.

My little lambs! he cried, falling to his knees near the feet of the transfixed Ruby. Oh, Lord, we praise Thy name! Oh, sweet, sweet little lambs! And to think I never hoped to see them again in this world! Oh, dear madam, if you was to know what travail—what a thorny crown I have borne in my search for these strayed chicks!

Rachel kept her eyes on him, her mouth thin as a string, and suddenly sat down in the warped old rocking-chair by the puzzle tree.

Oh, where are they, Miz Cooper? Where are my little lambs?

They've all went to gather black walnuts, she said, rocking fast in the dark August grass. Up in the woods beyond the Stalnaker place. My other two girls Mary and Clary's with them.

She fixed him still with that stare, her black eyes twinkling like berries and she thought: It's right for him to come for them if they is his own but there is something wrong here. There is nothing I can guess by looking at him but there is something I can feel in my bones, in my skin, in my hair, that is wrong. It is just like I could smell it on the poor dumb girl when she come in last night, that she had been with men. It is just like I can feel the thunder and rain in my arches and back a whole day before the purple thunderhead comes over the Ohio hills from the west.

Ruby, she said. Go call them kids!

Ruby minced primly off through the tall grass at the edge of the lawn, toward the pasture below the woods.

Preacher wiped at the tears on his leathery cheeks with the heel of his hand. That was when Rachel saw the letters of the Hate tattoo and shivered and the old mother-wit warnings raced and chattered like scared mice in the dark cupboards of her mind. He caught her staring and immediately commenced explaining. She listened, unmoved, as his rising voice described the war of good and evil in the human heart and his knuckles cracked and squeaked as the hands met and the fingers twined and strove together.

I am a man of God, he said at last.

And them kids, she said, is yours?

My flesh and blood! he said. My very heart and soul!

Where's your missus?

He bowed his head away from her and bit his lip and stared off into the far rainbow flicker of dragonflies above the puddles in the meadow.

She went the way of temptation, he whispered. Run off with a drummer one Wednesday night not an hour before I was to preach the prayer meetin'.

And took them kids with her? That's strange! If she took them then how come—

Yes, he said. Took them with her. God only knows what unholy sights and sounds those innocent little babes has heard in the dens of perdition where she dragged them! But at last it was too much for them. They run off from her—

Where's she at?

The Lord only knows! The good Lord only knows!

And them kids has been runnin' the roads since then?

Yes, he smiled softly. Before Jesus whispered in their little ears and led them to you.

Where'd they run from? I mean, where'd you figure the woman took them when she run away from you?

Somewhere downriver! he said, shaking his head grimly. Parkersburg, mebbe! Cincinnati! One of them Sodoms on the Ohio River!

Rachel rocked fast and hard, her eyes twinkling and strong in her face.

Right funny hain't it, she said, how they rowed all the way upriver in a ten-foot John boat!

Preacher's eyes flashed like summer heat lightning before the night storm.

They run north, he said. I been follerin' them all summer long. I reckon they stole the skiff and coasted downriver a spell to keep off the hot roads.

Rachel grunted sharply and listened to the flat, pale voice of Ruby hollering and hailing the children against the wind.

And now tell me about them! cried Preacher. Are they well?

They're a sight better than they was when I fetched them up from that mudbank where the river had throwed 'em. They was a sight to turn a body's stomach. Ticks in their hair and mud in their shoes and dirty as shoats from head to toe. Just skin and bones, too, and hungry as hogs.

Gracious, gracious! You are a good woman, Miz Cooper!

Now if you don't mind my askin', Preacher, she said, how you figgerin' to raise them two without a woman?

The Lord will provide, he said softly, and stooping chose an apple from the windfall beneath the tree. He tried it with his thumb and bit into it thoughtfully.

I don't reckon, he said, they had nothin' in the way of worldly possessions—except the clothes on their backs?

Not much more! snapped Rachel. And *they'd* hardly stand another washin'.

He eyed her again swiftly; the glance moving in a quick, feathering appraisal like the forked tongue of a copperhead.

That little Pearl! he crowed softly. Her and that doll of hers! Kept it with her night and day!

She still does, said Rachel and remembered the day she had

tried to get the doll away from the little girl to give it a scrubbing in the Monday wash and John had carried on as bad as she had.

And suddenly the children rounded the corner of the washhouse in a pell-mell rush of small faces: Ruby's towering above them all like a thistle above buttercups, and the face of the curious Clary and beaming Little Mary and the face of Pearl, just now awakening to the shock of love and remembrance at the sight of Preacher's face.

John, Pearl, said Rachel, rising. We got company today. Your dad has come to claim you.

For an instant none of them spoke, none moved. The group seemed frozen like figures in some quaint country tintype at a family reunion. Then Pearl gave a wail of happiness and, dropping the doll in the grass by John's feet, raced to Preacher's arms. He caught her up and kissed her and his face was twisting again in sorrowful happiness and he was crying out something about the mercy of the Lord. John stood still and looked straight into the old woman's eyes. And in that instant neither spoke and yet each told the other a thousand things, Rachel's eyes holding his and saying: What is it, John? What is wrong about all of it? What is it I can feel the same way I feel the gathering of tomorrow's storm before the west cloud comes? And then she read the dark and awful answer in his eyes. The years alone in the nights of river silence and river wind had taught her the wisdom of stable beasts; the cunnings of the small creatures of the woods. And now while she looked at the boy and listened while Preacher prattled and joked with the little girl Rachel felt the skin of her back bunch and twist like the hide of a frightened mare when something prowls the midnight yard and her new foal bleats with mortal dread. John lowered his eyes from hers then and stared at the doll at his feet. He stooped bravely and gathered it up, its loose, silly arms flopping against him. Preacher peered over Pearl's shoulder at him.

And there's little John! Ah, what a day this is! What rejoicing there must be in heaven just now! Come to me, boy!

But John did not move and the wind blew and the rope swing stirred gently under the gnarled branch. Rachel's mouth was a slit, her arms folded tight against her gingham bosom, her eyes watching Preacher.

Didn't you hear me, boy?

Preacher put Pearl down and he was still smiling.

John swallowed and lifted his eyes to the old woman.

What's wrong, John? she said.

Nothin', he said, smiling unaccountably because he knew how foolish it would all sound if he tried to tell her the truth of things.

What's wrong, John? she said again, bending to him a little. When your dad says come—you should mind him.

Her eyes twinkled and he read them and they said: You know this ain't true and I know it ain't true because there is something going on here that I don't know about but we must play the game out for a while till things get clear.

John? she repeated.

He ain't my dad, John said, and hugged the doll.

Preacher's smile was still there as he came toward the boy, and then Rachel moved between them and stood, thinking: And he ain't no preacher, neither, because I have seen preachers in my day and some was saints on earth and some was crooked as a dog's hind leg but this one has got them all beat for badness.

John! Have a heart! You'll have poor Miz Cooper here thinkin' I'm an imposter directly.

He turned his head to the little girl and smiled again.

Pearl, tell Miz Cooper who I am. Come on, now!

Pearl bent and pressed her fat knees with her palms and dimpled in a smile for them all. You're Daddy, she said. Preacher turned to Rachel again and threw up his hands at this proof.

There now. You see? The boy's a strange lad. The shock of all this—the mother runnin' away and all—he's a little *queer*.

Not so's a body would notice, snapped Rachel. Not so queer as some I've seen today.

And now the woodland warnings cried and skittered louder within her and she turned and moved, flushed and breathless, toward the washhouse.

Miz Cooper, you don't mean to hint you believe this boy!

I know him! cried Rachel. A damned sight better than I know you, mister!

The lights were there now, plain to see: the flickering fire rising behind his veiled eyes. His whole face began to sag suddenly, the smile gone; the whole mask of flesh melting quickly into a sallow leer of unveiled malevolence.

Well, they believed me in town, he said. And they'd understand it wasn't my fault if there's going to be any trouble about gettin' them kids back.

Old Rachel ducked inside the washhouse and John was alone as Preacher moved swiftly toward him. Soundlessly, John scrambled under the puzzle tree and disappeared.

Boy! Boy! Here! Here!

Squatting, Preacher peered through the leaves and saw that John had crawled under the low foundation of the washhouse. Preacher rose, dusting off his knees, and looked at them all accusingly.

Don't this beat all, now! A loving father come to claim his little lost lambs and one of 'em actin' up this way. Well! I reckon I'll just have to peel off my coat and scramble in there after him myself.

Old Rachel loomed above him then on the stone threshold: mottled and blue-stained with the sloshings of a half century's wash waters. The blue barrel of the pump gun was steady as doom in her old hands.

Just march yourself yonder to your horse, mister.

Preacher, on all fours beneath the puzzle tree, lifted his face slowly to the gun muzzle and then to Rachel's face. His features were yellow with it now: the raging, uncontrollable fury.

March, mister! I'm not foolin'!

He staggered to his feet and she saw then that he had the knife open in the palm of his hand, had had it out even as he started under the washhouse after John. Now he backed away from her, bouncing it lightly in his palm, the froth seeming to have gathered on his lips even before he started screaming at her; moving stiffly backward step by step, the bone-handled thing with its bright, winking blade still bouncing in his palm, his whole face suddenly going to pieces in a wash of madness.

Goddamn you! Goddamn you, I'm going! Yes, I'm going but I'll come back! Goddamn you, I'll come back! I'll have that bastard yet! Goddamn you, I will! You ain't done with Harry Powell yet, you Whore of Babylon!

Upon this outburst the children fell back to let him pass under the apple tree on his way to the tethered mare at the fence. His whole body was bent and racked with spasms of the roaring maniacal rage, the face a wrinkled mask of murder, the knife still bouncing like a carnival toy in his open palm. He led the horse away, shaking too badly to mount it and still screaming, and Rachel followed with the gun to the fence with all her little flock behind her, except for the still-hidden John.

I will wait until Almighty God sounds the trump of Doomsday! the voice roared across the silent fields. You'll wish you had never been born when I am done with you! The Lord God Jehovah will guide me to the hiding places of mine enemies! He will guide my hand in vengeance! Goddamn you! Goddamn you! I'll come back when it's dark. You devils! You Whores of Babylon! Just wait! You wait! Just wait!

And through the tranquil innocence of all that smoldering autumn afternoon the voice echoed across the fields, punctuated only by the thud of windfalls beneath the apple tree. When dusk fell Rachel lit the kitchen lamps and gathered all her lambs about her by the stove and sat with the shotgun across her knees, facing the night in the window. The sun had gone down in a blazing river rainbow in the yellow sky and it had been dark for only a few moments before the full moon appeared and lit the mists of early evening. They could see him quite distinctly from the kitchen window: sitting on a locust stump at the end of Rachel's garden, his whole body malevolently concentrated and fixed upon the silent farmhouse. Preacher's last siege had begun. Rachel sent the whimpering Ruby off to put the children to bed. John's eyes shone with an unflinching confidence that Rachel would save them. Incredibly, he slept.

The moon shone down on the field and against the pale luminescence of the mists the old woman fixed her smarting, weary eyes on the black shape of the hunter, thinking: Dear God, don't let me sleep. Dear God, there is something awful out there in my garden and I've got to keep it from my lambs. Dear God, don't let me sleep.

Once her head nodded and her lids fell for an instant and, catching herself, the old face snapped up and, peering through the deepening mists, she saw that the black shape of the man was still there. Now she thought for an instant that her wits were slipping, that her mind had begun to fail under the strain of the day. And yet the sound was quite distinct, quite unmistakable: he was singing a hymn: Leaning on the Everlasting Arms. And partly because she needed strength from God and partly because it would keep her from hearing the voice, her mouth began to shape the old words, too.

————

It seemed that her head had fallen only for a second. And yet when her eyes flew open again the moon had moved from the crooked elbow of the apple tree and swam free in the thin mists above the stable. The black figure was gone from the end of the garden. And the old woman thought in the first moment of real fear she had known: But he won't leave. No, he is up to something. If he had gone away I would have heard the mare, if he had gone across the river I would have heard the ferry engine or the bugle at the tree. He is closer now; sneaking in toward the house like a rabid fox with its belly dragging in the corn furrows, somewhere out yonder in the corn where I can't see him.

She was strong and she was old and there had been many things that had happened to her through the long years that had made her not so much brave as simply beyond fearing. But Rachel was frightened now, feeling again that hunch and twist of the skin of her neck and shoulders: the ancient, feral sense of something abroad among her flock. When the hoarse hall clock chimed three she gasped for breath and whispered: Oh, dear merciful God!

Then she thought: I had better fetch them all downstairs and we will stay here together by the stove till morning. Because I was a fool and fell asleep for a spell and even now if he was to get to the house I wouldn't know it.

She took the lamp to the doorway at the foot of the kitchen stairs and held it into the darkness.

Ahhhh, Ruby! Ruby! Ahh, Ruby!

An instant later there came a rustle of the straw tick in the room above and the dry hiss and pad of the girl's naked feet.

Yes'm?

Ruby, git John and Pearl up out of bed. Git Clary and Mary up, too. Bring them all down here to the kitchen.

Yes'm, Miz Cooper.

And she turned again and the long shadows stretched like

arms before the moving lamp as she came back to the table and sat down again with the pump gun facing the night window and thought: How many fools has that devil tricked with his lying, mealy-mouthed gospel and his prayers and his hymn singing? God, women is such fools! Such fools! And a widow with kids is the worst fool of all because she is the most alone and the quickest to cotton to a man like him.

The children padded swiftly into the kitchen from the stair door and circled her, wide awake and frightened and waiting for Rachel to tell them what to do. And looking into their round child faces she saw all the trust that was there and bit her tongue with hot, choking rage at the man in the mists.

Children, I got lonesome, she snapped directly, and wanted company. I figgered we might play games.

Pearl and Little Mary jumped up and down, patting their fat palms.

Will you tell us a story? Pearl said shyly.

I might, said the old woman with a swift, furious glance into the moonlit arena, I might tell a story.

And now she saw again in Ruby's face that stunned and simple smile, that glow of sweet wonder that had crept over her since Preacher's appearance in the yard that day. And when the girl saw Rachel looking at her she asked the question that had kept her tossing and burning under the quilt all that night.

Miz Cooper. Did that nice man go away?

Hush! Hush, Ruby! Just git a hold of yourself, young woman, and come back down to earth. Shame on you! Moonin' around the house this livelong day just hot as a fritter over that mad dog of a preacher! Shame, Ruby! Shame!

Ruby squatted on the floor boards by the old woman's knees and plucked reflectively at a callus on her long left foot.

That man! said Little Mary, moon-eyed and scary. He's bad, hain't he, Miz Cooper?

Yes, but hush up talkin' about him! cried Rachel. If we don't think about him he won't bother us half as much. Because it'll be sunup directly and he won't dare to come pokin' around by daylight. Ruby, run put the coffeepot on.

Can we have coffee? chimed the small ones.

Yes! exclaimed Rachel, with brisk, sudden cheeriness. I reckon a smidgen of good, strong coffee would do us all some good. Go long, Ruby, and heat the pot.

The girl padded to the stove in gawky, loose-limbed sullenness and shoved the full pot over the burner and lighted it.

John had spoken no word since coming into the kitchen. His eyes, fixed now on the night beyond the window screen, saw now another night by the wharf and his ears heard again the heels of the hunter ringing clear on the bricks of Peacock Alley in that hour when he and Pearl had fled the world. A moth thudded against the screen then, and Rachel bit her tongue to keep from crying out and her finger tightened on the warm flat trigger of the gun and she said loudly: All right! Who'll tell a story?

You! they cried unanimously. You tell a story!

John pressed forward so that the whole of his right arm was touching hers and he thought: Touching her is like something I forget: something long ago when the whole world was a blue wool blanket and the sun in my eyes and there was only two faces in the world only they are faces I can't remember no more.

Well, said Rachel, sipping the warm coffee that Ruby had poured for each of them. Mind what I told you last Sunday about little Jesus and his ma and pa?

They remembered. For how could any of them forget this tale of wanderers and of No-Room-At-AH and of those who took the wanderers in?

Well, now, there was this sneakin', no-account, ornery King Herod! cried Rachel softly, her lips pursed with indignation. And he heard tell of this little King Jesus growin' up and old

Herod figgered: Well, shoot! There sure won't be no room for the both of us. Ain't nobody wants *two* Kings and that's a fact. I'll just nip this in the bud. Well, he never knowed for sure which one of all them babies in the land was King Jesus because one baby don't look much different from another. You know that as well as I do.

Deep in the brush filth above the north pasture a rabbit gave the shrill death cry before the soft owl fell from the moon, and she thought: 'Deed, it's a hard world for little things. Rabbits and babies has a time. It's a cruel world to be born into and that's for sure.

—And so that cursed old King Herod figgered if he was to kill all the babies in the land—every last one—he'd be sure to get little Jesus and no mistaking. And when little King Jesus's ma and pa heard about that plan what do you reckon they went and done?

They hid in a broom closet! gasped Clary.

They run under the washhouse, said Little Mary.

No, said John. They went a-runnin'.

Well, now, John, that's just what they done! cried Rachel, angry all over again at what King Herod had done to all these little, helpless things. Little King Jesus's ma and pa took and saddled a mule and rode clean down into Egyptland.

Yes, said John. And that's where the queen found them in the billy rushes.

Pshaw, now! scolded Rachel. That warn't the same story at all. That was little King Moses. But just the same it does seem like it was a plagued time for little ones—them olden days—them hard, hard times!

And she listened to the ticking house and thought: I must keep talking and keep them listening because that will keep us from thinking about him. Because he is out there and he is closer now than I thought because I can feel the crawling stronger now,

I can smell it like I can smell burning brush filth in October even when there ain't no smoke on the sky to mark it.

It would have seemed the simplest matter in the world to go to the phone on the hall wall and take down the receiver and crank till Miz Booher answered and tell her to get the state troopers up here quick from Parkersburg. And yet this was the last thing that would have entered Rachel Cooper's mind. She had a deep, bottomlands mistrust of civil law. If there was trouble at hand it could most always be settled by the showing of a gun muzzle and a few strong words.

A gentle, steady wind rose from the river and the mists began clearing and the moon shone bright as twilight. And Rachel thought: Now, if I was to blow out the kitchen lamp I could see it all clearer: the whole of my farm from the barn down to the road and the river beyond it. That way I could sight anything moving out there under the apple tree; I could spot him if he should come creeping low under the puzzle tree through the yard toward the kitchen.

I sure could tell stories better, she exclaimed to the children, if we was to blow the lamp out! It's always more fun hearin' stories in the dark, ain't it, now?

Yes! they cried, shivering with excitement at this night game Rachel was playing. Yes, blow out the lamp!

So she cupped her palm against the smoking chimney and huffed once and suddenly the moonlight came pouring over the window sills in blue pools at their feet and in the soft wind an apple thudded dully among the windfalls in the yard.

Little Mary! cried Rachel cheerfully. Let's hear you do the Twenty-Third Psalm again. You and me has 'bout got that one learnt, ain't we?

Little Mary shut both eyes squint-tight and commenced lisping the words Rachel had patiently taught her through the strange and lonely Sabbath nights by the stove, and in her mind

Rachel could now see the small, intent face: the fumbling, racing little tongue trying so hard to say all of it right, to please her.

—He 'storeth my soul. He lea'th me in the paths in righteousness. For He—for He name's sake. He—

And the old woman's mouth shaped the words mutely with the child's voice because when you live for fifty years in a house you know every sound it is capable of making, and Rachel knew that the faint, soft outcry of the floor board by the marble-top table far away in the parlor was a sound that never happened unless a foot was there, pressing it. Yes, she thought, though I walk through the Valley of the Shadow of Death I will fear no evil for Thou art with me. Yes, she thought, he has come in through the west parlor window that I forgot to latch last Wednesday when I aired the room. Yes, he is in the house with us now and I dasn't get up to go to the stove for a match to light the lamp again because I don't know how close he is.

In the long, ugly pier glass in the hallway outside the kitchen door she could see mirrored the dusty square of moon on the dining-room floor and thought: When he comes through yonder archway I will see him no matter how softly he walks and that's when I'll start pulling this trigger.

Come, lambs! she whispered sharply. Come stand close by me! Mind, now!

They obeyed, and Little Mary, disappointed that Rachel's interruption had spoiled the climax of her recitation, put her thumb in her mouth and sucked it gravely. And then again it might have been Rachel's imagination: the tricks of an old woman's ears: that sound in the room of breathing that was not hers nor the children's. And she had turned her eyes cautiously again to the neglected window just as he spoke distinctly from the far end of the kitchen.

Figgered I was gone, eh?

Rachel swung the heavy gun, ready to start pulling the trigger as soon as she was sure where the voice was: hard and steady and angry as a man would have been and thinking: He's right yonder there behind the spice closet. He come in from the dining-room on his hands and knees so's I wouldn't spot him in the pier glass. I will say at least that he ain't no fool about his sneaking.

What do you want? she said, in a high, steady voice.

Them kids!

Yes, she said. I reckon so. But there's more to it than that, mister. There's somethin' them kids know—somethin' they seen once! What are you after them for, you devil?

None of your damned business, madam!

She ducked her face, whispering among the little faces for an instant.

Run hide in the staircase yonder! Run, quick!

And there was a quick scuffle of naked feet as they obeyed and yet through the corner of her eye Rachel saw that the girl Ruby had not moved: her face suspended like a moonflower in the half-light, like a moth clinging to a gray curtain.

Ruby! Mind me! Git yonder with the rest!

Trancelike, the girl obeyed, and now Rachel stood alone in the pale arena, the gun level in the crook of her arm.

Mister, I'm givin' you to the count of three to git out that screen door yonder. And if you ain't gone by then I'm comin' across this kitchen a-shootin' and I'll blast every winder and joist and shingle out of that end of the kitchen and you with it to Kingdom Come!

Silence. And the prickle and gather quickened in her flesh and even as she shaped her mouth for the count she sensed a motion at her feet; though it seemed no more than the shadow of a leaf on the floor where the moon's square of light ended, a delicate shifting of air and space a yard and a half from her naked toes and she knew suddenly that he had stolen that close in that space of seconds. And now he rocketed suddenly upward before her very eyes, his twisted mask caught for one split second in the silver moonlight like the vision in a photograph negative and she saw the knife in his fist rise swiftly as the bobbin of a sewing machine just as she began pulling the trigger while the gun bucked and boomed in her hands. After the scream and the thunder, the room rang with echoing stillness and she saw him reel backward through the affrighted air onto the threshold, screaming again and cursing, then stumble into the broken shadow and light beneath the apple tree in the yard and up the rough ground toward the open barn.

The children in the dark of the staircase had crouched in mute horror throughout all of it and now they listened as Rachel's footsteps padded to the kitchen door for a moment, and the screen door whined open and fell to again, and they heard her move grumbling into the hallway and crank the wall phone and wait. They heard her tell Miz Booher that she had better send to Parkersburg for the state troopers and get them out to her place right quick for she had trapped something up in her barn.

Yes, she quarreled to the darkness, banging the receiver back on the hook and shuffling to the kitchen door again and out into the yard to the rocker beneath the tree where she would begin the moonlight vigil before the barn door where the black figure had disappeared. Yes, and you can just bet those big, shiftless county court loafers will track up my clean hall floors to a fare-ye-well!

When morning shot its golden shafts into the mists of the trees in the yard Rachel stole softly into the kitchen to the stairway for a moment and stared in at the children on the steps, filled suddenly with the wonder that each of us must feel at least once in his life: the knowing that children are man at his strongest, that they are possessed, in those few short seasons of the little years, of more strength and endurance than God is ever to grant them again. They abide. They huddle together as these children now did: asleep in blessed faith and innocence beneath doom's own elbow, thumbs tucked blissfully between their sweet lips.

When the sun broke clean over the Ohio hills Rachel heard the cars in the lane and the voices of the men. And the children heard them, too, and awoke and went with her to the fence and saw the gathering cars in the lane beyond the north pasture, saw the men in the tan state police uniforms and the blue-coated city police from Parkersburg. Her hand was wound around John's cold fingers and when Preacher suddenly came staggering out of the barn door she felt the sweat spring in the boy's palm and heard the quick intake of his breath as the blue men stole in from the river mists and gathered under the branches of the apple tree.

Is that him, ma'am?

Yes! Up yonder in the barnyard! But mind where you shoot, boys! There's children here!

There'll be no shootin' if we can help it.

Now they moved together toward the man in the barnyard who did not now seem to see them or care if they came or not, and Rachel, towering above her huddled little flock, could not see the boy's face but heard the hiccuping whimper in his throat as he watched the blue men move solemnly toward the sway-ing man—Preacher, his left arm hanging useless in his shattered sleeve, the dried blood on his finger tips shining like dark drop-lets on a hare's nose when it hangs from the butcher's hook.

Harry Powell! You're under arrest for the murder of Willa Harper!

And John felt the scalding urine stream into his socks then and thought: It is them again and it is him and it is happening all over again or maybe this is it happening for the first time and it was only something I dreamed that time before. Now they are hitting him with the sticks again. Yes, and now he is falling down in the grass and trying to cover his head with the arm that ain't hurt. Yes, this is it. Yes, directly the little paper poke with the five-and-ten presents will fall out of his pocket and Yes! Yes! now they will drag him away!

John! John, wait! she cried.

But he was gone with the doll Jenny torn from his sister's arms and it was in his own now and he held it out in front of him as he ran toward them, holding it out for them to see. Even the blue men fell back when he came hurtling among them and arched above the man in the grass, his child's face twisted and clenched like a fist.

Here! Here! he screamed, flogging the man in the grass with the limp doll until his arms ached. Here! Take it back! I can't stand it, Dad! It's too much, Dad! I can't stand it! Here! I don't want it! I don't want it! It's too much! I can't do it! Here! Here!

Then the blue men seized him gently and one of them carried him back to the yard, limp and sobbing in his arms and when, at last, they had carried Preacher off to the cars, old Rachel bore the boy upstairs to her own big featherbed and undressed him and kissed his face and tucked him in—little and naked and lost—under the old gospel quilt that she had made when she was a girl in the mountains sixty years before.

John thought: They keep asking me to remember all kinds of stuff. The thing they don't know is that it was a dream and when you tell about a dream it is not all there the way they want it to be. They ask me the questions and all the people are looking at me. And the man with the gold chain on his vest leans over me and smiles. His breath is like a Christmas fruitcake and I think: What is it he wants me to say? What story does he want me to tell?

I had a dream once but you can't remember all the stuff in dreams and so when I start to tell him a little part of it the rest of it all goes away. When I look down there at the people all I can see is Miz Cooper and Pearl and that new doll baby of hers and Ruby and Little Mary and Clary and all I want to do is go home again because it is nearly Christmas.

The blue men came. I remember that part of the dream. And they took him away. Who? Well, I'm not so sure about that part. Only that he is a man and the blue men have him shut up in a big stone house up the street from Miz Cooper's sister's house. One day last week Miz Cooper taken us on the train to Mounds- ville for this here trial is what they call it. We are going to live with Miz Cooper's sister Lovey until the trial is finished and then we will go home again because it is nearly Christmas. Yesterday it was cold. The snow looked like the feathers when Miz Coo- per broke the bolster out in the back yard that time. They have this trial and they ask you questions. It is in a big place called Wellman's Opera House where they show movies. I heard Miz Cooper's sister Lovey say they don't usually have trials here but they are having this one here because the WPA's haven't got done building the new courthouse. When they have this trial they take you up on this big stage like they was going to put on a show and all these people are here on the stage and all those other people down in the seats like in church. And then the man who smells like fruitcake asks me questions and then another man with a gold tooth and bad breath, he asks questions, too. I can't much figure out what any of it is about except that this fellow with the gold tooth keeps saying something about Blue- bird. It seems like this Bluebird had twenty-five wives and he killed every last one of them and they been hunting him now for months and months and now they got him. I think it is some kind of make-believe story because nobody ever heard of birds with wives. But I do what they want and I try to figure out what they want me to tell them. Except there is one thing I cannot do. There is a certain place on that stage where I cannot look because I know if I look something terrible will happen like I think it did in that dream and every time they tell me to look over there at this place I get all out of breath and start to shake like I had a cold and then they stop. Maybe sometime I will make myself look but then I am afraid if I do that I will die or something. At night after Miz Cooper puts us kids to bed in that big soft, featherbed at Lovey's house I shut my eyes and after a while I can see it just as plain as day: the man who is there that I am afraid to look at on that stage. But then a funny thing happens and the next day I can't remember who it was and I am afraid to look and see, to remember. Pearl talks a whole lot when the men ask her questions. They sit down in the chair and take Pearl on their lap and talk to her real low and friendly-like and Pearl tells them all kinds of crazy stuff. Miz Cooper she talked lots, too, and somebody named Icey and a man named Walt stood up in the back of the crowd yesterday afternoon and commenced screaming and hollering and the old man behind the big box told them to shut up and when they wouldn't shut up he made the blue men put them people outside in the snow. This here woman Icey puts me in mind of a girl I used to know somewhere but I never seen the man. Today she got up again and commenced screaming and some other people started screaming and hollerin', too, and Miz Cooper taken my hand and held it. I reckon she was scared. This woman they call Icey she come up on the stage and answered some questions, too, and the gold-tooth man talked some more about the Bluebird and I reckon this got her riled up again because she went to shouting some more and when they made her go back down and set in them seats with the rest of the people she commenced hollering over and over again: Lynch him! Lynch him! This court won't never see justice done to that Bluebird monster! For he lied and he taken the Lord's name in vain and trampled on His Holy Book! And directly the old man in back of the box fetched his wooden hammer and beat on the box for a spell and he said: Madam, be silent or I'll order the Court! or something like that. But that don't hold her back and she hollers out: But he dragged the name of Jesus through the mud! And the old man says: Madam! We're trying this man for murder—not for heresy! And then this woman she screams out: Well, ain't that worse? Takin' His Holy Name in vain and tellin' all us good Christians he was a man of God? And then she went to screaming with her mouth open so you could see all the pink inside and the man who was with her started yelling at all the other men around him to do something that I can't remember what and with that the old man with the hammer told the blue men to put them outside in the street again. Last night we et peach cobbler for dessert only I had more than Pearl did and Pearl cried because there wasn't no more left in the pan and Miz Cooper said if we was going to act up like that we couldn't never come visit her sister no more. This is the biggest place I ever did see. They got lots of houses in this town and this here big movie theater only they ain't holding no movies now. They are holding this here Bluebird trial. Pearl has a new baby doll which Miz Cooper bought her at Murphy's five-and-ten the first day we come here. I just hate it. Every time I look at that doll I want to take it and break its head. And when Pearl comes to bed I won't let her take it in the bed with me and she cries something awful. Sometimes I just think to my soul I don't know what I'm going to do with Pearl. That's what Miz Cooper says when us kids is ornery—I just think to my soul I don't know what to do with you youngins! I love Miz Cooper. She says us kids is the little lost lambs of the Shepherd of Galilee. I don't know what it means but I reckon it's all right. She is nice except when she makes me wash all the time.

Yesterday they was a bunch of men out in front of the Wellman Opera House and they was selling little wooden things with strings hanging on them. I thought they was something to catch fish in the river with and I asked Miz Cooper to buy me one and she pulled me away and said I didn't want one of them shameful souvenirs because they was called a gallus or something and besides we didn't have the seventy-five cents to throw away. It is cold here. There is this big store across from the courthouse with a toy dog in the window and a great big Victrola record hanging out over the doorway and they have a big Victrola inside and every time you walk past you can hear this feller singing and playing the guitar like they do on the Wheeling radio we listen to up at Lovey's. Only this feller sings better and it's always the song that goes:

> *Oh, come and hear my story*
> *My tale of blood and gore!*
> *'Twas down at Cresap's Landing*
> *Along the river shore!*

Whenever Miz Cooper walks us past this store there is a bunch of fellers and women standing out in front listening to that song with their faces all kind of serious and crazy-like and when we are right close they sort of pull back from us like we was dirty or done something bad. And we just walk along and don't pay no mind but I can still hear this feller singing on the Victrola and the next part of the song goes:

> *'Twas there in Marshall County*
> *That rainy April day!*
> *When Bluebird Powell found her*
> *His weak and helpless prey!*

Sometimes Miz Cooper takes us all to supper at this big hotel across from the Wellman Opera House. I like hamburgs the best. I always eat more than Pearl does and she gets awful mad. Miz

Cooper won't let Pearl take her new doll baby around the dinner table when I am eating because one time she brought it to the table at Lovey's and I got sick and throwed up on the floor. Today when we was walking home from the trial that lady named Icey and her husband jumped out in front of us and like to scared me stiff. She just stood there and stared all goggle-eyed for a minute and then she stuck her finger out and pointed it right at me and Pearl and went to hollering and screaming at all the people around her like she done at the trial. Them's hers! she hollered. Them's her orphans! Them poor little lambs of Jesus! Them is the ones he sinned against, my friends! Yes, draggin' His Name through the evil mud of his soul! If the people of Marshall County don't string that Bluebird up to a pole then the Christian religion won't never be safe again! He lied! Do you hear me? Fooled us! Tricked us with his mealy-mouthed sermonizing!

Miz Cooper says don't pay her no mind because she is most likely one of them Duck River Baptists and probably a Republican to boot and we just went on home down the street. Halfway home there is a big stone house. And when we go past it big old Ruby grabs Miz Cooper's arm and hollers, Is that where they got him? and Miz Cooper says, Yes! Yes! That's where! and then she pulls us all off down the sidewalk as fast as she can and I start yelling at old Ruby real loud: The blue men got him! The blue men got him! The blue men got him! like it was some kind of big old joke or something except I don't know who it is they got there in the big stone house. Sometimes I think I can remember who it is and then the next thing I know it is all gone. Sometimes it is one face and then it is another face and when I dream about the faces I wake up sweating and grab Pearl and lay there in Lovey's big, soft feather-bed and outside I can hear the wind and a big icicle on the juniper tree scraping on the shingles like when you scratch your fingernail along the window and I think: Maybe it ain't an icicle sound at all but some other kind of sound like maybe a bluebird singing a terrible, scary bluebird song. This here trial sure is lively, all right. Everyone hollers and carries on. Today they had this old white-haired man named Thomas Steptoe and he runs a ferryboat or a wharf or something somewheres and he kept hollering and yelling that he never done it. They allus blames Birdie! he yelled. Ever' time somethin' happens they blame poor old Birdie! If only Bess was still alive! And directly he runs back down in the crowd and the old man behind the box hollers for someone else to come up and put on a show. I will sure be glad when this trial is done. Because then maybe Miz Cooper will take us all to a movie show. Sometimes when I am sitting on the chair up there in the trial and the man who smells like Christmas is talking to me, I try to think what a movie show must be like. Ruby went once and she told me all about it. Something wonderful.

Is that him? says the man who smells like Christmas. Will you identify the prisoner?

And he points. And I look at his finger. And I know he wants me to make my eyes go across that stage from the finger to what he is pointing at but I can't make my eyes do it.

Please, little lad, he whispers. Won't you look yonder and tell the court if that is the man who killed your mother?

Miz Cooper says that when Christmas comes if I am good she will buy me a pocket watch. I hope I am good but I don't know if I am or not.

A winter dusk.

Ruby?

Yes'm.

Run down to the little store across from the jail and fetch back a pound of butter. I clean forgot when we shopped today and Lovey's 'bout got supper ready. Run along now. Here's fifty cents.

Can I go? the children all cry out and Rachel shushes them

because she has told them not to shout because she realizes what a burden their being there really is on her sister Lovey who has bad enough nerves as it is. The children scamper away to the sewing room to play with the bright steel parts of the sewing machine that the old sister has given them as toys during their stay. Ruby pulls on the old coat, far too small for her, and the ugly toboggan that barely covers her shaggy hair. She moves into the crystal silence of the winter dusk, down the pavement, the coin clutched in her palm, the wind drifting sharp as a razor. The winter trees are naked and stretch like the fingers of poverty into the gray sky.

The blue men, Ruby thinks. John said it was them that has got him up there in that big stone house yonder. I reckon they won't let him out or else he would have come to see us again and maybe he would have told me again about my purty eyes. I love him. She don't understand that he is different from them others: the ones I done the bad thing with. She thinks he is just like them and she don't know that the reason he likes me is because I am so purty, and I'll bet if he was to get the blue men to let him out of the stone house he would walk right up to me right now and tell me so and ask me to marry him. He would love me I'll bet. Because I love him. And nobody really loves me—Miz Cooper and them kids. I love them, I reckon, but, shoot! I am so big and tall I don't fit things any more and I always have to lean over. When I am with her she treats me like them and they are babies and shoot! I can't be a baby and I can't be a grownup so what does that make me? I used to wonder who I really am and when I done the bad thing with them boys I just done it so they would like me—so they would love me. When you are too big for everybody nothing fits. This coat used to be Clary's and Clary is littler than I ever was so whenever I bend over I have to hold my shoulders up so's it won't rip. Rooms, too. Rooms don't fit. People don't fit, neither. Except him. Well, he don't make fun of me and laugh at me like them boys used to do and he don't want to do the dirty thing. That's the stone house yonder. That's where the blue men got him.

She lifted her eyes to the hard, yellow windows of the county jail and looked at the little bars and then she saw the tiny, black shape of shoulders and a head and thought: That's him now. If I wave my arms maybe he will see me and come out and we can get married.

She stood on the thin ice of the pavement and waved her hand and tried to smile the pretty smile like the beautiful girls in the movie magazines because maybe if he saw how beautiful she was again he would get the blue men to let him come out.

He is different, she thought, with a delicate smile on her poor mouth, and something stirred softly in the crackling cold of the night, a faint noise of thrashing like a restless beast moving in its hay in the stable darkness and she heeded it for a moment and then resumed her revery, thinking: A body just can't go around with people that don't fit. When I first come to live with Miz Cooper I was ten years old just like Clary and I had all my clothes in a cardboard carton tied up with a piece of clothesline just like Clary and I just sat there on top of it in Miz Cooper's hall, looking at them two other kids she had then before their folks come and took them away and I thought: Why, shoot! This ain't no better and it ain't no worse! I never fit. But when I seen him that night in front of the drugstore and he taken me in there and bought me that sody and that book I knowed he was different. Why, Miz Cooper she just taken on something awful about him buying me that there movie book. She was so mad she shot him with her gun and directly the blue men come and taken him away and put him yonder in the big stone house.

She turned her head, cocking it to the wind, as the stir and murmur grew like a vast, faint thunder in the town and her face screwed up cannily, heeding it, straining to fathom its meaning and wondering: Them's people shouting somewheres. All them people away off somewheres. This sure is the strangest place— the strangest town.

And then she shut her eyes and saw his face like it had looked at her in Ev Roberts's drugstore that night, all cruel and beautiful and angry, and she knew more than ever how unlike the others he was: them simpering, slobbering boys on the evening bench, them ones that used to take her down in the pawpaw thickets along the river road and do that bad thing to her. And now, opening her eyes again and turning her head she saw the bright flames and thought: Why, them's just like beautiful red flowers—like them poinsettias Miz Cooper had one Christmas— only that is fire on the end of those sticks the people are waving: that crowd that is marching up the street from the Wellman's Opera House.

They were walking slowly toward the courthouse yard before the jail and it seemed, curiously, as if their faces were not moving as slowly as their bodies were, as if, indeed, the faces were being propelled swiftly before them the leaping light of the red flambeaux. And now they were almost abreast of her in the middle of Tomlinson Avenue and she could see their faces more clearly and with a particular vividness the face of the big man in the lead, the man who waved the rope in his hands and shouted. Because it was the husband of the woman who had risen screaming and praying in the back of Wellman's Opera House at the trial just as she was screaming and praying at her husband's side now. And with a sudden sweet rush of knowing the girl understood why they were coming.

Sure! Sure! she thought. They're a-comin' to save him. They're going to make the blue men let him out of the big stone house.

And now she turned her eyes to the yellow windows of the

county jail again and saw that each square of yellow was swarming with black silhouettes of men now. She turned toward the trees in the yard at the shout from the courthouse steps, beneath the icy branches of the giant sycamores that embraced its ugly sandstone porch, and saw the blue men gathering there with the guns in their hands and still the saviors with their torches did not stop.

Yes! she breathed. Save him now! Let him free!

And she began to run, to catch up with them, wishing she had a torch, too, and then one of them turned and saw her and gave her a shove toward the pavement and told her to go home and said it wasn't any job for children and she stood there a moment watching with her dream eyes as the seething mob circled and moved in cautiously toward the porch under the trees where the blue men were knotted and she thought: I'll run back and get my things all ready: my other gingham dress and my shawl and my Mickey Mouse wrist watch that don't run and the straw hat with the flowers and I'll have them all packed up in that cardboard carton with the piece of clothesline around it and I'll tell Miz Cooper he is coming to marry me and she won't mind because she knows it as well as I do: I don't fit. I don't belong.

So she began to run back to Lovey's house while behind her the breaking, hoarse voice of Walt Spoon rose above the gathering chorus of the mob.

Because he tricked us! Because he tricked us! Because he is Satan hiding behind the cross!

And the mob roared its affirmation and moved up the steps and Ruby ran into the house and old Rachel met her by the umbrella stand saying: Why, where's the butter? Forevermore, Ruby, where you been?

EPILOGUE

THEY ABIDE

I say that we are wound
With mercy round and round
As if with air! . . .

—GERARD MANLEY HOPKINS

And Christmas came to blanket the black memories for a while: Christmas with a swirling two-day snowfall with flakes as big as summer cabbage moths. And now they were all home again, inside the warm, familiar house: old Rachel and her flock. She had been glad to come home, as much for being under her own roof again as for fleeing the scene of Preacher's last, terrible night on earth. And staying in her sister's house, even for a spell, had chafed her dreadfully.

She thought: Lovey is my sister and a good soul but she is old and I am old and when you are old and the house you live in is old you understand one another, that house and you, and nobody else's house is the same. Lovey's butter ain't fresh and sweet like I always want it: little things. Lovey has a way of running her finger around the inside of the cream pitcher and licking it off when she's redding off the supper dishes and I just can't abide that. Little things! Gracious, I'm getting old and queer!

She had bought a Christmas present for each of the children and for the season she baked a fruitcake and killed two fine fat Plymouth Rocks and opened Mason jars of the special holiday things she kept on the dusty cellar shelves: watermelon preserves and candied apples and peaches and strawberry jam. These were days when John had begun to smile again and had ceased to sit apart when Ruby and Clary and Rachel fetched down a greasy old deck of cards and played Hearts together on the kitchen table.

Christmas made Rachel angry. It made her think again of what the world does to children. If one listened well upon any night in history one might hear the running of their feet: the little children for whom there was no welcome door. Old Rachel banged pots and baking pans in her kitchen those bustling days before the Yule season, muttering to herself and scowling out her windows, angry at how it was with some child somewhere in the world that very winter day. On the afternoon before Christmas Day she had gone down through the snow of the path to the road, wearing nothing but her old gray wool man's sweater and her toboggan. When she saw that there was no mail in the RFD box she grumbled again to herself and stormed inwardly at the sweet old Christmas song that had kept finding its way to her lips all that day. There had been a card from Lovey the day before, but now she knew there would be neither card nor package from her son Ralph and his wife this year and she thought: Good! I'm glad they didn't send me nothing. Whenever they do it's never nothing I want nor need but something to show me how fancy and smart they've come up in the world. Though they might have sent a little box for them kids—yes, they might have done that.

And she labored back up the frozen ruts through the knee-deep snow, an old woman like a strong tree with branches for many birds, and bit her tongue with disgust at herself for being hurt, for caring that Ralph had sent nothing this year. Then the door to the kitchen opened under her hand and the warm, spice-fragrant steam of the indoors drifted against her face and she heard Ruby and Pearl whispering and giggling somewhere in the house as they wrapped the potholders they had crocheted her for Christmas gifts. Rachel shook herself angrily, more piqued than ever with herself, thinking: I ought to be ashamed. 'Deed, now! Caring about a fool thing like that! Why, *these* is my kids! A brand-new harvest! A brand-new brood! Ain't it always true that the last sowing comes up sweetest under the old autumn moon? Why, shoot! Them kids is all that matters.

She poured herself a sputtering-hot cup of black coffee and, squatting on the chair by the window, cradled the cup in her big, rootlike fingers and sipped it, listening to the winter wind that shrilled one moment against the window cracks and then fell silent again. Rachel watched the dusk of that Christmas eve gather over the stretching miles of white bottomland while amidst it the dark stream of the river flowed like the blood of the earth itself: old, dark Time coursing to the oceans and never stopping whatever the calendar or clock might say.

Rachel reflected about children. One would think the world might be ashamed to name such a day for one of them and then go on the same old way: children running the lanes, lost sheep crying in the wind while the shepherd drank and feasted in the tavern with never an ear to heed their small lament. Lord save little children! Because with every child ever born of woman's womb there is a time of running through a shadowed place, an alley with no doors, and a hunter whose footsteps ring brightly along the bricks behind him. With every child—rich or poor— however favored, however warm and safe the nursery, there is this time of echoing and vast aloneness, when there is no one to come nor to hear, and dry leaves scurrying past along a street become the rustle of Dread and the ticking of the old house is the cocking of the hunter's gun. For even when the older ones love and care and are troubled for the small ones there is little they can do as they look into the grave and stricken eyes that are windows to this affrighted nursery province beyond all succor, all comforting. To Rachel the most dreadful and moving thing of all was the humbling grace with which these small ones accept their lot. Lord save little children! They would weep at a broken toy but stand with the courage of a burning saint before the murder of a mother and the fact that, perhaps, there had never been a father at all. The death of a kitten would send them screaming to the handiest female lap and yet when the time came that they were no longer welcome in a house they would gather their things together in old paper cartons tied with a length of clothesline and wander forth to seek another street, another house, another door. Lord save little children!

They abide. The wind blows and the rain is cold. Yet, they abide.

And in the shadow of a branch beneath the moon a child sees a tiger and the old ones say: There is no tiger! Go to sleep! And when they sleep it is a tiger's sleep and a tiger's night and a tiger's breathing at the midnight pane. Lord save little children! For each of them has his Preacher to hound him down the dark river of fear and tonguelessness and never-a-door. Each one is mute and alone because there is no word for a child's fear and no ear to heed it if there were a word and no one to understand it if it heard. Lord save little children! They abide and they endure.

After supper that Christmas eve the children gathered round Rachel at the kitchen table and she told them the Christmas legend and they listened gravely because it was their own story, and while Rachel peered through her cracked old spectacles at the small Scripture words each of them stole solemnly in his turn and peered between cupped fingers through the moonlight of that crystalline winter's night toward the stable as if they had hoped to see there a lantern and paper cartons tied with lengths of clothesline where the Wanderers had laid down their burden at long last upon the threshold of a welcoming fold. Thinking then that they might not have understood the old words Rachel closed the book and gazed round their faces in the circle of the lamplight.

Now, did ye understand that story, children?

They nodded gravely and then Little Mary said: Can we give you your presents now?

Shoot! she said, rising and scurrying off to the stove for more coffee. You don't mean to say you got me a present? Shoot, now!

Oh, yes! they cried, and she chuckled and scolded herself for caring so much for them because one of these fine mornings the kinsmen would come to claim them or some fool county woman with a brief case and a head full of college words. And she stood waiting while they clamored away into the house after the messy little packages they had wrapped for her and when they returned they stood gravely holding them out for her to take. There were handmade potholders from each of the girls and though Rachel had helped them make them every step of the way she pretended now to be enormously surprised and pleased as a queen would be with kerchiefs of mandarin silk. Yet John had no gift half so fine as these bright, ragged potholders. His gift was a large McIntosh apple which he had taken from the barrel in the cellar and wrapped himself and prayed that she would not guess that it was not something for which he had paid a great sum of money in a rare and exotic market place. This, to be sure, was what Rachel pretended to believe and John smiled at her cry of surprise and then it was her turn and she gave them the packages which she had kept hidden in the top of the china closet behind the old Haviland china service she had not used in forty years. There were new calico dresses for the girls and sticks of peppermint candy for all and for John there was the dollar watch that he had wanted since that time long ago when he had seen one through the dust of Miz Cunningham's dreadful little ragbag window. The girls ran screaming now to the upstairs rooms to try their dresses on and Rachel, submitting at last to the spirit of the season, sat down smiling at the kitchen table. John had gone off to the cor-ner behind the stairs and stood listening to the watch in the pocket of his shirt, the stitch of its proud and magic heart beating against his own, its numerals that shone in the dark of his pocket burning with a sweet, soft ecstasy against his breast. And he thought: If I keep it here in my shirt pocket for a while it will be all right because it is so big and so much that it makes me scared when I hold it and look at it. Because things go away in the world, they fall sometimes and they break, they are there one minute and then gone. And Rachel knew what was in his mind just then so she grunted and her eyes twinkled in his direction.

I declare, John! That watch sure is a fine, loud ticker!

He cast her a swift, burning look and then could not hold back the wide, proud smile though still he could not find a word to say that would be just right.

My! It sure will be nice, she cried, to have someone around the house who can give me the right time of day! That old Seth Thomas in the hall just ain't what it was once upon a time.

And then he waited until she stopped looking, until she seemed busy again with her mending of the child's stocking from the rat's nest of her sewing basket and walked softly to her, standing very quiet, hoping she would not notice him, because if he might be allowed to stand there unseen for an instant then there would just be the two of them, and then he might find the words to speak his heart. And Rachel paid him no mind, frowning and pursing her lips, and then bit off the yarn and held up the stocking on the gourd to see if there was any hole left and that was when John reached out his hand and touched her shoulder.

That there watch, he said, is the nicest watch I ever had.

Well, good! Good, John! she said. I'm mighty glad to hear that! A feller can't just go around with rundown, busted watches in his pocket! Especially when folks is countin' on him for the right time of day!

So he went away again and stayed for a while in the pitch-dark parlor, among the white specters of the muslin-cloaked furniture, and stared at the little glowing numerals that winked and burned softly like the eyes of golden mice, and listened to the measured ticking of the watch, as solid and steady and fine as the beat of his own stout heart, and above him in the bedrooms the voices of Clary and Pearl and Little Mary whooped and screamed over their pretty dresses while the low, shy voice of Ruby asked them all if hers looked pretty, too.

He thought: You have to be careful or things go away. So I will take a big piece of butcher twine from the kitchen drawer and tie it very tight around the little link on top and then I will tie another knot with the other end so's it will be a loop and I can put it around my neck when I go to bed. If it is still there in the morning then I will feel a whole lot better about it. I'll bet she paid a lot of money for it because it is gold or something like that and if Pearl ever tries to take it away from me I'll push her even if she is a girl. She give me the watch and I give her an apple because it is the day when you give things to people because the Lord is born. And there wasn't no room for Him at the inn so Him and His folks put up for the night in a barn. I went and looked out the window at the barn while she was reading but I never seen no one so I reckon it is just a story. Or maybe they ain't got here yet and they'll be getting set up in the barn after we're all in bed asleep. You never know what they tell you. You never find out if it's real or a story.

And again he pressed his face to the cold pane in the parlor window and stared across the white sheen of fresh snow that blanketed the valley under the winter's moon.

Because someone is chasing them, he thought. That's why they picked up and started running. I reckon that's what she meant because there was another story she told us about the bad king and the children who ran. I wish I could remember stuff. It all gets mixed up inside you. And sometimes you can't remember if things is real or just a story. You never know.

In the kitchen now he could hear Rachel hollering about how pretty Ruby and the rest of them all looked in their dresses and directly she yelled for him to come, that it was time they all got to their beds. But there was no sleep for John for a long, ticking time that night. Crouched beneath the bright, heaped quilts he stared at the watch on the string; watching the circuit of the creeping golden hands until they marked the passing of an hour. Pearl hunched warm and sleeping beside him. In the other bed Clary and Little Mary smiled and wriggled in their dreams. And John lay listening to the faint, bright ticking and then he heeded some secret and forgotten bidding of his memory and looked at the place where, on the ancient, flowered wallpaper of the bedroom, the moon cast its square of pale light through the windowpane. The branches of the apple tree shook their naked winter fingers in the gusts of harsh wind from the river. And in that new, pale proscenium of light John saw again the dancers, the black horse prancing and the brave little soldier and the clown with his toothpick legs. Now when John shut his left eye the soldier waved his sword gaily and the charging mare frollicked and tossed her forelegs to the stars. And yet something else awaited its cue in the wings of that arena: the shape of a man who had stood there in a lost time long ago. Silently John slipped from beneath the covers into the icy air and stole shivering across the cold floor to the window sill. Then he saw that the black shape had, indeed, returned, standing as it had before, as he had known it would be. John lifted an arm and the specter did the same. He twisted his body that way and this and lifted his arms above his head and wiggled his hands and the shadow mimicked every finger, every nodding lock of bushy hair. Then John felt the cold watch pressing against his naked breast.

I ain't afraid of you! he whispered to the shadows. I got a watch that ticks! I got a watch that shines in the dark!

And with that he scurried back into the bed and lay still for a long while, heart thundering, daring not look to see if the shadow man had been angered as before and had stayed, fixed to that white square of moonlight: watching, waiting, speculating before he moved on, singing down some fateful country lane among dream meadows that were breathless beneath the affrighted moon. At last he forced his eyes to turn again and look and he saw that the man was not there. Only the others remained: the horse dancing and the soldier waving his sword at the circling winter galaxies and the clown pirouetting on his spindly legs. But the night of the hunter was gone forever and the blue men would not come again. And so John pulled the gospel quilt snug around his ear and fell into a dreamless winter sleep, curled up beneath the quaint, stiff calico figures of the world's forgotten kings, and the strong, gentle shepherds of that fallen, ancient time who had guarded their small lambs against the night.

THE BITTER TEA OF GENERAL YEN
by Grace Zaring Stone

This groundbreaking novel was the basis for Frank Capra's shocking drama starring Barbara Stanwyck and Nils Asther. Traveling to Shanghai to marry her missionary fiancé, Megan Davis finds herself caught in the toil of civil war between Republican and Communist forces. Determined to save the inhabitants of an orphanage in a Communist-occupied city nearby, Megan joins a rescue mission that ends up under attack by a mob. She avoids death thanks only to the intervention of General Yen, who brings her to his palace. As violence outside the palace walls escalates, the motives behind various associates of the General are called into question, leading to an irreparable betrayal.

Fiction

BACK STREET
by Fannie Hurst

In the bestselling story behind Ross Hunter's classic melodrama starring Susan Hayward and John Gavin, gorgeous socialite Ray Schmidt meets Walter Saxel in Cincinnati and their attraction is instant and everlasting. As their bond deepens, Ray finds herself envisioning a future with Walter, until one fateful day when her family affairs interfere with their plans to meet, and his relationship with another woman forms.

Fiction

ALICE ADAMS
by Booth Tarkington

The Pulitzer Prize–winning novel that inspired George Stevens's celebrated film starring Katharine Hepburn, Fred MacMurray, and Fred Stone is set in a small Midwestern town in the wake of World War I. Alice Adams delightedly finds herself being pursued by Arthur Russell, a gentleman of a higher social class. Desperate to keep her family's lower-middle-class status a secret, she and her parents concoct various schemes to keep their family afloat.

Fiction

SHOW BOAT
by *Edna Ferber*

The classic tale behind MGM's blockbuster movie brings to life the adventurous world of Mississippi River show boats, the grittiness of turn-of-the-century Chicago, and the majesty of 1920s Broadway. Magnolia Hawks spends her childhood aboard the *Cotton Blossom*, growing up amid simmering racial tension and struggling to survive life on the Mississippi. When she falls in love with the dashing Gaylord Ravenal and moves with him to Chicago, the joy of giving birth to their beautiful daughter, Kim, is offset by Gaylord's gambling addiction and distrustful ways. Only when Kim sets off on her own to pursue success on the New York stage does Magnolia return to the *Cotton Blossom*, reflecting on her own life and all who once called the show boat their home.

Fiction

THE GHOST AND MRS. MUIR
by *R. A. Dick*

Burdened by debt after her husband's death, Lucy Muir insists on moving into the very cheap Gull Cottage in the quaint seaside village of Whitecliff, despite multiple warnings that the house is haunted. Upon discovering the rumors to be true, the young widow ends up forming a special companionship with the ghost of handsome former sea captain Daniel Gregg. Through the struggles of supporting her children, seeking out romance in the wrong places, and working to publish the captain's story as a book, *Blood and Swash*, Lucy finds in her secret relationship with Captain Gregg a comfort and blossoming love she never could have predicted.

Fiction